Hot Dutch Daydream

gr 7 +

Also by Kristy Boyce
Hot British Boyfriend

KRISTY BOYCE

An Imprint of HarperCollinsPublishers

HarperTeen is an imprint of HarperCollins Publishers.

Hot Dutch Daydream
Copyright © 2023 by Kristy Boyce
All rights reserved. Printed in the United States of America.
No part of this book may be used or reproduced in any manner whatsoever without
written permission except in the case of brief quotations embodied in critical
articles and reviews. For information address HarperCollins Children's Books,
a division of HarperCollins Publishers, 195 Broadway, New York, NY 10007.
www.epicreads.com

Library of Congress Control Number: 2022943667
ISBN 978-0-06-316030-9

Typography by Michelle Gengaro
23 24 25 26 27 LBC 5 4 3 2 1

First Edition

To Mom and Dad, for your
endless love and support

chapter

1

I am frazzled. And I'm not one to get frazzled easily. In fact, I pride myself on my unflappable demeanor, but an eight-hour overnight flight next to a teething baby means I'm flapping all over the Amsterdam airport.

I'm in such a sleep-deprived state when I get off the plane that I leave my laptop bag on board and have to go back to get it, then get turned around trying to find a bathroom. At least I've now found my way to baggage claim. I tap my foot and pull out my phone even though only two minutes have passed since I last checked the time. Dr. Reese, who I'll be living with for the next two months, will be here to pick me up soon, and I'd really like to retrieve my luggage and swing into the bathroom to wash my face first. But just as the baggage carousel jerks to a start, my phone buzzes with a text.

We're here and waiting in arrivals.

I just need to grab my bag, I type back quickly. Next to me, a young couple chatter away in Dutch, but I can't understand any of it. I studied the language when I realized I'd be working as Dr. Reese's nanny this summer, but I only had a few weeks and languages aren't my forte. My brain is much happier living in the STEM fields.

I run a quick hand over my dark pixie cut and then down my shirt. I'm wrinkly, disheveled, and exhausted, but hopefully she'll understand. I don't want to keep her waiting, so I grab my gray bag as soon as it comes into view and head through the exit into the rest of the airport.

There's a small crowd waiting for passengers, including a man holding a bouquet and a family with smiley-face balloons. I scan the group and find Dr. Reese off to the left, looking as pulled together and professional as she always did in the lab last fall. Her auburn hair is cut in a stylish bob that frames her face and her blue silk scarf is both elegant and summery. Most moms I know—including my sister—are lucky if they're wearing a clean shirt, but somehow Dr. Reese pulls off the *working mother* look perfectly.

Her three-year-old sits in a stroller fisting a messy sippy cup. To my surprise, he has bright red hair. So this is who I'll be watching every day? I eye him dubiously. He does the same to me.

"Dr. Reese, it's so good to see you again." I'm not sure what to do so I put out my hand.

She smiles and shakes it. "I can't tell you how happy I am to have you here."

"Thank you so much for inviting me. Working in your lab was the highlight of senior year, so it's a real dream to be helping again."

Last fall, I studied abroad in England and used the opportunity to volunteer as a research assistant in Dr. Reese's oncology lab while she was on sabbatical there. Working in her lab was the best part of those four months—though I know my friends from the trip would say that's blasphemous. It was hard and overwhelming, but I loved every second of it.

"It hasn't been the same without your enthusiasm around the lab. You put my grad students to shame." She winks at me. "Though this summer will be quite different—I hope you're up for the challenge. If you thought research was difficult, then wait until you're watching a three-year-old every day!"

She laughs at the joke, but my stomach twists with nerves. I'm willing to do just about anything to get more experience in her research lab, but to say I'm not a kid person is putting it lightly.

As if he knows what I'm thinking, her son takes this moment to throw his cup across the vast arrivals terminal like he's an NFL quarterback. It sails past the Burger King and the wooden tulip shop before cracking an old man on the head.

The man yelps and Dr. Reese and I share a horrified look before I realize a second too late that I should run and grab it. It's possible that I'm *not* cut out for babysitting.

I dash over and pick up the cup. It's sticky. Ugh, gross.

"I'm so sorry. He didn't realize . . ." I gesture back at the toddler.

The man glares at me and turns away.

"Diederik, no throwing," Dr. Reese says in a singsongy voice when I return. "Sage, let me make the formal introduction—this is Diederik." Her wide, doting smile is so different from the serious face of the medical researcher I worked with in London.

I hand him back the cup. "Um . . . nice to meet you, Diederik."

He throws the cup again.

I try to pay attention to Dr. Reese's commentary as she drives us through Amsterdam to their place in the Jordaan district. People stroll down the sidewalks, bikes whiz past, and the gabled rooftops of narrow buildings loom over us. Unfortunately, my brain is fuzzy from lack of sleep. I'd planned to take a sleeping pill and get a full night's rest on the plane—just as I had in the fall—but the last six months have shown me it's impossible to sleep when a baby is crying.

I've spent those months living with my mom, my older sister, Wren, and Wren's one-year-old daughter, Maddie. I'd originally thought I'd have the house to myself this year since Wren would be gone and in college, but plans changed when Maddie came into the picture. Coming here means I'm basically switching up one kid-centric house for another, but Diederik is three, so at least he won't be up all night crying like an infant.

"How are things at the lab?" I ask, because I know this topic of conversation will keep me awake.

She brightens at my question. "They're going really well. It was a bit of a transition back after my sabbatical, but we're in the flow of things now. Actually, we've just started a really exciting collaboration with another researcher looking at the psychological effects of cancer diagnoses for patients and their families."

I have to stop myself from cringing. I know all too well how the diagnosis can affect families. I don't say that to Dr. Reese, though.

I don't like talking about private stuff with people, particularly not my boss.

She turns to me, her serious researcher expression back. "Once you get settled, I'd love some help pulling together the references for a paper we're working on, and I'd like to see a rough write-up of what you're thinking for the Berlin poster. Also, I want to start training you in data abstraction immediately. Katina is over-whelmed right now, so I'm going to rely on you for that."

I nod eagerly. "Yes, absolutely."

Joy blooms in me. *This* is the real reason I agreed to spend my summer babysitting. At the end of July there's a huge international oncology conference in Berlin. Dr. Reese is giving a talk and also had several posters accepted, including one on the research I helped conduct last fall. Ever since I found out, I've been drooling over the idea of getting to attend with her and present the poster. I'm imagining it'll be somewhat similar to the state science fairs I've attended where each person creates a poster to explain their research and then describes it to the attendees. Except for the small detail that I'll be surrounded by some of the most well-respected cancer researchers in the world instead of kids who still need to be dropped off by their parents. Presenting at a conference like this is more than most students will do after four years of college, let alone before they've even moved onto campus. This kind of experience could seriously help my chances of getting into a top med school once I finish my bachelor's at Johns Hopkins.

The problem with the conference was money—I'd never make enough shelving books at the library to cover my flight and hotel in Berlin. Particularly now, since Mom has been putting every penny into helping Wren and Maddie. Babies are *expensive*. I'd given up on the possibility until Dr. Reese asked if I'd be willing to nanny in exchange for her flying me to Berlin for the conference.

She pulls into a spot in front of a brick canal house with a shiny black double door. "Here we are."

The street is charming, with big trees that extend over the canal and arched bridges that connect this side with the opposite. Bicycles are strewn everywhere—locked to posts and leaning against trees—and all the narrow houses that line the canal have decorative gables on the rooftops in various shapes. It's just like in the travel guides.

"I love the bell gable on your house."

She shakes her head. "You never miss a trick. I should've known your wide array of knowledge would extend to architecture."

I smile sweetly. Knowing everything is my specialty.

Dr. Reese gets Diederik out of the car and pops the small trunk so I can get my bags. "I hope you packed light. We're heading up to the third floor."

I follow her up a set of enclosed stairs, similar to a staircase in an apartment building, and through a door into a long bright room that serves as the living room, dining room, and kitchen. It's not a huge space, but it feels large because there are big windows at the front and back of the room.

"Welcome home," she says with a smile. "We're on the third, fourth, and fifth floors." She settles Diederik on the ground with a basket of toys—which he promptly ignores in favor of something across the room—and waves me toward the stairs. "He'll be fine for a little bit. Let me show you your room."

The stairs are so steep and narrow that my tired legs are shaking by the time we hit the next floor. I've never really been into exercising, but it looks like this house will also function as an at-home gym.

"Here we are." She opens a door at the end of the fourth-floor hall. "This is where you'll be staying."

I poke my head in. The room is tiny, and there are large wooden support beams cutting into the space, but it's functional. Except for the boxes piled on the floor and all over the bed. Just the sight of the clutter sends my heart beating faster.

"Oh." She takes a step into the room. "Berend was supposed to clear this out this morning. I'm sorry." She looks me up and down. "And I bet you were hoping to get a little nap."

I shrug as if it had only just occurred to me.

She frowns for a moment and then her eyes light up. "Actually, follow me." We walk up yet another flight of stairs that would never pass American building codes. "The attic will be a perfect place for you to sleep. There's no one to bother you and you won't hear any of the noises downstairs."

The attic has a steeply pitched roof and walls that slope down so that it's hard to walk upright unless you're in the center of the room. Mismatched carpets cover the wooden floor and bookshelves overflow with bottles, brushes, piles of fabric, and pads of paper. Any open wall space has been covered by sketches, and a center table takes up the majority of the room. Some people might (incorrectly) describe the room as charming, but really it's just a mess.

Dr. Reese picks up a paintbrush thoughtfully.

"I should've asked him to clean before he left." She holds up the brush. "This is my older son's workspace. As you can see, he's an artist. He keeps telling me artists are messy, but I don't see why the two have to go hand in hand." She gestures to the back corner, where a couch hides amid the clutter. It's definitely seen better days, but it looks soft.

"Are you sure? I don't want to take over his workspace."

"Oh, don't worry about that, he's away traveling this summer. That's why we felt comfortable inviting you to stay." She looks around the space. "Berend and I never come up here, so feel free to use the space whenever you like. It could be a little office for you since your room downstairs is small." She turns to leave. "I should get back down to Diederik. He's in a very curious phase and if I leave him for long, even with toys around, he tends to get into something he shouldn't. You'll see soon enough." She smiles and waves. "Make yourself at home."

As soon as she's gone, I lie down. I know everyone back home is going to freak out if they don't hear from me immediately, so I text my mom and my closest friend, Ellie, to say that I'm safely at the house. I can already imagine Ellie checking and rechecking her phone, anxiously awaiting updates. She's more than a little jealous that I get to spend the two months before freshman year of college in Amsterdam while she's stuck at home in DC. As she's reminded me *many* times, the least I can do is send her constant texts and pictures. I close my eyes as soon as the texts go through, even though I know a reply from Ellie will be here momentarily.

When I wake up, the shadows have shifted. I look at my phone and groan. *Noooooo*, how did I sleep for *five* hours? Now I'll be awake all night.

I've missed dinner, though Dr. Reese left a plate of food for me. At least her husband cleared the boxes out of my room so I can unpack, which immediately makes me feel better. I like having everything in its place.

I could go search for Dr. Reese and introduce myself to Berend, maybe watch some TV with them, but I'm not in a social mood. Instead, I go back upstairs to the attic with two of the latest research articles Dr. Reese has published. I might have lost the afternoon, but I'm determined not to waste any more time today.

At second glance, the attic is cozy, but there's stuff *everywhere*. It makes me itchy. If her son is going to be gone while I'm here, what would it hurt if I cleaned up the space a little?

Or a lot?

I clear out all the paint bottles and papers and knives and— dear god, how many brushes does one person need? Then I think better of it and put them back as close as I'm able to. I should take photos first, so I can remember where all of this went. I don't want him coming back in August and realizing some stranger messed with his stuff.

After I've taken photos of everything—feeling very much like a forensics expert documenting a crime scene—I start again. Peace fills me as the clutter dwindles.

The door to the stairway opens. I freeze and look up to find a teenage boy at the door.

"Wie ben jij?"

"What?"

He's very pale, though his cheeks are flushed, and he has on a blue screen-printed shirt of dueling paintbrushes. But what really stands out to me is his hair. Soft waves of bright red hair fall to his shoulders, framing his face. The same color as Diederik's hair. He has to be Dr. Reese's older son, except he isn't supposed to be here.

"Who the hell are you?" he asks with an offended expression.

"I'm the nanny."

He drops a huge bag on the ground—the kind people use for backpacking across Europe—and I cringe as the crash reverberates through the room. "And what is the nanny doing up here in my space?"

I narrow my eyes. Oh no, he doesn't get to act like *I'm* the one out of place in this scenario. Dr. Reese gave me permission to be here. He's the one who needs to explain.

"And I could ask what you're doing here. Given your hair color, backpack, and presupposed authority, I'm assuming you're Dr. Reese's son. But you aren't supposed to be back until the end of summer and I was told I could use the room in your absence."

His eyes widen and for a second I think he's going to tell me off, but he laughs instead. "I can't believe this. I struggle back to my house, exhausted and defeated after the worst trip of my life, only to find an aggravated nanny has taken over my workspace. *And* you're American."

"Very perceptive."

He laughs louder, his hair bobbing. I've never seen someone with such shiny red hair.

"Fair enough. And what's your name, American Mary Poppins? I'm—" He breaks off as his eyes scan the room. His jaw drops. "Wait! Where's all my stuff?!" He turns in a circle. "Everything's gone. Did you—" He points at the paint tube in my hand. "Are you *throwing away* my supplies?"

I can feel my cheeks heat, but I only roll back my shoulders. "Of course not. Your mother said I could use this space when I needed to get away, and I tried but I couldn't relax with this mess, so—"

"Mess! That's my art, thank you very much!" He moves through the room, inspecting the shelves. "Where is everything? It'll take me all night to put it back and I'm already so exhausted."

"Oh, stop complaining." Lord, he's whiny. Like a very tall toddler. "I have it all over here. And I took pictures so I could put everything back before I moved out."

"You . . . took pictures of my things?"

I pull them up on my phone. "See? No need to throw a tantrum. I'll put it all back if you insist. Though it is a mess."

He plucks the tube from my hand, but I think I see a hint of another smile. "Oh, okay, so you're out of your mind. Does my mother already know or will I have to break the news?"

I sniff and we start to return everything, him from memory and me with my *very* useful and not at all weird pictures to help. It turns my stomach to re-create the chaos.

"You never told me your name," he says.

"Sage."

"Like the herb."

"Like the American nanny who hates clutter."

He chuckles. "I can already sense we're going to get along well." He swings around and sticks out his hand. "Ryland Hayes."

I shake it, noting the different last names. I don't know a lot about Dr. Reese's personal life, but I believe this is her second marriage. Maybe Ryland is her son from her first one.

We work silently, and in a few minutes everything is back into its whirlwind place. If I wanted to, I could probably see why he had things laid out this way. But I don't want to. I gather up my articles and head for the stairwell.

"Where are you off to?"

"Well, now that you're unexpectedly back, I won't bother you in your space. I'll go read in my bedroom." It's too bad. I'll have to work on my bed now, and that always gives me cramps in my shoulders.

Ryland flops onto the couch dramatically. "Mom is *not* going to be happy when she finds out I'm back."

I look at him sharply. "She doesn't know?"

"No, I came up here directly. She and Berend are watching TV. I'll tell them later."

"Where were you backpacking?"

He raises an eyebrow. "The better question is 'Who was I backpacking with?'"

"Actually, in that case, the better question is 'With whom was I backpacking?'"

He groans and covers his face with a pillow. "You're not going to be here all summer, are you?"

That brings up a good point. Will Dr. Reese need me now that Ryland is back? She mentioned only inviting me here because her son was gone. If my babysitting skills (whatever those might be) aren't required anymore, then I might be headed home before I've gotten a chance to work more with Dr. Reese, let alone go to the conference.

"I guess I'll be here until your parents don't need me."

"You mean my mom and stepfather."

I smile—I was right. I love figuring things out before I'm told. I'm anxious to get back to my quiet and solitude—I've already lost so much time—but first I need to know. "Are you Diederik's usual babysitter?"

He barks out a laugh and peeks from under the pillow. "Uh, no. Mom wouldn't trust me alone with him for long."

Huh. I wasn't expecting that, but I guess my job is still secure. "Okay. Well, good night."

"Wait." His voice sounds a little strangled. "You could stay. I don't actually mind. I could use the company—I've had a hell of a day."

"No thanks." Staying means being pulled into whatever drama he's got going on, and that's a horrible idea. "I need quiet to study and I'm already getting the impression that I won't get any of that here."

He sits straight up.

"*Study?* What in the world are you studying? Diederik's eating habits? I'll let you in on a little secret—he loves bananas and bread. Have fun trying to get him to eat anything else."

"I'm not studying eating habits, I'm reading research papers."

He gives me an incredulous look.

"Nice to meet you, Ryland."

I quietly make my way back to my room and close the door before I can call any attention to myself. I don't want to have to explain to Dr. Reese that her son is home, especially when I'm still processing that fact myself. So I'm going to be living in close proximity to Ryland all summer? I hope no one freaks out when they hear about this. Well, let's be real, Ellie will absolutely freak out. She's been trying to convince me to date someone since the moment we met, and this development will only encourage her wildest daydreams about my love life. But where Ellie will see this change as something to be celebrated, I'm worried Dr. Reese may have the opposite reaction. I don't need anything jeopardizing this summer and the Berlin conference.

I take a calming breath. This doesn't have to be a big deal. The important thing is to make sure I stay as focused and dedicated as possible so she has no reason for concern. This is no different from living with boys last fall. Ryland and I will be on separate floors, doing separate things, living separate lives. I know myself. I've never allowed anyone to distract me from my work before.

I won't let Ryland be the first.

chapter 2

I don't fall asleep until almost one a.m. and then wake up again at five a.m. with the sun. I try to lie in bed but I'm too restless. I'm not good at sitting still and doing nothing. I don't even know how that works.

I glance at my phone to see that Ellie wrote me approximately ten million texts while I was sleeping. I hesitate. It's only eleven p.m. back in DC, and I'd like to get her take on Ryland . . . even though I know exactly what it'll be. Her squeal will be so loud she'll damage the hair cells in my inner ear. But I still want to hear her voice.

She picks up after half a ring.

"Sage! Omigod, I'm so glad you called! I was just telling Dev that if I didn't hear from you before I went to bed I was sending you fifty vomit GIFs when I woke up in the morning."

"I guess it's a good thing I called, then."

"Exactly. Now tell me everything," she continues. "Is everyone nice? How is the house? Did you get to explore Amsterdam yet?"

"I haven't been here for twenty-four hours."

She huffs and I can imagine her rolling her eyes. "Sage, I know you. And I already made you promise—multiple times—that you'd get out and explore. Please, please tell me you aren't going to stay locked up in that lab all summer."

"I don't know if I'll have much time in the lab. Remember, I'm going to be on kid duty."

"Oh, I haven't forgotten. That's the only thing making this palatable." She laughs. "How is he?"

I think back to the throwing incident in the airport. "He's . . . fine. Actually, I was calling because there's another boy at the house who I'm more worried about."

"Wait, what? Did she drop secret twins on you or something?"

I stand and walk to the window. The street below is quiet, but a boat glides slowly down the canal. "Not exactly. It turns out she has another son. Ryland."

There's a moment of silence and I know Ellie is processing this information. Her voice is practically vibrating with excitement when she whispers, "And how old is this newly discovered son?"

Here it comes.

"I don't know exactly, but if I had to guess, I'd say . . . eighteen."

Her shriek is even louder than I'd imagined and I jerk the phone from my ear.

"Sage, are you *kidding* me? You already get to live in freaking Amsterdam and now you're spending the summer with a cute Dutch boy? Please tell me he's cute. Never mind, I already know he is. He has to be."

"I didn't notice."

She snorts. "Of course you didn't. Are you okay with this? It's weird that Dr. Reese didn't tell you about him."

"He wasn't supposed to be home." I shake my head. "But I'm fine with it. It doesn't matter to me if there's an extra person in the house, but I'm wondering how everyone else is going to act. What if Dr. Reese doesn't like the idea of me living in the house with Ryland? I don't want to come home yet."

"No, you can't! Just act cool like you always do. Dr. Reese knows how responsible you are. That's why she flew you all the way from America to watch her son. So do your job and—you know—wait to flirt until she goes to sleep."

We both laugh at that like it's the funniest joke we've ever heard. Because it is. I do *not* flirt.

"I should take a shower," I say. "But tell Dev and everyone I said hi."

"Of course. And you better—"

"I know, I know. Send constant updates and pictures."

"And what *kind* of pictures?"

I shake my head. "Pictures of Ryland?"

"There's that genius friend I know and love."

I wait until a respectable seven a.m. before I go down to the kitchen. Berend is sitting at the table in a suit. He's drinking a cup of coffee and looking at his phone.

"Morning," I say quietly.

He fumbles his coffee and some of it spills on the table. None of it gets on his suit, luckily. I grab a dish towel and hand it to him.

"Oh, good morning! You must be Sage. I'm so glad to have you

17

here." He stands to shake my hand, then gestures at the wet table. "Sorry, I need to get used to having someone new at the house. It was just the three of us with Ryland gone, but now we're back to four again." He nods. "That's a good number, though. A nice round number."

I look at him for a moment and then nod and turn to the coffee maker. I'm going to let Ryland be their discovery to make.

"Your flight was okay? And you slept well?" he asks.

"Pretty well, though I'm still dealing with some jet lag. Thank you for having me. My room is very charming."

"I'm glad to hear that." He looks around the apartment with fondness. "Actually, my family has lived here for generations. Your room was my sister's growing up, so I'm pleased it has a good purpose again."

I hear Dr. Reese and Diederik's little voice from the other side of the stairway door. I plaster a smile on my face and wave as they walk in.

"Good morning, Dr. Reese. Good morning, Diederik." I try for an extra happy kid-centric voice.

He looks up at me with his huge eyes and then totters past me and into the living room.

"Sage, good morning. I can't tell you how much better I feel knowing that Diederik is with somebody I trust."

I think for a second about Ryland's comment that his mother doesn't trust him to watch his little brother. It's odd that she would trust me more than him, but then I didn't just return unannounced from some strange trip.

"I'm so happy to be here." I pour a second cup of coffee and pass it to her.

"Ah, thank you. Berend and I both have pretty busy days, so I think we're going to have to throw you into the deep end. I know you can handle it, but please call if you have questions. I'll try to get home earlier than usual today."

The deep end? Shouldn't we have at least one onboarding day? But I don't want her to see my nerves, so I only ask, "What does Diederik like to eat for breakfast?"

She sighs. "Well, Diederik is . . . particular about food. It could be a bit of a problem, but usually toast works, or bananas."

"Toast and bananas it is," I reply, thinking of Ryland's advice last night.

I start to work on breakfast and Berend stands up. "All right. Long day ahead for me." He leans in and kisses Dr. Reese with more gusto than I'm expecting. I turn and stare down at the banana. It's oddly off-putting to watch two grown adults kiss. Dad used to kiss Mom like that. He was constantly pulling her in for hugs and kisses and whispering who knows what to her. Sometimes I think he did it just because he knew how it made Wren and me squirm, and he loved to tease us. A small ache thrums in me and I push it away with a frown. What a stupid thing to be thinking about on a morning like this.

"I should go too," Dr. Reese says. They both give Diederik a hug and kiss.

"Mama!"

She kisses him on the nose. "I'll be home soon," she says, then gives him one more kiss and heads out with Berend. I half expect Diederik to break down in tears, but luckily he only stares at the door for a few moments before walking over to the toys.

I guess this means I'm officially alone with Diederik. Well, except for Ryland, wherever he might be. I swallow down a bubble of nerves—I hope this babysitting goes well.

A few minutes later I've figured out where they keep the butter and how their toaster works. It's not exactly a five-star breakfast, but it looks edible. "Diederik!" I call cheerfully across the room. "Time to eat now."

He looks up. "Nee."

I don't need to speak much Dutch to know what he's saying. Dr. Reese wasn't concerned that I don't speak Dutch, but now I'm wondering how big of a deal this is going to be. Most children in the Netherlands grow up learning multiple languages, including English, and she told me they're particularly motivated for him to learn since she's British. But still, how is this going to work? What if he says something important to me in Dutch and I can't understand him? I have a small English-to-Dutch translation book I bought online, but that's mostly stuff like *How much does this cost?* and *Where's the restroom?* I think I'm going to need something heftier than that.

"I made your favorites. Toast and banana." I shake the banana at him like it's a treat and he's a dog. It's not my finest moment.

He gives me a scrutinizing look and then leaves his toy train and comes over to the table. He takes exactly two bites of toast and three bites of banana before standing up. I barely have a chance to drink my coffee.

"No, you need to eat more than that."

"Nee! Niet meer."

"But you're going to be hungry."

He walks back in the living room and I look between the food and the toys, conflicted. Then I shrug and follow him. I have a strong feeling I'm going to have to pick my battles.

I sit down on the ground and point to his toy train. It's one of those old ones that make a click-clack sound when you roll them on the ground. "Who is this?"

"Geel." He takes the train and chugs it back and forth before pointing to the bright yellow roof. "Geel." He hands me another train. "Tjoeke tjoeke tuut tuut!"

I blink in surprise before realizing he must be mimicking a train's *choo-choo* sound. Then I grab my dictionary and do a quick search—yep, *geel* is "yellow" in Dutch. I smile at his highly creative name and follow him, chugging my train up over sofas, onto the carpet, and over the windowsills. It's mind-numbingly boring, but it's doable. Maybe I'll just spend the summer taking his lead. I can play what he wants to play and keep him happy and then I'll have nights to do work for Dr. Reese.

And, most importantly, I'll get to go to the conference.

Unfortunately, within fifteen minutes he's bored of that. I get exactly two more bites of banana into him, but only by following him around the room and giving him bits when he isn't otherwise entertained.

I point to another basket of toys that they keep at the bottom of the bookshelves. This one is full of pretend food. "What about this?" I take out the top toy, which is a fabric strawberry.

"Look, Diederik, a strawberry!"

His eyes shine. "Aardbei!"

"Strawberry?" I ask, and hold it out.

"Strawberry," he repeats. And then takes it and throws it all the way into the kitchen. He should be a freaking baseball player when he gets older. Or maybe an Olympic shot-putter.

"No throwing." I shake my head and stand up to get it. As soon as my back is turned, there's a clatter. I swing around to see the big basket overturned, stuffed foods and miniature plates and cups everywhere. He's ecstatic.

"No, no! Let's not make a mess."

He picks up another toy and giggles delightedly. "Vis!" A stuffed fish goes flying. "Koekje!"

"Not the cookie!"

"Cookie!" He laughs maniacally and throws it over my head.

Somehow we make it through the morning, but I don't get a second of rest. If Diederik isn't throwing things, then he's trying to climb up the bookshelves, or opening the kitchen cabinets despite the childproof locks, or scrambling up the kitchen table and trying to drink my cold cup of coffee. I get him to eat a quarter of a sandwich for lunch, but then he accidentally knocks his milk to the ground and I have to clean up the mess. I don't have the energy to make myself anything, so I just eat the rest of his sandwich before he can squish it in his fingers.

By one p.m., I can't take it anymore. It's time to employ everyone's favorite babysitter: screen time. Dr. Reese left out an iPad for him, but I got the impression I should only use it as a last resort. Well, it's day one, this whole floor is trashed, and I'm throwing in the towel.

I drop onto the couch next to Diederik, who is perfectly content and quiet now. He's surprisingly adept at the rocket ship game I pulled up for him.

The door to the upstairs opens and Ryland strolls in. His hair is mussed from sleep and he's still wearing the same T-shirt from last night. He sits down on the couch and points at the iPad.

"Oh good, a babysitter after my own heart. And I thought you might be an overachiever."

I tamp down my annoyance that he's caught me using screen time to placate Diederik. "Your mother left it especially for him. Everything in moderation."

He chuckles and rolls his eyes. "I can already see why she chose you. You two are just the same. You're like the daughter she never had."

I shrug, unsure how to reply to that. He stands and walks into the kitchen.

"Exhausting morning, then?" he asks over his shoulder.

"We're just getting used to each other."

His phone, which he left on the coffee table, vibrates with a text from someone named Evi. Maybe that's the *someone* he went on that trip with. I close my eyes with exhaustion. I wish Diederik still took naps, but unfortunately Dr. Reese told me those ended when he was two. The phone vibrates again. I peek at it, my love for knowing everything winning out over my desire not to get sucked into conversation with him. This text is from someone named Mila, followed quickly by another from Evi and then a call from Lillie. I cough out a laugh.

"Do you have any popular girl bands in the Netherlands? Because if so, I think they're all trying to contact you at once."

He closes the refrigerator door and walks back over. "What? Oh. Yeah, they're all realizing I'm back home."

"You have a lot of friends."

"I'm very popular." He winks and pops open a blue bottle of water labeled *Spa Reine*. "Do you have plans when you're done with this one?" He ruffles Diederik's hair, who completely ignores him. "A group of us are getting together tonight for dinner. You could come."

"No thanks." Ellie's going to kill me for turning down the offer to get out into Amsterdam and make friends, but that's not why I'm here. I still have a reference section to compile, a poster to write, and a stack of articles from Dr. Reese that I want to read. Maybe there'll be time once I'm more settled, but for now I need to keep my head down.

"You can't stay cooped up in here forever."

I can't help but notice his wording—*cooped up*. Is that an internationally popular phrase? I know better than to ask questions that will lead to more conversation, but I'm too curious so I plunge forward.

"Did you grow up here? Because your accent would suggest yes, but sometimes . . ." I pause. "Some of your wording makes you sound American."

His mouth falls open. "You *are* perceptive. Yes—to both.

My mom met Dad when she lived in America for school. He's a researcher too. He's still there, so I usually spend my summers in Philadelphia with him, his second wife, and my half sister. Anyway, I should go." He waves at Diederik. "Have fun."

"Just make sure you build in some family bonding time soon. I'm sure your mom will have lots of questions when she realizes you're back."

"Wait, you didn't tell them? I thought you'd go to them directly." He groans. "Actually I was counting on it so I wouldn't have to do it myself. They bought my Eurostar ticket."

"I'll leave that fun treat for you."

"You're no use at all."

"Not to you. You're not paying me."

He raises an eyebrow. "And what use might you be if I were willing to pay?"

My cheeks heat at his possible meaning. "You wouldn't have enough money if you owned Amazon."

He bursts out laughing, which makes Diederik jump in surprise. Ryland stands. "We definitely need to hang out more."

I suppress a sigh. That's the opposite of what I was hoping for.

chapter

3

I wake up the next morning set on making my day with Diederik a good one. Yesterday wasn't the best, but I should have expected that. He's still getting to know me, and I should have been much more prepared. I pull out a notebook, and soon I have a beautiful color-coded schedule for the entire day. We'll start with trains, then move to stacking blocks and dress-up. We can have story time and maybe I can even teach him some of the songs that Wren is always singing to Maddie. Plus, they have tons of art supplies, so—if I'm really on top of it—maybe I can put together a little art project for Dr. Reese and Berend this evening. Parents love their kids' art.

Diederik has little interest in breakfast, but otherwise the first half of the day goes better. I half expect Ryland to stroll into the kitchen around lunchtime, but there's no sign of him today. If I weren't uncompromisingly logical then I'd think he was a ghost only I could see.

After lunch, which Diederik spends pouring water back and forth from his glass to a used coffee mug, I stand to clear the table.

Diederik walks to the door. "Buiten, Sage! Outside."

"Oh, um . . . that's not on the schedule today. We'll go tomorrow. Why don't we color right now?"

"I want outside!"

I lean back in shock. That's the most English he's spoken to me yet. And his lip is quivering in an ominous way. I cringe and walk over to the window. I guess I can't keep him inside forever. And if I don't explore Amsterdam soon, Ellie's going to send me those vomit GIFs she was threatening.

"Okay." I kneel down and smile, hoping to head off any tears. "We'll go outside for a bit."

"Outside!"

He wraps his chubby arms around my neck and squeezes. I'm taken aback and almost pull away in surprise before giving him a little squeeze back. He's pretty adorable . . . when he's not chucking stuff all over the house.

He runs over to the door and I laugh. "Hold on."

It's a good thing they installed a lock that's too high for him to reach, because otherwise there would be no keeping him inside. I open the big storage closet on this floor and hesitate before pulling out the stroller Dr. Reese had at the airport. I get the feeling it doesn't get a ton of use. Earlier, she showed me where the family keeps their bicycles outside, including one that has an attachment so a child can ride along, and she was so enthusiastic that I couldn't say no to riding it. Secretly, though, I knew there was no way in hell I was getting on that bicycle. I haven't ridden one since I was ten and I do *not* feel comfortable doing that in a city of bicyclists with a child riding with me.

Diederik practically runs down the stairs when I finally open the door. At least it's a beautiful day out. Sunny with blue skies, but cooler than a usual June day in DC. We're in a residential area of Amsterdam, so it's quiet, but there are more people on the street than the last time I was out. I take Diederik's hand and bring him toward the stroller.

"Okay, time to get in. We're going on a walk."

"Nee. I walk."

I shake my head vehemently. "No, no, you have to be in the stroller. Otherwise you could get lost." All I need is for him to go shooting off down the road and fall in a canal or something.

Unsurprisingly, he doesn't see it my way. After several more minutes of fussing, I eventually get him strapped in. He yowls in anger, but I decide to start walking and hope he'll calm down. I don't have a direction in sight, so I just stride down the narrow brick road.

The city is enchanting. Mismatched gabled houses line the canals and people gather at outdoor restaurants to chat and watch the boats go by. I find myself crisscrossing over the arched bridges just so we can walk over the canals. Bicyclists zoom past us silently. Their bikes are laden with all sorts of things—grocery bags, briefcases, and, yes, plenty of children. The land may be very flat here, but I still don't have the strength to pull Diederik across the city.

Diederik is pretty content for the first twenty minutes, but then he starts to twist in his seat.

"I walk now," he calls.

"No. You can't do that."

The stroller suddenly jams into something and my chest slams against it.

"Ahh!" I swallow down my shock and come around to the front to investigate. The stroller didn't catch on the sidewalk. Diederik has somehow stretched out so that his feet are planted on the ground.

"Diederik!" I exclaim. "Don't put your feet down like that. I could have hurt you!"

He says something I don't understand and I shake my head.

"No. Keep your feet up." I move his feet back in place.

He says the same thing again and touches his stomach.

I squint at him, trying to decipher his words. "Are you . . . hungry?"

He nods and rubs his stomach.

I roll my eyes. "Well, of course you're hungry. You didn't eat anything today. All right, let's go back home and I'll get you a snack."

I start to turn the stroller around and he shrieks, making me jump.

"Hungry! Out!" He screams so loudly that several people at a nearby café turn and stare at me with judgmental eyes.

I smile nervously and bend down. "No, no, everything's okay, we're going home right now."

I bustle off, hoping I can get home quickly. I shouldn't have gone so far the first time. He cries louder and I cringe. "Keep your feet up!" I call to him.

Why didn't I bring any food with me? Everyone knows the

stereotype of moms with their huge purses filled with snacks and toys. My sister is living the stereotype right now. I kick myself, but there's nothing to be done about it. Best to just hurry home as fast as possible.

Diederik grows louder the farther we go. His screams burrow themselves into my head in a primal, painful way.

"Mama! *Mama!*"

I lean over the front of the stroller as I jog. His face is bright red, tears streaking down his cheeks. Oh my god, this is bad. I just need to get him home and put something in his stomach and sit him in front of the TV. Then he'll calm down and everything will be fine before Dr. Reese gets home.

I sprint down the last block, ignoring the passing glances and my own heavy breathing. *Get home, get home* is all that runs through my head. I pull to a stop in front of the house only to find Ryland outside talking to a girl. I have to suck in a few breaths before I can speak. His flirty expression drops as soon as he sees us.

"What happened?" He stares at his brother in horror. "Didn't my mom tell you she frowns on torturing Diederik? It's one of her top rules."

I fumble for my key. I don't have time for his jokes. "He's hungry."

I get the key out of my pocket, but drop it on the ground. It's impossible to think with all this screaming. It's like a knife through my brain. Ryland pulls out his own key and unlocks the door.

"Evi, ik spreek je later. Oké?" he says.

The girl's face falls and she looks at me with a jealous expression.

Seriously? As if I have time for shade from this random girl when Diederik is bucking like a demented animal and about to lunge for my jugular. I ignore her and manage to unclip him from the stroller without losing an eye. Ryland swoops in to pick him up and trots up the stairs. I fumble to collapse the stroller and reluctantly follow. I thought there'd be less crying with a toddler compared to a baby, but clearly I was mistaken.

However, when the stroller and I get up to the third floor, sweat dripping down my forehead, the apartment is blissfully quiet. Diederik is already plopped on the couch in front of the TV, watching a cartoon bunny I don't recognize.

Ryland rummages around in the kitchen. "I assume you don't approve of TV, but it's best to just let him watch Miffy. You won't get any peace otherwise." He pulls a sleeve of cookies from the pantry and sits down next to Diederik, handing him one.

I open my mouth to argue—I know Dr. Reese would want him to have a healthier snack—but Ryland lifts an eyebrow, as if to say, *Really?*

Fair point. I drop down on the couch next to them. "I thought you didn't babysit," I say after a moment.

He points at the TV. "This isn't actually babysitting. And you looked like you could use some help."

I frown, but I don't argue since he's 100 percent correct. I hate that he found me in such a wild state. I'm never like this.

"I have to say, you don't really strike me as much of a babysitter. When you said you were from America, I assumed you were some sort of nannying goddess, but . . ." He chuckles. "Well, it seems I was mistaken. Why did my mom fly you over here?"

"We worked together last fall in England." I tuck one of my legs under the other and wipe my brow. "I volunteered in her lab and helped with some of the research that she'll be presenting at a conference in Berlin. She needed a babysitter and I couldn't afford the flight to attend the conference on my own, so . . ." I shrug.

"So you're using my baby brother to get a free trip to Germany?"

My eyes widen, unsure if he might be serious this time, but of course he grins at me.

"Well played," he says. "I'd do the same."

I snort. "I was wondering . . ." I hesitate. I have to admit I'm curious about Ryland, but I don't want to give him the impression that I'm falling for his charming smiles and shiny hair like all the other girls in his phone. Luckily, I've developed a thick mental wall that keeps boys out so I can focus on my work . . . even when their hair is falling into their eyes in a way they *must* know is alluring.

"You said your mom wouldn't trust you to watch Diederik. Why is that?"

"Oh, don't get me wrong. I've watched him plenty of times when my mom and Berend were in a crunch. But she doesn't exactly think of me as responsible. It's probably something about the art."

"Or maybe secretly coming back from trips and hiding from her?"

He waves away my words. "I'll tell them tonight. I'm just . . ." He shakes his head. "I can get into my own head. When I'm thinking of a new design or working out some detail, I tend to kind of . . . forget everything else around me. And that's not so good when you have a three-year-old terror living with you."

I nod, surprised that I know exactly what he's talking about. There will be times when I'm working and it's like the whole world falls away. I don't talk to people or pay attention to conversations. I'm totally immersed in my task. Those are my favorite parts of the day.

"Well, thanks for getting him settled."

We both glance at Diederik, who is giggling at the show with cookie crumbs all over his front. We share a look and laugh.

"It gave me a good excuse to get away from Evi. I really need to get back to work. I have so much I want to do with my block printing and mural painting, but people always want to hang out and it's hard to say no."

"No, it's not. You just say no. See, like I did there."

"Oh yeah? Well, if it's that easy, then you can say no to Evi the next time she won't stop calling."

I think of the girl on the sidewalk. I didn't have time to get much of an impression, but the arch of her perfectly manicured eyebrows told me she isn't used to people telling her no.

His phone buzzes with a series of texts and I laugh. "You better get that. You don't want to miss Evi."

chapter

4

I'm so grateful when dinner with Berend and Dr. Reese is over that evening and I can finally retreat to my room. I thought Ryland might make his presence known at dinner, but no. I didn't eat much—I was worried about whether I should go ahead and say something. I don't like keeping information from Dr. Reese, but it's also not my place to get involved in their family dynamics. I don't want to start this summer by rocking the boat. Plus, I'm utterly exhausted. All I want to do is curl under my blankets—I have the fluffiest down comforter on my bed—and sleep away the rest of the night. But I know I need to work while I have the chance.

I settle into the bed, trying to get the pillows just right, and lay all my articles and highlighters around me for easy access. I'm missing the attic and all that extra space right now, but this will do.

I get into a groove, my mind settling into the esoteric terminology in the articles. Ellie would absolutely kill me if she knew I was sitting on a bed reading when I could be exploring the city. But no amount of sightseeing is as important as my future, and I think Dr. Reese might be the key to even more amazing things to come. She's already insinuated that if things go well this summer then I can keep working with her remotely during undergrad. We'll be on different continents, but there's a lot I can still help with, like entering data and running simple analyses. Maybe, if I *really* impress her, she'll even let me write some portion of a future article. I don't care if there are ten authors on the paper and I'm listed dead last; having my name on a paper with *the* Dr. Reese would be a dream come true. Her work is so influential, and it's exciting to think that something I do might have an impact on cancer treatments in the future.

I pick up one of the articles Dr. Reese gave me about the psychological and social outcomes from genetic counseling in oncology. It's not my favorite topic. I'd rather be in the lab developing an actual cure, but they don't exactly let high school grads help with that. I'm lucky to be getting any research experience at all.

I skim the introduction of the paper where the authors review the substantial evidence that social support significantly mitigates the negative psychological effects of a cancer diagnosis. I hope that was true for Dad. I think it was—he was so cheerful, all the way from that first horrible doctor's appointment, through the rounds of chemo and radiation, until the very end. Honestly, he was the most positive of us all, but I'd like to think having us around him helped.

Actually, I'd like to think of anything in the entire world except Dad.

A loud yell comes from downstairs and I jump, causing all my highlighters to fall on the ground. *Dammit.* Trying to work on this bed is so annoying. I stand to pick them up and then walk to the door. A deeper voice bellows. The words are muffled, but intuition tells me that Dr. Reese and Berend have finally discovered Ryland is home. I laugh a little despite myself. The voices become rushed and loud—not exactly angry, but not happy either. I'm *definitely* staying in my room tonight.

I fall back into the article, rereading a section that cites a new prescreening questionnaire for genetic counseling. I make a note to look up that original article, as well as figure out how they operationalized anxiety. I find it's best if I write down everything as I go. The material is too dense for me to remember if I don't keep a constant stream of notes.

Someone knocks on the door and I sigh and get up. What now?

I find Dr. Reese frowning in the doorway. "Sage, I need to talk to you about something. Do you mind if I interrupt?"

"Of course not," I say, flipping to the polite professor voice I always use with her. I step back to let her in. "What's going on?" I ask innocently.

"Well . . ." She sighs. "There's been an unexpected change. Do you remember I mentioned my son before? The one who was on the trip for the summer?"

I nod.

"He's actually back home. I guess the trip didn't—er—work out and he's back much sooner than I expected." She beckons someone from the hallway. "Ryland, come here."

"Yes?"

"Sage, I want you to meet Ryland." He appears, his eyes way too innocent right now.

"Ryland, this is Sage Cunningham. Berend and I hired her for the summer to help take care of Diederik since things fell through with Lotte. Of course, I didn't realize you would be home when I made that choice." Her eyes are a little sharp, and Ryland rubs his toe into the carpet. "Sage only got here a few days ago and she was planning to stay until the end of July, when I have that conference in Berlin."

I blink and try to keep my face serene. I *was* planning to stay? As in past tense and no longer relevant? Is Dr. Reese coming here to tell me that my services are no longer needed? I thought Ryland said he wasn't a babysitter. I'm suddenly nervous that I didn't tell Dr. Reese immediately that Ryland was back. I didn't want to get involved with it, but maybe that'll look like I'm an accomplice? I really don't need her upset with me.

I plaster a smile on my face and give Ryland a little wave. "Hi, Ryland, it's so nice to meet you. I hope you had a pleasant trip while you were abroad."

He schools his features. His smile is much too polite. "Sage, right? Good to meet you as well. And how are you enjoying our little Diederik?"

"Oh, he's wonderful. He's at such a fun age."

"The best age, definitely. So full of energy."

Dr. Reese glances between us, but she doesn't seem to suspect anything.

"Yes, well, I need to talk to Sage. Ryland, why don't you go clean up that attic, since you'll be spending much more time there."

I give him a small triumphant look before he turns away. I guess I'm not the only one who thinks he needs to clean up.

Dr. Reese takes a step into my bedroom and closes the door behind her. She sits on my bed and picks up one of my articles. "Oh, you're reading the Keller article. What do you think?"

"I'm not finished yet, but it's really intriguing so far. Though I was confused about their operationalization of anxiety."

Her eyes light up. "So was I! We were talking about that at a lab meeting last week." She cocks her head and looks at me fondly. "You are so exceptional, Sage. So bright for your age. I can see such great things for you, and that's one of the reasons I wanted you to come here. I really would love to continue mentoring you this summer." She twiddles her thumbs—a telltale nervous gesture.

My stomach twists and I sit down next to her. It feels like a big *but* is coming next, and I don't want to hear it.

"Sage, it was one thing for me to ask you to live here and babysit when it was only going to be you and Diederik all day, but it's a very different thing for you to stay now that Ryland is here. Not that he's a bad kid or anything. He's great. He always makes me laugh when I come home from a hard day, and he's so talented. My brain doesn't work like his at all." She shakes her head. "But nonetheless, there is now an eighteen-year-old boy living in the house. I would never ask you to do anything that makes you feel uncomfortable."

I don't need to hear more.

"I'm not uncomfortable, Dr. Reese. I honestly don't think it'll be a problem. I'll be with Diederik every day and I'm sure Ryland will have his own plans. In the evenings—I think you already know me well enough to know that I'll be working." I gesture to the bed. "I don't think this changes anything." I try to put all my persuasive and logical power into my words.

She purses her lips. "Well, it's certainly true that Ryland has never shown much interest in being with Diederik, so I doubt you'll see him. But he'll still be living here."

"That's fine. I have this room and he has his own. It's not like you're asking us to sleep in the same room or anything."

She coughs out a laugh. "I would certainly think not. So . . . you're sure you don't mind? And it won't bother your mother?"

I pause, thinking about it. Mom is a planner like me, so she won't be thrilled about this change to the agreed-upon arrangement, but she's too caught up with Wren and Maddie to get upset.

"I'm sure," I reply.

She blows out a breath. "It's a huge relief to hear you say that. I don't know how we'd manage with Diederik otherwise." She stands. "Just one thing . . . I'm sure I don't need to say this, but to be clear, there can be nothing"—she hesitates—"*romantic* between you and Ryland. You're our employee while you're here, and I'm also using grant money to fund your flights and attendance at the conference. I wouldn't want anyone to think I'm misusing my funds by giving out flights or research opportunities to family friends. Now, of course, you can still be friendly—actually, I hope seeing your work ethic will finally inspire Ryland to reach his potential—but your relationship needs to stay absolutely platonic."

I reel back in shock. "Of course. Believe me, that's the absolute *last* thing on my mind right now. I came here to work and that's what I intend to do."

"Good. I already knew that, but I still had to say it. You're such a diligent student." She pats my arm. "Speaking of which, let's plan to spend tomorrow evening training you on the data abstraction I mentioned earlier. It's very detail-oriented and a little tedious, but I know I can trust you with it."

I nod enthusiastically. If I'm being honest, there's a small part of me that flares with nerves at her words. I've already been given three other projects for this summer, and I had no idea how mentally (and physically) exhausting it would be to babysit all day. I thought it would be fairly mindless, but my brain isn't exactly chugging on all cylinders right now. There's no way I'm saying no to Dr. Reese, though. I'll just have to figure something out.

"All right," she says, "I'll let you get back to it. Thanks for your understanding about Ryland."

"No problem. Good night, Dr. Reese."

I heave a deep breath and settle back onto the bed when she's gone. Wow, that was close.

It takes me thirty minutes to get refocused, and as soon as I do, there's another knock on my door. *Crap*, please tell me she hasn't changed her mind. I jump up, ready to defend my place here again.

"Dr. Reese, it really won't be a problem," I say as I open the door.

Ryland stands there instead, looking annoyingly amused. "What won't be a problem?"

I roll my eyes at him. "You."

"Are you sure about that?" He leans against the doorway. "In my mother's eyes I'm almost always a problem."

"She's worried about me staying at the house now that you're living here."

His mouth drops open. "Really? Does she think I'm some sort of sexual predator?"

"No. But she's concerned I'll be uncomfortable with you here."

He raises an eyebrow flirtatiously. "And are you uncomfortable?"

I move to close the door.

He puts up a hand to stop me, laughing now. I want to be more annoyed, but his whole manner is so carefree that it's hard to work up much emotion. He would get along with everyone back home so well—particularly Ellie. I'm not surprised that he's so popular.

"I'm *not* losing my place at this conference because of you."

He holds both hands up in surrender. "I'm not asking you to. I only wanted to make sure everything was okay between you and my mom."

"Yes, it's fine."

"Are you liking your room? Getting a lot done?" He peeks inside.

"I'd get a lot more done without all these interruptions. And aren't you supposed to be working on your art?"

"Actually, speaking of that, I wanted to give you a formal invitation to study up in the attic whenever you want. I was maybe a little . . . short that first night, but I really don't mind."

"Thanks, but like I said, I need quiet and no interruptions. And you're basically a walking interruption."

I expect him to be irritated, but instead his eyes flash with delight. He points at me. "Ooh, I like that. I'm going to use that." He tilts his head against the doorframe. "You really don't need to worry about me. I'm fine with quiet after what happened this afternoon. I need all the quiet I can get."

He clearly wants me to ask what happened—or react in any way—so he can tell me all about his drama, but I have zero interest. Actually, it's more like a palpable lack of interest.

"Good night, Ryland."

I close the door more firmly this time, but not before I see his mouth twist in displeasure. He's not used to having girls close the door on him. But he's going to get used to it with me.

chapter

5

It's not a good day with Diederik.

Actually, I've been here for a week now and none of the days have been particularly good. And it's not for lack of trying. I had everything perfectly planned out for today. We were going to have a rainbow-themed day—three different rainbow crafts, rainbow-colored food, and a science experiment showing how to "grow your own rainbow" using markers, paper towels, and water. I've been staying up extra late every night, trying to pull together ideas from the internet and laying them out into a schedule, in the hopes that my planning will make the days go smoothly.

It has not.

As it turns out, Diederik doesn't like rainbows. He only ate the strawberries out of the rainbow fruit plate I made for lunch, smeared all the paints together when we were painting our spring rainbow scene, and spilled the water for the experiment all over the table.

By the time everyone is back home for the evening, I'm so exhausted I can't think. Between eight hours of Diederik a day and trying to churn out this data abstraction task for Dr. Reese in the evenings, I'm barely holding it together. I slump into a chair at the dining room table and lay my head down. All the work that still needs to get done tonight presses heavily against my chest.

I know I can't complain. *I'm* the one who desperately wanted to sign up for more work the summer before college. I'm the one who's agreed to every task Dr. Reese mentioned. I've always been able to juggle it all. But my kinesthetic sense must be fading, because now I'm dropping balls all over the place.

"Dinner's here!" Berend calls as he walks in holding two large bags. "Thought we'd go French—crepes and quiche from Chez Lorraine tonight!"

That does sound good. I sit up and put a smile on my face before anyone notices how I'm feeling.

Dr. Reese comes over from where she was playing with Diederik, kisses Berend on the cheek, and starts pulling plates and cups from the cupboard. A second later, Ryland walks in like he's a bloodhound smelling a rabbit. I'm surprised to see him. He's mostly been MIA around here, only eating dinner one other time with the family in the last week.

I stand to help set the table, careful to be pleasantly neutral around him. I don't want to give anyone the impression that I'm unhappy—or overly happy—with him being here.

"How was your day, Ryland?" Dr. Reese asks as we all sit down and she cuts up pieces of a cheese crepe for Diederik. She misses the puking face he pulls.

"Good. Very productive."

She levels a glance at him. "I hope your productivity has included finding some employment."

"Don't worry about that. Espen always wants my prints and Dan needs me more than ever."

"But those things aren't steady work. Are you sure this isn't the right time to find something more permanent? Isn't your friend Tom able to sculpt while still working at the bank?"

"I don't want a job like that. I make enough money to get by as it is."

Dr. Reese shoots him a skeptical look and sighs. Berend focuses on his food. It hadn't occurred to me to wonder what kind of job Ryland might have or what he's planning to do in the future. He doesn't strike me as the kind of guy who wants to go to college, but it's also hard to imagine him not going given Dr. Reese's focus on education. I almost want to ask him . . . but that just opens me up to more conversations I don't need.

"Still working on your murals too?" asks Berend. He has some food stuck to his mustache, but hasn't noticed.

Ryland glances at it, then at me for just a second, and I smile into my spinach quiche. "Yes. Now that I'm home I'll be able to focus more on it."

"Good, I'm glad to hear it."

"Dear," Dr. Reese whispers, and subtly wipes her upper lip. Berend smiles and does the same.

I glance over at a large mural that covers the kitchen wall. It's similar to a traditional still life filled with vases of flowers, fruit, wine, and cheeses, except this one has modern items like Heineken beer and stroopwafels. It's really well done. I figured they'd hired a professional.

I turn back to the group. "Wait, did you paint that?" I ask Ryland.

"He did it last year," Berend says. "I wasn't sure about it, but I'm glad he convinced me. It freshens up the space."

"Thanks, Berend." Ryland takes a last bite and pushes away from the table. "I'm headed out now."

Diederik farts just then and starts laughing hysterically. Ryland and Berend both chuckle while Dr. Reese and I shake our heads.

"Say *excuse me*, Diederik," Dr. Reese says. "And eat those three pieces." He pushes a crepe square off his plate as soon as she returns her gaze to Ryland. "You're off again? But you just said you're focusing on your work more."

"I am, but now that I'm home for the summer everybody wants to see me." He looks over at me. "Do you have any interest in coming, Sage? I could show you around Amsterdam a little bit."

The others turn to me, except for Diederik, who is covertly pushing the rest of his food onto the floor. He's smart, I'll give him that.

"No thanks, but I appreciate the offer."

Dr. Reese looks relieved.

"Another big night planned, then?" Ryland asks with a smirk.

"Only the biggest nights for me."

After dinner I help clean up, and then I'm officially off duty. I head back to my room to call Mom and catch her up on the latest news. Instead, Wren picks up.

"Oh, hey. Where's Mom?"

"She's taking a shower. I saw your name pop up on her phone so I figured I should pick up. She'll be annoyed if neither of us talk to you when you call."

"Okay." I hesitate. I'm thrown off that Wren is on the phone even though I know it's silly. She's my big sister and we've lived together our entire lives, but it's been a while since we were close enough to have a real conversation. When we were young, it was different. We'd spend hours coloring and putting on plays. We even started our own jewelry business in junior high. We had an online shop and everything. But now . . . I don't know what to say to her.

"How's Maddie?" I ask. My niece is the only subject to bring up.

"She's good." Her voice brightens slightly, but she sounds tired. "She's cruising like crazy now. She'll be walking soon."

"Cool." I look up at the ceiling, thinking of something else to say. "Anything else going on?"

"Nope. Being a mom is pretty much taking up my whole life right now. Is everything going well over there? Are you finally coming around to little kids?"

"I think it's having the opposite effect, actually." I fill her in on some of our recent escapades. "But he is really cute. I'll figure it out."

"It's so weird thinking of you spending entire days with a toddler. Have you ever watched Maddie for more than a few minutes when I had to go to the bathroom?"

I grit my teeth. "Of course I have. Though mostly I was too busy finishing high school."

"I still can't believe you're going to be over there for the whole summer. And once you get back, how long will you have until you pack up and move to campus? A week? Ten days? You're missing so much with Maddie, all so you can go babysit some stranger's kid."

The bitterness in her voice can't be ignored. I really don't want to get into this right now, not when I'm already spent and have so much I still need to do tonight. I just spent the last six months living with her. Am I not allowed to have my own life?

"You know I'm not here because of the babysitting, Wren. And Dr. Reese isn't exactly a stranger."

"You're going to miss her first steps. Just like you missed tons of firsts in the fall when you were in England."

I roll my eyes and start pacing the few open steps of my room. "I thought you'd be proud of me. Do you know how rare it is for a high school student to be involved in a research lab like this? It's a big deal."

"A bigger deal than having a niece, obviously." Her words are so quiet I can barely hear them.

I bite back a sigh. We've been having this same fight ever since Maddie was born last June. Wren has it in her mind that I've abandoned her or something, but that's not true. I was in the hospital room when she gave birth. I took middle-of-the-night shifts last summer when Maddie wouldn't stop crying and Wren needed to sleep. And that's not to mention the entire year before, when Wren was struggling with her pregnancy and finishing her senior year of high school. Who kept her homework organized, made sure she finished every assignment, and checked in with her teachers? Who froze out her former friends when they made horrible jokes about Wren missing senior prom because she couldn't fit into a dress? It's not fair for her to turn around and be angry at me for going after my goals now. I've put in my time.

"You know I love Maddie." I try for a reasonable tone. "She has nothing to do with this. All I'm doing is thinking about my future the way I should be. The way Dad would've wanted."

"Don't bring up Dad."

I flinch, the sting of pain and anger hitting me simultaneously. Why can't I bring up Dad? Isn't it worse to dishonor his memory by never talking about him again? I know he'd side with me if he were listening. He always wanted us to dream big. Of course, the only reason I'm here is because he's not anymore. I don't know if I'd even care about oncology research if he hadn't died from lung cancer. But it's dangerous to start imagining how different life might be if Dad were still alive. Would I still be premed? Would Wren have Maddie right now or would she be getting ready for sophomore year of college? I don't know. And there's no point wondering.

"I should go," I reply.

She's quiet for a moment. "You know, you can't plan for everything, Sage. And you shouldn't try."

I roll my eyes. That's rich coming from her, who plans for absolutely nothing. Of course I know you can't plan for everything. We hadn't planned on losing Dad. But just because some things are uncontrollable doesn't mean you can't dictate other parts of life.

"Thanks for the advice. I should really get back to work."

I can almost hear her shaking her head through the phone. "I'll tell Mom you called."

I drop my phone onto the bed, annoyed and wishing I hadn't called. I was already exhausted, and talking to Wren for five minutes sucked the last tendrils of energy from me. Maybe I should schedule a weekly time to call Mom in the future to avoid conversations like this again. I don't need anything making me upset, especially during the evening, which is my only free time.

I look at the floor where my laptop, pile of articles, and supplies are stacked and then glance at my bed. I can already tell that if I lie down with the idea of working, I'm going to fall asleep immediately. I guess I could use the dining room table, but it's open to the living room, so I'll hear Dr. Reese and Berend watching TV and they'll be able to see me as well.

But Ryland is gone tonight . . . maybe I could work up in his attic for a few hours? He would never know I was there. Decided, I gather my things and head to the attic space. Sure enough, I'm all alone. I spread my things out across a low table that sits in front of the couch and curl my legs up under me. It's *very* soft.

I need to focus. Dr. Reese's grad student, Katina, needs me to pull out twelve different data points from each patient file and it's a very slow process. My (ambitious) goal is to finish twenty-five more patients tonight. I complete three before my eyelids start to droop. I shake myself and gently slap my cheeks. If I'm not careful then I'll miss an important detail and all the data will be messed up.

My brain is so slow, though. I sit back against the couch.

Sometimes it feels like high school was a marathon, but rather than eating a banana and getting wrapped in a silver blanket at the end, I just kept running faster. I close my eyes. I'll rest for a minute and then keep pushing. It's better to do that than make a mistake.

I put my laptop on the table and lean my head back.

Scratch, scratch, scratch.

I crack my eyes open at the noise. I sit up a little bit and realize I'm covered with a blanket. A *blanket*? Did I have a blanket before? I don't remember grabbing one.

"Sorry. Did I wake you?"

I spin around, then groan at the sudden movement. My brain wasn't ready for that.

Ryland is at his work desk. He doesn't move, just lifts his eyes to look at me through his hair, which has fallen in front of his right eye like a small screen. "Diederik must be even more exhausting than I imagined."

I blink, still disoriented. Does this mean *Ryland* put the blanket on me? "I wasn't taking a nap. I was just closing my eyes for a few minutes."

"You sound like Berend."

"What time is it?"

He looks at his phone. "Almost midnight."

"What?! *Midnight?* That means . . ."

"That means you took a nap."

I groan. "Nooooo. I wasted a whole night." I rub my eyes with the heels of my hands and then run them through my hair. Now

I'm even further behind than I was. Plus, I was hoping to write a rough draft of the intro and methods sections for the poster. I imagine my planner in my mind and start shifting the to-dos, inwardly cringing as I see the work piling up even more.

"I'd say you spent the night perfectly."

I shake the planner from my mind and narrow my eyes at him. "When did you get back?"

"It was a quiet evening. I got back around eleven."

Something flutters in my stomach at the knowledge. "So you've been up here for an hour while I slept?"

"Lucky you're a quiet sleeper. If you snored then I would've rustled you awake immediately."

"You should have woken me up. I wasn't planning to be here when you were here. I know this is your space."

He rolls his eyes. "Like I've already told you, you're welcome up here whenever you want. It doesn't bother me. And clearly you must like it if you're sneaking in when I'm gone."

My cheeks heat. Once again, he's caught me off guard. I do feel better, though, more rested. Maybe I can get a bit more work done tonight since I won't be able to get back to sleep quickly. I pull my laptop back over.

Ryland points to an electric kettle on the corner of his table. "If you're staying, do you want some tea? I tend to forget what I'm doing once I get going so Mom got me this a while back." Before I can answer, he grabs a cup, pours the water over a tea bag, and pops in some sugar cubes from a bowl on the shelf.

"You keep cups and sugar up here?"

"I try to keep as much stuff up here as possible. I don't like to leave and get interrupted. Sometimes I sleep there, actually." He points to the couch and a tingle runs up my spine. He hands me the cup and goes back to his work, picking up a weird-looking tool that has a wooden ball on one end and a metal tip on the other and starts carving into a gray block.

"What are you doing?" I ask before I can think better of it.

His whole face lights up. "I'm working on a block print." He holds up the block and I can see a silhouette of the iconic Amsterdam canal houses carved into it. "It's one of my favorite ways to work. I carve my designs into the linoleum blocks, then roll them with ink and transfer them to paper. It's a slow process, but I love it. I like getting to control every step."

"Oh . . . that's really cool."

His mouth quirks in a smile. "You sound surprised."

"No, I just didn't know what you were doing. I don't know much about art. But that's impressive."

"Thanks." He stands, pulls stacks of fabric off a built-in shelf, and holds up a few. It turns out they're T-shirts, each with a different design. "Screen-printed shirts. Another passion project." He hands one to me and I run a finger across the graphic of a bike with butterfly wings before I catch myself and look up guiltily.

"I probably shouldn't touch that, huh?"

He laughs. "It's just a shirt. Though it's a favorite of mine."

I meet his gaze and recognize the shine in his eyes. He's not faking it when he says how much he loves to do this. His excitement awakens something in me as well. Not that I'm an artist, but

I understand what it's like to care so passionately about something that it takes over your thoughts. I don't find a lot of people who are that passionate. Ellie's like that with her fairy gardens, but most people I know don't *deeply* love anything. It makes me like Ryland much more to see how excited he gets.

"I'll make you something," he says.

I hand back the shirt. "No, please don't. I wasn't trying to—"

"I know you weren't. You won't be able to stop me, though."

His phone buzzes.

"Is that Evi again?"

I grimace, take a small sip of tea, and try to shake the questions from my brain. I should put down this tea and get back to work immediately. Or go back to my room. But instead, I take a second sip. Maybe it's the extra sleep, or the combination of the tea, blanket, and tranquil setting, but I'm not feeling my usual urgency to move and be productive. It's nice to have a real conversation with someone who isn't throwing toys around the room or asking for reference lists.

He looks at the phone. "Not her."

"The backpacking friend?"

He shakes his head again. "No, not her either."

"How many girls do you know?"

"Too many," he says with a chuckle, and puts his phone back in his pocket.

I pull the blanket around my legs. "So what happened with the backpacking trip?"

"It was a horrible decision. I never should've gone."

"Yeah?" I take another sip. I've found that people will keep talking if you just stay quiet long enough to let them think.

"She was all wrong for me. I knew that. But we went to school together, and she's moving to Scotland in the fall, and . . ." He looks up. "She had this whole plan. We were going to start in Paris, then work our way down to Nice, then over to Italy. She was so excited." He shrugs. "I think we got more caught up in the trip than each other. Or, at least, that's true for her."

His voice is tinged with sadness, so it's hard not to feel bad for him.

"Did she come back to Amsterdam with you after?"

"No." He runs a hand through his hair and it falls right back into place around his face. "It turns out that her old boyfriend lives in Nice. She texted him to say hi, they started chatting, and then— shockingly—my presence on the trip was no longer needed."

"Oof." I laugh and then feel guilty. "Sorry."

He smiles good-naturedly. "It's okay, it's pretty funny. Actually, you're the first person I told that to."

"Really? I thought you had a billion friends around?"

"Oh, I do, but it's a horribly embarrassing story."

"And you don't care what I think?"

"I care. I just know there's no impressing you."

I snort. I mean, he's not totally wrong.

"Honestly, the thing I'm most upset about is that I gave up on entering this art competition when I decided to go on the trip, and now that I'm back I don't think I have time to pull something together. Particularly with these new commissions." He spreads his arms wide over the table.

I cock my head and raise an eyebrow.

"There's that look again." He picks up a pencil and starts sketching.

"What look? You don't know me well enough to know if I have 'looks.'"

"I think I know one look. It's the *I'm not impressed by you* one. And if I had to guess, most everybody you know recognizes it."

I'm not sure what that look is, but I try to intensify it. "Weren't you the one who was out until eleven tonight?"

"But it was my friend Dan's birthday. I couldn't skip that now that I'm back in town."

"And the night before? And during the afternoons?" I say before he can argue with me.

"Like I said, it's hard for me to say no."

I take a sip of tea.

He sighs. "Go ahead. I can tell you're dying to tell me how I should live my life."

"You need to get your priorities straight. I bet you could enter the art competition if you just focused on your work and stopped going out constantly. Dating, in particular, is too time-consuming." I think of Wren and how all her plans were derailed because of a relationship. A relationship that doesn't even exist now. "It makes you forget about everything else you care about, which means you can't be productive, then you break up and what are you left with? Nothing but wasted time and bad memories. Whereas if you'd spent that time doing something useful that you actually love"—I gesture at his table—"the time would never be wasted."

He scowls. "Are you talking from experience?"

"I most certainly am not, because I'm logical. I have no time for or interest in relationships right now. When I'm older, sure, but right now I'm about to start my freshman year of college, and I have so much I want to do there."

I expect him to fight me, but he just shrugs.

"You're right, I need to sit down and focus. No excuses." He puts his pencil down and waves his hand at me in a frustrated way. "You make it seem easy, though."

"Don't blame me because I have superior self-control."

"Actually, that's a very good point. . . ." A wide grin spreads across his face and my nerves spike. Whatever he's got in mind, it's not good. "You could help me."

"No."

"You don't know what I'm going to say."

"I know I'm not going to like it."

"I think you might enjoy this idea." He pauses dramatically. "You can stop me from dating."

"What?!"

He claps his hands together excitedly. "I'm so bad at saying no. I always figure, what's the harm in one date? But then I get sucked into more dates and relationship drama and suddenly another week has passed and I've done nothing. You can shut it down."

"Ryland, I am not going to . . . to . . . *break up* your dates or something. I barely know you. That's the most bizarre thing I've ever heard of."

"Why? I think it's a great idea."

"Because the last thing I want is to get caught up in the drama of your personal life. You're on your own for this one."

Any thoughts of staying here to finish more work fly out the window and into the night. I take the last swig of my tea and gather up my things. I spend ten minutes talking to him and suddenly I'm getting pulled into supervising his *dating life*? Oh, hell no. This is what I get for trying to be social.

chapter
6

"Sage, we have some good news for you," Dr. Reese says as we're cleaning up the dishes after dinner that Thursday.

"Oh yeah?" I try to look interested even though I'm pretty sure she's about to tell me they have a new toy for Diederik, or something else babysitting-related.

"I have the day off work tomorrow," Berend says, "and I thought I'd take Diederik so you could have the day off as well."

"And if you'd like, you're welcome to visit the institute," Dr. Reese adds. "But I understand if you'd rather have the day to yourself to relax or explore the city. You haven't had much free time since you arrived."

"No, I'd love to come!" I practically yell.

Everyone, including Ryland, who came down for dinner again, looks at me in surprise. I don't usually get so excited, but this is one time when I feel like shouting.

"Well, great! I'm glad you're up to coming. I have some meetings in the morning, but maybe you could come after lunch? I can show you around the institute and then you can sit in on our lab meeting."

"That sounds fabulous."

Ryland is staring at me like I'm an alien, but I ignore him. This is exactly what I need. The last few evenings since my nap haven't gone much better, but a day off to visit Dr. Reese's lab will reinvigorate me. My mind races with everything I'll need to do before tomorrow. I'll want to review research articles for the meeting and work a bit more on my poster write-up. It's best to be prepared in case anyone asks for an update from me.

"Will you be comfortable traveling on your own?" Dr. Reese asks. I shut off the inner list-maker in my brain so I can concentrate fully on her.

"I'm sure I can figure it out. Is it in walking distance?"

"No, it's quite a bit south from here, but it's not hard to get there. Let's see, I'll pull up a map." Dr. Reese looks around, presumably for her phone. Diederik's delighted shrieks fill the space. Berend is tickling him.

"Don't worry about it. I'll take her."

I swivel to Ryland, surprised. "That's not necessary."

"I'm heading that way tomorrow anyway. I have some prints to drop off."

"Yes, go with her, Ryland," Berend says. He's got Diederik on his lap now and is bouncing him so much he's about to fall off and crack his head on the wooden floor. I cross my arms in disapproval but stay silent. I'm off Diederik duty for a few days. "The city may be easy to get around, but you still need a little time to learn. I don't want you getting lost, Sage."

Dr. Reese nods, though she doesn't look as sure as her husband. "That's probably true. You don't mind, Ryland? And you won't get distracted and forget about Sage?"

He narrows his eyes. "I'm capable of getting her to the institute without accidentally dropping her down a canal or something."

Dr. Reese nods. "All right then."

She turns away to focus on Diederik, who is practically hysterical with laughter now. Ryland just barely tilts his head toward the stairs. I know that's his way of asking if I'm coming up to the attic tonight.

I shake my head. I've got way too much to do to be ready for tomorrow.

I spend the night and the following morning reading and prepping for the day. Hopefully this will be the beginning of even more trips like this. I flip through my clothes, wondering how dressy to be. I want to make a good impression, but I also know that most academics aren't walking around in full suits and heels. After some debate, I choose a black skirt and blousy gray top. It should be sufficiently casual while still looking professional. I also go ahead and study the tram route on my phone to make sure I know where I'm going, just in case Ryland bails on me.

But, to my surprise, he's actually dressed and in the kitchen by eleven. And wearing—

"What's that?" I point to his shirt. It has the word *Interruption* printed on it, in bold fat lettering, but the word is turned on its side like it's standing on one end. Below the word are two legs. It's a bizarre shirt, and not just because it's blinding neon green.

"Do you like it? The legs need a little work, but overall I think this one turned out pretty well."

I stare, waiting for him to make sense.

"Don't you remember? You said I'm a 'walking interruption.'" He puts his arms out to the sides.

My words from days ago in the hallway come back to me. "You made a shirt based on that?"

"If sales are good, then we can talk about giving you a cut, but don't get your hopes up."

"I appreciate your generosity."

Ryland gestures to the door. "I thought we'd bike over to the institute. It's the best way to see the city."

My eyes go wide. "Oh, no, I don't think so. I'm not a bicyclist."

"Then you won't fit in here."

I lift up my phone. "Well, I'm a tourist, so I guess that's okay. I'm taking the tram. And don't feel obligated to come—I'm sure I can figure it out on my own."

He rolls his eyes. "You're more stubborn than Diederik. Come on."

It's only a four-minute walk to the tram stop. I buy a ticket from the driver and validate it at a little machine by the tram door. It's simple enough, but I have to admit it's comforting to have someone with me the first time.

The tram is more packed than I was expecting, but Ryland maneuvers through the crowd and finds two seats in the back. I pull my bag up on my lap and look out the window, having a sudden flashback to my England trip last fall. Back then it was Ellie and me together, headed to the nearby city, her bouncing with excitement and me making lists of school supplies I needed. I never would have guessed that I'd be here now, in a different country but still volunteering in Dr. Reese's research lab. It's more than I could have possibly expected.

I wonder what my father would think if he saw me here. He never got to travel. He was a civil engineer—always busy. He talked about going on a big family vacation some year, but something always came up. I think he'd be really proud of everything I'm doing . . . though I'd easily give this all up in a second if he was still with us.

"You okay?"

I shake my thoughts away. "Yeah. Thanks for taking me to the institute. You really didn't have to do this."

"I don't mind. I need to drop off prints anyway." He lifts the large bag in his hand.

I must look a second too long because he asks, "Do you want to see them?"

I have to admit I'm curious.

He opens the bag and pulls out a few. They are the block prints he was working on earlier in the attic. The design is the same— four canal houses in a row—but each is unique as well. He printed the first one with layers in three colors—blue, green, and orange. It's beautiful, simple and psychedelic in the overlapping colors. I pick up the next one in shades of red and yellow.

"I'd rather sketch something else, but tourists love the canal houses." He shrugs. "And right now I need money so Mom and Berend will stop nagging me about everything."

I turn over the print and see his signature on the back. I can understand why these would get scooped up immediately by visitors looking for something unique and artsy, but still a reminder of the trip. In fact, I bet Ellie—and particularly her art-loving boyfriend, Dev—would really like one. I make a mental note to ask about buying some eventually.

"They're really great. Very vibrant."

"Well, *I'm* very vibrant."

That's true. With the neon shirt, bright red hair, and constant energy, he definitely stands out in the tram crowd.

"Why did you add this?" I ask, noticing a small cat hidden on the left corner of the print.

He beams. "You noticed! Most people don't." He sits back. "I love drawing cats. I started doing it when I was young—now it's almost like a game trying to hide a cat in my prints with each design. It keeps it interesting for me."

"Huh. Cats as art."

"Have you ever seen Louis Wain's work?"

I shake my head.

He taps his phone and then hands it to me. On his screen is a psychedelic cat drawn with geometric shapes, bright stripes of colors, and huge eyes. He flips to another cat and, although this is weird to think, the cat looks a little . . . paranoid. Like he's looking for something right off the page.

"I'm obsessed with these," he says. "He was known for painting cats. When he started his career, he painted little delicate ones having tea and playing golf. Very popular." I think of Ellie and nod. She'd love that. "But his mental health deteriorated and he was put in an asylum. These are some of the cats he created while he was there. People have said that he developed schizophrenia, and that his cats show his changing perception of the world." He taps his phone again and shows me another picture. This one is mostly colored lines in the general shape of a cat. "I don't know if that's true, but they're amazing. I love the energy and color in his work."

It might not be everyone's inspiration—to paint psychedelic cats like someone who was in an asylum—but it fits Ryland.

"So, is that the goal, then? To be able to paint cats to your heart's content?"

He side-eyes me. "My goal is to support myself solely from my art. I want to start selling my T-shirts, expand my block printing from tourist prints into textiles and art prints. And I want people to commission my murals." He shrugs. "I'm still thinking about that contest I mentioned before. It would really help . . . if I could pull it off."

"What exactly is this contest?"

"It's through the Amsterdam Arts Council. They're looking for a series of eight pieces depicting the 'charms of Amsterdam' to display in Centraal Station. Millions of people come through that station every year—it could be huge exposure for me. But it's also hugely competitive. Evita Sprik and Rois Baatz are judging it." He stares out the tram window, his eyes narrowed and his voice more determined. "That would bring me the recognition I need. Winning it could be life-changing."

"How many pieces have you done so far?"

He presses his lips together. "Well, none. Yet."

"How long does it take to do a piece?"

"For me . . . it can be a while. Three or four days often, maybe a week. It depends on if I have to redesign and rework things." He shakes his head. "I know, I'm far behind. But I *do* plan to spend the rest of this afternoon working."

I don't say what I'm thinking—that if he really wanted to do it then he'd already be working. I have no time or patience for people who are endlessly *saying* they want to do things, but never do them. However, I don't want to risk saying more, just in case it reopens the conversation about my involvement in his dating life. I am starting to understand why he'd ask for my help, though—it's a shame he can't focus. His art is beautiful.

The tram slows and I turn my focus to the screen that displays the tram's route to see what stop we're at. We've been stopping every few minutes and it's hard to keep track.

"The next stop is mine."

He squints. "Uh, yes. How did you know that? Did you memorize the tram route?"

I just smile. I didn't exactly memorize it, but it's pretty easy for me to remember things once I've seen them.

"Thanks for coming with me," I say as we slow at the next stop. I stand and he stands quickly to let me pass.

"Can you find your way back or should I come pick you up later?"

"I'll be fine getting home. You should use the time to work." I shoulder my bag and push into the crowd before the tram moves on with me still inside. I have a feeling Ryland might want to come back for me—or feel obligated to—but that's not a good idea. I like Ryland, but I don't want him thinking we're close.

I step off the tram and look around, pretending confidence. We've clearly left behind the canals and charming inner city. This looks more like an industrial park with rows of brick apartments and larger buildings. I head down a wide walkway and soon I'm standing in front of a modern building with *Nederlands Kanker Instituut*—Netherlands Cancer Institute—spelled out in large letters. Excitement and nerves fill me.

I text Dr. Reese and a few minutes later she meets me in the foyer.

"I'm so glad this worked out so you're able to come today." She smiles at me. "Let's go up to the offices so I can introduce you to the others."

The space is larger than I'm expecting. There's a meeting room in the center, with her office to the right and several smaller cubicle-like offices to the left. And I see that all the offices have partial glass walls so you can't hide out in them.

"Everyone!" she calls when we walk in, and three heads pop up from the cubicles. She's clearly got them trained.

I immediately recognize them as they come out to the center even though I've only met one of them before. I studied Dr. Reese's lab extensively and know everyone's names, academic backgrounds, and specific research interests. What stands out most to me is how old they are. Or how young I am. They're all either PhD candidates or postdocs, and seeing them in front of me heightens my already keen awareness of how unusual my position is.

Before Dr. Reese can say more, one of the women rushes over to hug me. "Sage! I'm so glad to see you again."

I pull back and grin at her. Katina. She was in London with us in the fall and we worked together a lot. I guess I was kind of her lackey—finding references, proofreading, cleaning data sets—but Katina was really wonderful and took time to explain procedures to me, help me run analyses, lots of things. I'm so glad to see her again. As much as I respect Dr. Reese, this is the first time I've felt like I have a friend in Amsterdam. I'm surprised at how good it feels.

Dr. Reese smiles fondly at us. "Obviously, you both know each other. Ezeudo and Jacqueline, this is Sage, the student I'm mentoring. I invited her to sit in on our meeting this afternoon."

Ezeudo sticks out his hand. "Nice to meet you. I've heard great things."

I shake it, understanding why Katina was always talking about him in London. I have a feeling Ezeudo isn't hurting in the dating department. His black skin and bright white smile pull you right in. In contrast, Jacqueline is so pale I can almost see the veins beneath her skin. She must spend a lot of her time in the lab. She shakes my hand, looking a little taken aback by me. She's probably close to thirty, so I must seem like a child to her.

We all sit down at a conference table and each person goes around updating Dr. Reese on their current work. Luckily for me, although her students are from around the world, English is a common language for them all, so I'm able to follow along. Well, mostly. They have so many concurrent projects that it's hard for me to keep them straight.

"Katina, have you confirmed when Ben wants to roll out the new social support questionnaire?" Dr. Reese asks.

"He said we could start by the end of the month if we're ready."

"Oh, really?"

Dr. Reese notices my confusion and turns to me. "I haven't had a chance to tell you about this one," she explains. "We're partnering with local hospitals and oncology specialists on a new project to survey cancer patients and families throughout diagnosis and treatment on perceived communication with physicians, distress levels, and social support. It's the first time we'll be working directly with physicians at the hospitals, but I'm hoping this might lead to even more collaborations." She turns back to Katina. "That's a lot to get done in a short time. Is it possible?"

"Yes. It's just . . ." Katina shakes her head. "I'll make it possible."

"Ben was hesitant to partner with us on this research project to begin with. I don't want anything to damage that." Dr. Reese frowns and looks between Katina and me. "Would it help if you had someone entering all the questions into Qualtrics? Maybe Sage could work with you on that?"

Katina smiles at me. "That would be a big help if you can manage it."

"Are you up for it, Sage? I know you already have a number of projects you're helping out on."

"Absolutely. I'd love to help."

I don't hesitate, even though a little voice in my mind is yelling and pointing at my already overflowing planner. It doesn't matter. I'm not going to turn down an opportunity to contribute to this project. *This* is why I came to Amsterdam and I'll find a way to work it out. Somehow.

chapter 7

Dr. Reese and I take the tram back together at the end of the day. My mind is still whirling with excitement and nerves about being added to this new project when we walk into the apartment and find we're not alone.

Ryland is standing at the dining room table with three other people. They're all laughing about something but swing around to look at us.

"Hallo!" a girl says, and waves. Her blond hair is so long I think she's sitting on it. She turns back to Ryland and says something in Dutch.

"Yes, this is Sage. And you know my mom."

"It's been a while since I've seen you all," Dr. Reese replies. "How have you been?"

The other guy in the group shrugs. "Same as always."

"We've been insanely busy," says the blond girl, gesturing to the East Asian girl next to her.

"Glad to hear it. Are Berend and Diederik here?"

"They went to the park," Ryland says.

"Okay. Well, I'm going to change. Good to see you."

Ryland waves me over when his mom is gone. "Sage, let me introduce you."

Reluctantly, I walk over. Making small talk with a bunch of strangers is the last thing I want to do. I'm going to need a serious planner overhaul and I won't be able to relax until I've done it. But I guess it's best to get this out of the way.

"Hi."

"These are my friends. This is Dan." He gestures to the blond girl.

"It's short for Danella," she says. She has thick black-rimmed glasses and her arms both have sleeves of tattoos, mostly colorful flowers and butterflies. I remember Ryland mentioning a birthday party he went to for someone named Dan. Is this the same person? Or is this one of the girls who's so interested in him? But then I look down and realize she's holding hands with the girl next to her.

"I'm Maiya," the other girl says. She has purple highlights in her long hair and almost as many tattoos as Dan. She looks me up and down. "Aren't you a fun addition to the household?" She raises an eyebrow at Dan.

"And this is Tom. But we call him Twitch," Ryland continues, gesturing to a white boy with a buzz cut and oversized T-shirt of a bear playing PlayStation.

"Nice to meet you all. I didn't realize Ryland was hanging out with friends this afternoon." I give him a quick glance so he knows I haven't forgotten what he said on the tram about working today. I really don't care either way, but I do find it annoying on principle.

Twitch shrugs. "I had the day off—"

"And we had a break between clients," Maiya adds.

There's a short knock at the entrance and then someone pushes it open. A girl pops her head around the door. "Ryland?"

She steps in and I realize who she is. It's Evi, the girl who gave me the evil eye when I interrupted her and Ryland on the street. Her eyes sweep over the large room, landing on Ryland before narrowing in my direction.

Dan and Maiya both cough out laughs.

"Evi? What are you doing here?" Ryland doesn't sound happy to see her.

She blinks in surprise, and I realize she's probably confused about why he's speaking English instead of Dutch. She scowls and walks over. "You didn't return my texts or calls today. And when I texted Twitch, he said you were all here. Why didn't you invite me?"

Ryland shoots Twitch the quickest of angry glances before turning his full attention to Evi. "I haven't been paying attention to my phone today. I had to take Sage across town." He points to me, and I glare at him. I do *not* want to be pulled into this. "You remember Sage, right?"

She doesn't take her eyes off him. "I've missed you."

Dr. Reese comes back into the room, now wearing jeans and a blouse. She frowns. "More people? Ryland, Berend and Diederik will be home soon. We'll need to start getting ready for dinner."

Maiya stands and Dan follows suit. "We need to go anyway," Dan says. "We both have evening appointments. Nice to meet you, Sage." She winks at Ryland. "Have fun."

Twitch claps him on the back. "Later." And they all head for the door.

Ryland raises his eyebrows at me, and I have the distinct impression that he wants me to run interference and save him from Evi. Yeah, no thanks.

"See ya." I twiddle my fingers at them both and make my escape.

First, I head to my room, but then decide I want a bigger escape. Dr. Reese mentioned they had a small rooftop deck. I haven't been out there yet, and this sounds like the perfect time for it.

It turns out that *deck* is a very strong word for this place. My imagined version of a deck implies space, and that is not true here. This is really a tiny square of wood perched between two peaked roofs of buildings. There's enough space for two chairs and that's about it. But it's nice to have different scenery at least.

I pull out my planner, correction tape, and colored pens. Past Sage was a little too cocky, writing the schedule in pen, and now I'm going to have to correct everything. I should probably give up my old-school planner and put everything into my phone like the rest of the world, but I prefer the tangible weight of my daily planner. I usually like that I can't immediately delete a reminder or due date once I've written it. Except for right now.

Some amount of time has passed—I'm not sure how much because I'm so engrossed—when I hear a jangle of the door to my right. I look up and am disoriented to see that the sun is much lower in the sky now.

"You finally found this place," Ryland says.

"Your mother mentioned it." I push down a sigh. Looks like my work time is done for a while. "Are you coming to kick me out so you can spend a romantic evening with Evi up here?"

He rolls his eyes. "No, she's gone now, but the entire thing was extremely annoying. This is exactly what I was talking about before. I really could have used you in there."

"Ryland, let's not get started on this again." I close my planner. "I'm going inside. There's not enough space for the both of us out here. There's barely enough for me."

He sits down in the chair opposite me, as if to prove me wrong. "So, you're not going to ask what happened to my afternoon plan?"

I smirk. "I think I already know the answer."

"I *did* turn in my block prints and Espen was very happy with them. In fact, he's commissioned another fifteen. But then the group texted about getting together and it's so rare our schedules line up . . ."

"I see."

He leans toward me. Given how little space is up here, he's suddenly *very* close. "Listen, I know you think I'm ridiculous, but I'm not. This idea can work for both of us. I need your help and I bet you need mine too."

"Why would you think that?"

He gestures at my planner. "You've got about twenty highlighters up here and an expression like you're trying to crack an unsolvable calculus problem."

"I'm excellent at calculus."

"I'm sure you are. And you'd be good at this too. Just think of me as your next homework project. I need to stay single and focused this summer. If you see me slipping up, then give me one of those patented judgmental looks you're known for."

I sputter. "I'm not *known* for those looks."

"We've already established that you are. But either way, lock the doors, turn off my phone, do whatever you need to do."

"I'm already babysitting one person in this house. I don't need to babysit two."

"It won't be babysitting. In fact, it'll be the opposite of that. Do you remember when you tried to take Diederik on a simple walk and changed him into a fire-breathing toddler? And do you remember how relieved you were when you found me at the house, and I swooped him up and shoved cookies at him to make him happy? Don't deny it, we both know it's true. Well, if I'm home more, then I'll be around if something comes up. You'll have built-in backup for the next disaster."

"I don't need backup."

"Oh, really? So, it wouldn't be helpful if I made his lunch every day? Or found his favorite TV shows and toys when he's throwing a tantrum? Or helped with your future outings so you could avoid another meltdown on the street?" He sits back and crosses his arms over his chest. "You need me."

I bite my lip. I hate to admit how nice it would be to have someone else around. Just to have another pair of eyes on him so I could run to the bathroom without worrying that he's about to get himself killed. But still . . .

"If you're helping me with Diederik, then you won't be working, which contradicts your entire argument."

"Don't worry, I wouldn't spend the entire day at his side. I'd just come down to help when I'm needed."

I look down at my overflowing planner. Maybe this isn't the

worst idea in the entire world? I'd get extra help with Diederik, which would hopefully translate into calmer days for me and more energy in the evenings to devote to work. And there's something strangely appealing about getting to dictate Ryland's social calendar. There have been so many times I've wanted to do this exact thing with Wren and Ellie, but they were too hard to reason with. This time I'd actually have the power to tell someone no for their own good. But I can't drown out the other arguments spinning in my mind.

"I don't think your mom would approve."

"Because I'm helping with Diederik? She doesn't mind that—she just doesn't want me being solely responsible for him."

"No, because . . ." I pause, unsure how to word this without making the conversation extra weird. "I guess she didn't tell you, but she doesn't want us spending a lot of time together."

He smirks. "Oh, *that*. No, she already made her feelings on that subject very clear to me. But we're following her rules perfectly. Not only will I not be dating *you*—I won't be dating anyone."

I hesitate.

"Please? Think of yourself as a mentor, teaching me how to achieve my goals for once. I'd really appreciate it."

I suck in a deep breath and point my finger at him. "If we're going to do this, then we need a real agreement." I flip to the back of my planner and try not to think about how foolish I am to say yes to this.

"Wait, we're doing this? You're actually agreeing?" He jumps up, hits my knees with his own because we're sitting so close, and sits back down. "Yes, let's make it official! I bet I can find a calligraphy pen so it looks fancy. And maybe we should write our names in blood for extra oomph?"

I bite my lip so I don't laugh. "A red pen will be fine."

"Doesn't sound nearly as exciting, but all right."

"Okay, so let's nail this down. What exactly am I doing?"

"I don't know, just keeping me on track."

I put my pen down and sit back. If he doesn't want to set the terms, I will. "Great, then here's what you do: wake up, work, sleep. You can eat and clean yourself, but let's limit that to no more than fifteen minutes at a time. No more seeing people until the project is done. Agreed?" I smile serenely.

"But . . . I have to see my friends sometimes."

"Fine. Once a week."

"That's it?"

I stand as if I'm going to walk inside.

He pulls me back down. "Every other day."

"Every *three* days, and only in the evenings, after you've made sufficient progress."

"Better make that afternoons only, then. I do my best work late."

I swallow down a smile of recognition. Although I like getting up early, I'm most productive after dinner when the day is done and I can focus in peace.

I make a show of slowly writing this in the planner using my best cursive. "And no dating at all until the pieces are complete."

"Agreed. Occasional outings with friends only."

"And what about when you inevitably break protocol and I find you leaving with Evi or someone else?"

"Hey now, that's not inevitable! I'm serious about this." He pauses. "But if I *were* to slip up, then feel free to drag me back inside the house and lock the door behind me."

I huff. "I'm not going to fight you all summer. I will . . . remind you to prioritize yourself. But if you choose not to listen, then this whole thing is off."

"Fair enough. And in exchange I'll help with lunch every day at twelve—"

"—eleven."

"At eleven, as well as soothing his tantrums, assisting with outings into the city, and doing other tasks as needed."

Our eyes lock and we both give brisk nods, as if we're finishing up a corporate negotiation. I write these last notes in my planner and Ryland reaches out to shake my hand with a grin.

"Good doing business with you."

His hand wraps around my own, his skin warm against my palm, and I pull away quickly. No touching. I should add that as an addendum to the agreement.

"I already feel better!" He stands and gestures for the door. "Okay, time to get started. Do you want to work in the attic with me? I promise not to interrupt anymore."

Ha-ha-ha.

"No thanks. I actually need to work." I give him a pointed look behind his back.

"Me too. Oh!" He turns to look at me. "And this offer holds for you too, by the way. If you meet anyone and it looks like you're getting distracted, I'll make sure to send them packing."

I burst out laughing. "Believe me, I'm *more* than capable of sending them packing myself. I'm the last person who needs a guard."

He quirks up an eyebrow. "You really think so? Even if the perfect person came around, you don't think you'd be the least bit interested?"

"No. Once I've finished my residency I'll start thinking about dating and relationships. Not before." I lift my chin defiantly.

He regards me, the smallest smile brightening his face. Maybe he's trying to play it cool, but I can read his expression. He thinks I'm full of crap. Well, Ryland, if you think you're going to prove me wrong, then go ahead and try. I'm *always* right.

chapter

8

To my surprise, Ryland keeps his word and focuses on his art all weekend, which means I'm able to work all day Saturday and am up early Sunday to keep going. By the afternoon, my brain is mush and I give myself permission to take off some time to wander around the city. I need to do some shopping for everyone back home, so Dr. Reese suggests I head to De Negen Straatjes (the Nine Streets), which is a twenty-minute walk. It's absolutely beautiful, with a wide canal cutting between two roads lined with narrow houses, small restaurants, and stores. But even when I'm supposed to be relaxing, I have my to-do list in the back of my mind. And there's one item I've been putting off for too long.

"It's so good to hear from you," Mom says when she picks up my call. "I was worried you were never going to call back."

"Well, things are pretty busy over here. If I'm not with Diederik then I'm trying to keep up with all my tasks for Dr. Reese."

"How is it going? Are you happy to be working with her again?"

"Definitely." I pause in front of a shopwindow, making a mental note of a bracelet that Mom would love. "Actually, they just added me to their newest project. It's great experience."

"Wonderful! We sure do miss you around here, so I'm glad to hear that."

"I miss you all too."

"Is it lonely over there with no one your own age to talk to?"

I clear my throat. This is why I've been putting off this call, but it's time to rip off the Ryland Band-Aid. "Well, actually, I'm not the only one here. It turns out that Dr. Reese's older son is living at the house as well. Ryland."

"A boy your age? Why didn't she tell you about this earlier?"

"There was a last-minute change of plans. You don't need to stress about it."

"I wouldn't usually, but I'm surprised you didn't tell me earlier. That's so unlike you."

"I did try calling before but got Wren instead." A group of laughing women carrying shopping bags barrels toward me and I step to the side. "Everything is fine. I'm really busy with my babysitting and I work on research every evening." I think about explaining to Mom how I'm actually helping Ryland to stop dating, but I don't think she'd get it. Probably best to say as little as possible.

"I'm glad it's going well. But I was young once too. I remember what it's like being away from home, in close proximity to a cute boy. He's cute, isn't he?"

I stop on a bridge and stare out over the canal, where a single duck is floating serenely. A cool breeze ruffles my hair. "He's . . . vibrant."

She chuckles. "That means cute in Sage speak. Just wait until your sister hears."

"Do you have to tell her?"

"I think it'd be better if you told her yourself, actually. She's been struggling lately. She's lonely." She lowers her voice. "None of her friends come over, Sage. No one messages. All of them—all those little shits who used to crowd our kitchen and eat our food—have dropped her."

Anger and sadness flood through me. I wish all her so-called friends were standing in front of me right now so I could tell them again what selfish, faithless, horrible assholes they all are. When I told them that exact thing during Wren's senior year, I made one of them cry. And she deserved it.

"Maybe Wren doesn't care anymore?" I ask hopefully, and keep walking across the bridge to the other side of the canal. "She's probably too busy or too tired to notice."

"Oh, she notices. But you're right, she has plenty to occupy her mind. Just . . . just don't forget about her. You know, she's really proud of you."

I scoff. "No, she's not. She's bitter at me."

"Can you blame her? And people can be multiple things at once. She's jealous, but she's also proud. She told me so."

I bite my lip, surprised. "Well, tell her I'm proud of her too. Watching Diederik is no joke, so I have no idea how she's doing it with Maddie."

"I'll tell her." Mom's voice softens. "And maybe you can tell her sometime too?"

"I will. I'll call her sometime."

Although I think passing messages through Mom is a safer bet. I'm scared if I call again then we'll get into another sparring match, and neither of us needs that.

"Now keep your head on straight. I trust you, but . . . just be careful, okay?"

"Of course. Love you, Mom."

I might not be ready for another call with Wren just yet, but maybe a care package will do the same job. Then she'll know I'm thinking of her and Maddie, with the bonus of no snide comments and no losing time on the phone.

I don't see a lot of kids' stores, but eventually I find a shop with some stuffed toys and picture books. Wren won't be able to read them since these are in Dutch, but they can look at the illustrations together. In another shop, I find a fuchsia scented candle I know Wren will like. I also grab her some fun costume jewelry. She always loved dressing up in high school. I wonder when she did that last? Probably not since the last time she saw Marcus. The night she told him she was pregnant.

I see red just remembering it. They'd been so popular—everyone's favorite couple. Always together, voted Most Likely to Get Married their junior year. I know Mom used to worry about why I never dated in high school. Well, this is why—because relationships lead to trouble. Romance? Commitment? No. They distract you when you're happy and decimate you when you're not.

Wren had so many plans. She wanted to go to school to become a dental hygienist. She wanted to move out west. She wanted to travel. And now what is she doing? Changing diapers and searching for part-time jobs. Oh yeah, and mending the heart Marcus broke when he ran away to his freshman year at Penn State. No responsibilities. No stigma. Of course not. There never is for the father.

I pick up a scarf for Wren as well. Screw my budget, she deserves it.

Monday morning I'm back to my new normal. Dr. Reese and Berend are out early and Ryland is still sleeping. Diederik and I go on our now-usual rounds. Today our theme is supposed to be butterflies. I printed out some coloring pages and thought we could use them to review colors.

I pull out a basket. "How about coloring?" I take out paper, crayons, and stickers. Instead, he goes for the glue. And scissors. I should have known.

"Look, let's draw a flower for the butterfly to land on." I take a red crayon and try my best approximation of a flower. It's less than impressive.

"I want to cut!" he exclaims, and starts cutting little pieces and littering the floor. At least his English is improving.

"Okay, how about you draw some things and then we can practice cutting them out. And we can glue them onto another page when we're done."

I read that "scissor skills" are important for kids going into school, so at least if we're going to make a mess, we should be learning as well.

He relents and draws another flower-shaped thing, followed by a circle for a sun. I convince him to color them. Maybe if I can keep him on task we'll have a cute drawing at the end of this to show Dr. Reese.

"You two look busy this morning."

I glance up to find Ryland walking into the kitchen. I expect bedhead and sleep-crusted eyes, but he looks awake. He's wearing a yellow shirt that has giraffes forming a heart with their necks. All his clothes are so bright they make me squint. Joy flashes in his expression. "I got up early to work. Thanks to you!" He pours some old coffee into a mug and lifts it in my direction. "This deal of ours has really gotten me focused. I already had some inspiration for the pieces."

"That's great." I try not to look surprised, but I am. I kind of assumed he'd blow this whole thing off within a few days.

"I feel accountable now. Like I need to produce something to show for my time. I'm getting back at it until lunch. Though—" He pauses and fishes his phone out of his pocket. "Take this." He hands it to me. It's warm from where it lay against his upper thigh. "I can't take the distractions."

I look down at it and see a half dozen text messages. I don't want to read for fear of invading his privacy, but I can see at least one request to meet for lunch.

"I don't want it." I hold it up to him. "This wasn't part of the agreement. Just put it under a pillow or something."

"I tried that. My brain is primed to listen unconsciously for the vibrations. Every time I hear something I feel a compulsion to check. It's ruining my flow. If something really serious comes up then let me know, but otherwise just keep it away from me."

"How am I going to know if something serious happens? I

don't know any of these people."

"Like, if Mom or Berend text about something important. Or Espen texts about the commissions." He waves away the phone, looking completely relaxed.

"You don't feel weird having me see your texts and notifications popping up?"

"Well, we could exchange phones and I could read all your texts if that would make you feel better." He smirks. "What have you been telling your friends at home about me? I wonder how you described me . . . the derelict living in the attic? The useless artist? Or maybe the cute big brother?"

I press my lips together and control my features. He will not get a reaction from me, no matter how much he works for it. Though, good lord, what would he think if he saw *one* text from Ellie?

"I'll keep my phone to myself, thank you. I'm not the one looking for help."

"Not yet, at least." He winks. "I'm a very trusting person."

"Very."

He looks beyond me and laughs. "And you're even more trusting than me if you're willing to give Diederik a glue bottle. The furniture looks like it's judging us."

I spin around and see that, while I was focused on Ryland, Diederik managed to find little plastic craft eyes in the bottom of the basket and glue a half dozen to the back of a chair.

"I have to say, it really adds something to the room. I might need to play with that for an art installation."

"Ah!" I leap up.

"Does this count as an emergency you need my help with?"

"No." I wave him off. "Just go away and stop distracting me."

"Don't worry, that glue is water-soluble. It'll come out. With time." He raises his mug again and heads for the door.

I manage to clean the back of the furniture with a wet washcloth enough that I don't think anyone will notice the big glops of glue in the upholstery, assuming they dry before Dr. Reese and Berend get home tonight. Despite the mess, Diederik and I manage to create a cute scene of flowers and a sun, with blue dots as raindrops. I take a picture to send to Mom, Wren, and Ellie. Maybe they won't be so skeptical about my babysitting skills if they see what we're making. We're doing so well, in fact, that I give myself permission to let him watch some TV after lunch.

And, throughout all of this, Ryland's phone keeps buzzing. It's mildly distracting, but I don't care about reading his messages. I'm actually starting to be happy that I agreed to help Ryland. This situation is out of control and I'm just the right person to shut it down.

There's a knock on the apartment door around three that afternoon. I gently wiggle out from under Diederik. He's been sitting in my lap for the last twenty minutes as we read Paddington Bear books together. I figure we might as well practice our English since Dr. Reese wanted me to help with that.

I open the door to find a girl about my age, looking very restless and perturbed. This one has blond hair so pale it's almost white and is wearing rainbow-striped clothes. Her eyes pop open at the sight of me and she says something in Dutch.

I shake my head in confusion. "I'm sorry, my Dutch is really bad."

She starts again. "I came here to see Ryland. Is he home?"

"Oh." I size her up. There are more girls coming to the door for him? This is too much. "Actually, I think he's busy right now. But I can tell him you came by. What's your name?"

"I'm Sanne." She narrows her eyes at me. "Who are you?"

"I'm Sage. The babysitter." I shift so she can see Diederik behind me. Luckily, he's still looking at the books and not hanging from the ceiling or painting the walls with food in the two seconds I looked away from him.

Her whole demeanor relaxes. I guess it's easier to be nice when I'm not a threat. "Is he really busy? And not . . . out with someone else?" she whispers, and looks around my shoulder as if expecting Ryland to be lurking inches away.

"Well, as far as I know he's not out."

Which is actually a good point. His first days here made it clear that he can come and go without me knowing, but if he really wants to sneak out, then more power to him.

"Ah, good. If he's here then he'll want to see me." She tries to walk past me, but I don't move.

"I think he's pretty caught up right now. He asked me to send people away."

"He did not. He wouldn't do that." She looks at her phone. "I don't understand, he always replies."

"Like I said, he's busy." I'm about to lose my patience. We were all doing so well and now she's interrupting.

She eyes me suspiciously and then types something into her phone. A second later, Ryland's phone beeps on the coffee table. I try to suppress a laugh.

"He also left his phone here so he wouldn't be distracted."

Now she looks completely affronted. She pokes her head into the living room and looks around for Ryland. When she doesn't see him, she turns on her heel and storms down the steps.

I shut the door, then lock it in case she tries running back and shoving the door open.

I can't help but look at Ryland's phone. The latest text is in Dutch. Against my better judgment, I get out my own phone and translate it.

A very rude and dull girl is saying you aren't available. You need to fire her.

I laugh louder than I have in weeks. Rude and dull. I look down at my gray shirt and shorts. Fair enough.

chapter
9

Ryland is down for dinner that night, even coming early enough to help his mom cut up vegetables for the salad. I'm still very cautious about how I act around him in front of Dr. Reese. I know she was nervous about us being in the same house, and I don't want to give her any reason to doubt that we can coexist without incident. Ryland must have the same understanding because he isn't nearly as chatty and flirty with me.

Most of the conversation at dinner circles around a big advertising client Berend is finding extremely difficult to work with. Toward the end, Dr. Reese asked Ryland how his day was.

"Great, I got a lot accomplished." He catches my eye. "Actually, Sage has been really motivating me."

She looks between us. "She has? I didn't realize you two were spending time together."

The look of concern is back on her face, and I want to kick Ryland. He's lucky it's a big table.

"Well, I just noticed how dedicated she's been to her work here and I thought maybe I needed to take a page out of her book."

Her face clears. "Really? That sounds fabulous."

"And we did chat a bit and she told me how I really need to prioritize my work over going out. So that's what I'm doing."

Dr. Reese shares a surprised look with Berend. "Well . . . great. You're so talented and I've always said you just need to apply yourself more if you want something to happen with your art. I'm not sure why it took someone you just met to get that into your head, but whatever it takes." She smiles warmly at me. "I guess this really is going to work out well."

I nod encouragingly. "Definitely. I'm loving it here."

"Good. Well . . ." She stands from the table with her plate. "I should let both of you get back to it. I'm glad you're getting along well and being a good inspiration to each other!"

We clean our plates, and I can almost feel Ryland's gloating wafting into my air supply. "You know that was risky," I say under my breath when Dr. Reese and Berend are caught up with Diederik.

"Not if you know my mom well enough. If she thinks you're a positive influence on my work ethic then she'll have us spending every day together." His eyes sparkle triumphantly. "This way we don't have to pretend to be indifferent strangers anymore."

"How do you know I'm not an indifferent stranger?"

"Oh, I'm sure you're indifferent. But you can be my indifferent bodyguard instead of a stranger. Speaking of which, nice job with Sanne this afternoon. I got an earful when I finally called her."

"You called her after I gave you your phone back? You should have been working."

"I can't work every second of the day! And we didn't say

anything explicitly about no phone calls."

I scoff. Already trying to get around the rules.

"You'll be proud to know that I told her I couldn't go out. She's very annoyed." He chuckles. "And, shockingly, she's not your biggest fan."

"Well, she and I can definitely be indifferent strangers."

"So, are you coming to the attic to work tonight?"

I shake my head. Despite dedicating almost the entire weekend to work, I have lots to do tonight. I don't want to complain to Dr. Reese and seem ungrateful, but I'm still feeling burned out.

He frowns. "You don't trust that I won't interrupt you."

"It's hard to trust without evidence."

"Spoken like a scientist. Okay, fine, come up one last time and I'll prove it to you. If it's too distracting then I won't offer again."

I regard him closely. A small warning bell goes off in the back of my brain. This is getting to be too much. Too much chatting, too much time, too close together. I'm not trying to be friends with Ryland. But then, it would be nice to have a comfortable place to work this summer. And it's not like Ryland is looking for more girlfriends. That's kind of the whole point—he's staying away from girls. And friends.

I nod. "All right. Just tonight and we'll see how it goes."

"Deal." He winks. "See you up there."

I sigh. He's much too flirty for his own good. At least he's this flirty with everyone.

Ryland is at his desk with headphones on when I arrive. The attic is as comfy as ever. Evening light pours through the slanted skylights, illuminating the wooden shelves and art supplies. I narrow my eyes at him, expecting him to start talking, but he only glances up long enough to give a quick smile before going back to his work.

All right . . . let's see how this goes.

I open my laptop to work on my poster for the Berlin conference and soon lose myself in it. The purpose of the poster is to succinctly describe our research project in a way that's easy to digest so people can understand without reading the whole paper. It might not seem like a lot of work to write up a few paragraphs on the methodology and results and throw it up on the wall with a graph, but it's actually extremely difficult to summarize so much information. Trying to condense ten pages of research background into three sentences makes me want to drop my laptop off the roof deck.

When I look up again, an hour has passed. I glance over at Ryland, but his head is down, hair falling all around him so I can't see his face. I roll back my shoulders and smile. This is what I'm talking about. I turn back to the *Future Research* bullet points, feeling an extra push. There's something motivating about working next to another person, knowing you can't speak. Knowing he's working makes me want to work harder so I can prove how much I accomplished by the end of the night.

Another ninety minutes later he stands, but I can tell he's trying to move as gingerly as possible. He grabs bottles of paint and tiny rollers. Is he painting? It doesn't look like it, but I can't tell what he's doing. Screw it, I need to stand up and stretch anyway.

"What are you doing?" I ask.

"Mm, hold on." He lays a piece of paper on top of one of the carved blocks he showed me before, rubs it with something, and then slowly pulls it off from one corner, revealing a large canal scene. "Sorry, who was the first person to speak tonight?"

I blink in surprise and then glare at him when I understand his meaning. "You were the one walking around."

"As quietly as possible. And you didn't answer the question."

"Fine. You've made your point. It was me."

He bows. "Thank you."

"So you made progress?"

"Tons. I have the idea for the project now and the first two pieces sketched out. They're supposed to illustrate life in Amsterdam to pull in tourists, but also show the city in an unorthodox way. So"—he grabs his sketch pad to show me—"I'm showing Amsterdam through the perspective of a cat."

I laugh, but lean in to look closer.

"It'll be eight interconnected pictures, showing different parts of Amsterdam during the changing seasons, but the viewer will be pulled through the images by the cat."

"Don't you mean a cat's butt?" I ask, pointing to the two sketches. In both there is a cat at the edge of the sketch, ready to walk off the page, tail high up in the air like an exclamation point and butt out for all to see.

"*Exactly!* It's perfect. Fun and irreverent. I think the judges, particularly Rois, will like it. His work has a similar tone." He sighs longingly. "I haven't decided on all of the sketches, but I know I'm going to do one of people ice skating on the canals and the cat half sliding across."

"That doesn't sound realistic. I bet a cat would never go down into the canal, frozen or not."

"You're probably right, but that's why it's called artistic interpretation."

"Fair enough." I yawn and stretch toward the ceiling.

"How about you? Did you get anything done?"

"A lot, actually."

"See, I knew this would work. It'll be a competition to see who can accomplish more." He gestures over his shoulder. "I'm going to make a cup of tea. Do you want one?"

"Do you have Irish breakfast? That's my favorite."

He shakes his head. "No, sorry. How about chai?"

"Sure."

He makes it and hands it to me, along with sugar packets and a little cup of cream. I pour it in and watch as the cream slowly swirls into the tea, softening the color and looking like a dream.

"Um, what are you doing?"

I look up. "Watching the first few seconds as the cream mixes in. I like how it billows."

"Billows?" He quirks his head, looking at me. "You *are* a surprising one." He takes a scratch pad and scribbles something on it.

"Please tell me you aren't going to make a shirt about that."

"I'm already designing it."

Ryland and I work companionably each night for the rest of the week, and I'm surprised how much I'm able to get done in his presence. It does become a competition over who can work the longest and quietest each night and there's *no* way I'm losing to Ryland.

He gives me a run for my money, though—I'm not sure I've ever seen someone get so absorbed in their work. By the time I go to the institute Thursday evening to meet Katina, I'm feeling good. For the first time since I arrived in Amsterdam, my to-do list is manageable. It makes me even more excited to help with the new project now. Katina is waiting for me at the door.

"It's good to have you back!" she exclaims. I'm struck by how perfectly straight and shiny her hair is. It's different from how she had it in England, but she's always been super stylish. "I'm so grateful that you're able to help me."

I follow her up the cold metal stairs and into the office space. Ezeudo and Jacqueline wave from their cubicles.

Katina gestures to the meeting table where a laptop and water bottle already sit. "I'll show you how the system works and then you can try entering a few of the questions to make sure you understand it."

Basically, I have to type each question into Qualtrics and then set up a number of possible answer choices like True/False or Likert scales depending on the question. There's a lot of detail to make sure that all the data is collected correctly for analyses, but it seems straightforward. It'll be tedious, but I bet I can get it done by the end of the week.

I'm beaming when I leave the institute. I'm really proud that I'm now a part of this new project, even if my part is pretty small. While it's not research that's explicitly focused on *curing* cancer, I like the idea of collecting data on communication and social support in families and then using that to minimize distress in patients. Dad had a great team of doctors, but I remember times when there was confusion about his treatment plan, and it really helped that Mom was there to ask the doctor. I can't imagine going through it all without an amazing support system.

I get off the tram a few stops early and meander around the Jordaan district. It's surprisingly quiet here. Above me, a woman sits in her window ledge, smoking and listening to a song I don't recognize on the radio. Up and down the streets, people have planted huge containers of flowers. I pause in front of an especially beautiful scene where someone has trained blooming wisteria to grow above their arched windows. I take a picture for Ellie, knowing how much she loves plants, and then decide to call her. I haven't told her about my new agreement with Ryland, but she's definitely going to want to know.

"Hi!" she squeals as soon as she picks up. "I'm so glad you called!"

"Is this a good time?"

"Um, it's always a good time to talk to you! I need to hear everything!"

I update her on visiting the lab and how Diederik and I are doing. She listens patiently, and asks questions about Diederik and my research, but I know she's just biding her time until I get to Ryland. It makes me want to drone on about data entry just to keep her in agony.

"I think that's about it over here," I finally say when I can't think of another detail to add. "How are things back home?"

"Sage, you're evil and you know it. Is that really all you have to tell me about? There's nothing *else* going on?"

I laugh. "If you're asking whether Ryland and I are spending every night in his attic making out, then I have nothing to report. In fact, we're doing the opposite."

"What exactly *is* the opposite of that? Are you two fighting? Or are you just sitting together and staring at the walls?"

"We're not fighting. I've actually motivated Ryland to swear off girls and dating so he can focus on his work."

"He's research-obsessed too? You two really are made for each other."

I laugh. "No, definitely not. He's an artist. But he has a big competition coming up and he's realized he needs to take it seriously. I've inspired him." I can hear the pride in my voice and I feel a little silly, but I am proud. Ryland is talented—despite his ridiculous T-shirt designs—and he deserves to give himself every chance to make this dream come true. I love helping people realize their potential.

"Um, okay. That sounds good, I guess."

"And you'll get a kick out of this. He's actually recruited me to 'guard' him. I'm supposed to keep other girls away so he doesn't—"

Before I can finish, Ellie screams so loud that I have to pull the phone away from my ear. I knew she'd think that was funny, but I wasn't expecting yelling.

"Whoo!" she screams, but her voice sounds far away. I hear a slap like she's high-fiving. I squint. Am I on speakerphone? Is she high-fiving someone about the Ryland agreement?

"Ellie?"

"Sorry! I'm back!" She laughs. "Dev is giving me a death glare right now. I'm over at his house and we're all watching cricket together."

"Do you finally like that sport?" Last fall, Ellie recruited Dev's help to teach her cricket so she could win over a British boy. It had the opposite effect, though—she and Dev have been head over heels for each other since we left England.

"No, but I've found a new way to make it fun. Sahil and I team up to root against whichever team Dev is cheering for. The New Zealand national team just scored, so Sahil and I had to do our victory dance. I choreographed it. Dev *loves* it."

I laugh. He probably does secretly love it even if he pretends to be grumpy. I spent almost all my free time with them during senior year, and it was pretty clear that Dev loves everything Ellie says and does.

"Anyway, sorry, back to you! So, wait, let me get this straight—you're supposed to *stop* him from dating?"

"Yes, I'm helping him manage his time."

"But if he's not dating anyone, and you're both spending time together . . ." I can almost see her pointed expression. "Are you sure this couldn't lead to something between the two of you?"

"I'm positive."

"Well, all right. You *do* sound perfect for this job."

"Right? I have no problem saying no to people."

"Truer words have never been spoken. I hope you're still leaving yourself time to enjoy Amsterdam?"

I look around at the tall brick buildings on either side of me, people chattering together as they pass me on the sidewalk, boats drifting down the canal. "I'm definitely enjoying it."

"I'm so glad." I can feel the warmth of her voice through the phone. "And don't think I forgot that you still haven't sent me a photo of Ryland!"

"There haven't been many photo opportunities. But if I take a photo, you'll be the first to see it."

"Thank you. That's all I ask for."

"Tell Dev and his family I said hi."

"Will do! Miss you!"

"Miss you too."

I end the call and put my phone in my pocket. It really is beautiful here. Maybe it's time I see even more of it.

chapter
10

When Ryland comes downstairs Friday to work on lunch, I'm busy double-checking the entrance times to various attractions while Diederik plays on the floor. It's been almost three weeks since I arrived and I know I need to get Diederik out into the city, but I'm not sure how much risk I'm willing to take. I can't handle a complete toddler meltdown.

Ryland looks over my shoulder. Today he has on a pink shirt with a cat sitting inside a wooden clog and the words *Puss in Clogs* below. I wonder if this is one of the images he sells to shops for tourists.

"The Little Orphanage?" he asks. "Are you suddenly becoming a tourist?"

I look down at my list. That one does sound bleak to me—it's a museum that teaches kids what it would be like to be a seventeenth-century orphan in the Netherlands. Not exactly a lighthearted day out, but the guidebooks love it.

I shrug. "I'm not, but everyone wants me to see more of the city while I'm here, and I can only spend so much time in the house with Diederik."

"Yeah, I'm usually good after five minutes." He reads my list, nodding and making little sounds.

"What?"

"No, it's fine. It's a good list."

I glare at him. "These are all the top sites in Amsterdam."

"Sure. Although I believe I should have been consulted on this list given our arrangement. But if you'd rather go it alone, then have fun with that."

I cross my arms. I don't really need Ryland for this. I know how to make itineraries and travel plans. I bet any travel guide would love my list . . . though he *has* lived here his whole life. I put my pencil down and turn to him.

"All right then, what are your suggestions?"

"Actually, your timing is perfect. I'm getting ready to leave for a little research trip of my own, and you two are welcome to come with me."

"Research?" My eyes pop. I do like research.

"For my art project."

"What kind of research? Will it be Diederik-friendly?"

"Of course. That's my role, isn't it? Though I'm not sure how Sage-friendly this will be."

"You have to tell me where we're going."

He smiles. "No, that wasn't agreed upon in the contract. It'll be much more fun to surprise you. Or, of course, you can go check items off your list."

I look down at the paper and then back at him, feeling both frustrated and intrigued. I know he's just doing this to needle me, but it does sound a lot less stressful to explore the city with a two-to-one ratio of adults(ish) to impulsive toddlers.

"Fine, you win." I throw my hands in the air. "Diederik? Do you want to go on a trip with me and Ryland?"

"Yes! Trip, trip! Let's go!" He jumps up and runs over to where his shoes are. I laugh and shrug. I guess I'm outnumbered anyway.

This time I'm smart enough to bring a big bag with extra food, clothes, and toys. I even throw the iPad in there for good measure. But my stomach sinks when Ryland starts unlocking bikes out on the sidewalk.

"No, I didn't agree to bike riding. This is a walking trip only. Maybe a tram if I think I can manage it with him."

Ryland shakes his head and keeps unlocking them. "Nope. You've got to ride a bicycle here. I don't blame you for not wanting to do it alone with Diederik, but if it's three of us then we're definitely riding."

I eye the bicycle suspiciously. I can just imagine it toppling over or bucking me off like a horse. I don't like anything about it.

"I'll ride with Diederik and you can manage for yourself. I promise you'll love it."

I want to argue, but I'm embarrassed to admit just how scared I am to fall off the bike. I've noticed that none of the locals wear a helmet here, but luckily Ryland is able to rummage up an old one for me. I don't care if I look dorky as long as I don't get a concussion.

We take off and I'm wobbly at best.

"You have to pick up a little bit of speed," he calls out. "Just follow me."

My mouth is clamped tightly from anxiety and concentration, but I do what he says. There aren't special bike lanes on the smaller roads, so we have to ride on the brick streets with the cars. It's very unnerving, and I have to focus to make sure I don't slam into a car, another bike, or a pedestrian walking in the street. Multiple times I have to ring my bell to get people's attention.

However, after a few blocks, it's not *quite* so terrifying. I'm lucky that there aren't a ton of people out. I risk looking around as I pass by overflowing pots of flowers that line this street. Bright red shutters gleam at me across a canal. As much as I hate to admit it, this really is a beautiful way to see the city.

Out of the blue, a memory of riding bikes with my family comes back to me. When Wren and I were little, we'd sometimes go to a local park to eat lunch and ride on the paths. I was *always* the slowest, but Dad would keep pace with me so I didn't fall behind and get lost. I can still see him cheering me on as I did my best to chug my legs and keep up with Mom. A wave of searing grief passes over me and I force myself to squeeze the handlebars instead of squeezing my eyes shut the way I want to.

I don't like remembering him. I don't want to forget him either, but it's so hard to remember. Most of the time I can keep the memories in a little twilight space in my mind—just at the cusp of awareness but far enough away that I'm not overwhelmed by the pain—but sometimes my brain slips up and the memories flood back in. I can't predict when they'll hit me until I'm knocked over by their power.

My feet slow and Ryland surges off in front of me. I push myself to catch up, but my legs are weak all of a sudden. A moment later, he turns and sees me in the distance. Immediately, he slows his bike and maneuvers off the road and onto a narrow sidewalk. I force myself to ride over to him.

"Are you okay?" His voice is soft and concerned and it makes me defiant. I don't like people seeing me like this. Vulnerable.

"I'm fine."

He cocks his head. I'm not fooling him. "Should we turn around and go home? It's no trouble."

"No, we'll never hear the end of it if we do." I gesture to Diederik, who is already looking restless at our stop.

"True. Okay, well, call out if you need to stop again. We aren't far now."

We make our way onto a bike path that's wider than the walking path. People of all ages zoom by, most focusing on themselves but some waving or smiling, particularly when Diederik waves to them. The canal houses blow past, and I see tiny glimpses of the inside of each house before I'm on to the next. Soon Ryland is slowing and I'm pulling off to the side. I come up beside him and step down.

"Why are we stopping?"

He beams. "We're here."

"We're *where*?"

I thought we were going to some sort of Amsterdam attraction, but this is just another street. There are no museums or parks or playgrounds, just a canal and lines of brick homes like so many places in the city, although these houses seem grander than the ones where Ryland lives.

He points to one of the buildings, and I can tell he's enjoying my confusion. At first glance it looks the same as every other house . . . and then I see a small oval sign with a black cat on it.

"I told you this was a research trip for my project. Lucky for you, my art only focuses on the most interesting things in life, so"—he dramatically flourishes his hand toward the building—"I give you KattenKabinet! The best art museum in the world."

My jaw drops to the floor when we walk inside. It is, as far as I can tell, a very grand and traditional canal house. There are beautiful carved moldings, inlaid wooden floors, and antique-looking furniture. In fact, in some ways it reminds me of the English manor house I lived in last fall. There's just one small difference. . . .

Every open space is decorated with art dedicated to cats.

There are paintings of cats from the floor to the ceiling, covering every wall and filling the stairway. If there is a shelf, a nook, or a piece of furniture, then you can be sure they've topped it with a cat painting or sculpture. They even have a cat figurine—right next to a costume from the musical *Cats*—attached to the wall as if it's climbing and hissing down at us.

It's the wildest—and most amazing—thing I've ever seen.

"Ryland, *what*?"

He's so happy the joy is practically blinding me. "Isn't this the best? I didn't want to give it away because I really wanted to see your expression. This might be one of my favorite places in the city."

Diederik doesn't like staying in one place very long, so we circle through each room, both of us holding hands with him while

Ryland points out pieces and keeps up a running commentary.

"Have you ever paid attention to how cats are depicted in art throughout history? Like the way they drew cats in medieval times? It's as if they had no idea what a cat even looked like. And look at this one." He points to a painting on my right. "Look at that expression on its face, like it knows your secrets."

"Or how to kill you in the dark," I say.

"True."

After a bit, Ryland leaves to sketch some of the pieces. It's a little nerve-racking to have Diederik here because everything is fancy, but he's surprisingly good as long as I hold his hand and talk to him about the art. We wander through the back courtyard (also filled with cat art), play a few notes on a piano that's open to the public, and check out their cat Plinko game. Eventually, I pick him up and carry him around on my hip, talking about the colors we see and the other objects in the paintings.

"There's an apple!" he exclaims in his adorable high-pitched toddler voice.

"That's right, good job!"

His English is getting better and better. I give him a little hug. He turns to me and kisses me on the cheek. I take a small breath, my eyes flying open.

"Thank you! What was that for?"

He giggles and gives me another kiss on the cheek. Ooh, he's going to be a flirt just like his brother.

"Can I pet?" he asks, and points at the ground.

I'm about to tell him we can't touch the art until I realize that he's pointing at a real cat that's wandering through the room. *Of course* they have actual cats here as well.

"Let's see if he's nice," I tell Diederik.

I put him down and we follow the cat to a window bench, where it jumps up and settles onto a cushion. It turns out he's very sweet—and sleepy—so we both sit at the window, giving little pets and watching the world go by on the street outside. This particular afternoon is one I never thought I'd have in life, but maybe it's okay not to have every single hour of my life planned. Because this is a pretty cool experience.

We're still at the window when Ryland comes to find us. "So, you've officially seen the best of Amsterdam. Ready to pack it in?"

"As fun as this cat-themed site is, I have a feeling there's still more to see."

Diederik rubs his stomach as soon as we're back on the street. I'm not playing this game again. In two seconds flat, I've grabbed fruit gummies from my bag and handed them to him. He happily gobbles them up, but I know that won't last forever.

"On second thought, maybe we should head back."

Ryland shakes his head. "No, I have a better idea, come on. We can walk from here." A minute later, he's walking into a casual restaurant and ordering at a counter. The person hands him drinks and a paper cone of fries covered in mayonnaise.

"Fries?"

"Not regular old American fries. These are a national delicacy."

Ryland leans down and we both watch to see if Diederik will take one. He's still an incredibly picky eater, but he devours his fry eagerly. I'm not sure about the mayo, but I take a fry anyway because I know Ryland will tease me if I don't, and stare out into the canal. A group of people sail past on a boat, chatting and relaxing with drinks. Farther down, a larger tour boat with a glass ceiling floats lazily.

"You should take a ride on one of those before you go," he says, and points at the tour boat. "Another classic outing."

I nod, but don't agree. That looks a bit romantic for my tastes.

Ryland crumples the empty paper cone in his hands. "Those are good, but my favorites are by the Rijksmuseum. They fry theirs in sunflower seed oil."

I stare at him. "You can tell what kind of oil they use?"

"Of course. I'm a man of many tastes."

"What does that mean?"

"It means I'm a supertaster. I have a very refined palate."

As usual, I can't tell if he's being serious or screwing with me. I narrow my eyes and try to discern his expression. It's frustrating that he's so hard to read because usually I can read people easily. We start to meander down a busier street, me holding Diederik's hand firmly so he stays close. Luckily, today's outing is so different from usual that he seems content to walk and take in all the sights.

"I'm actually serious," Ryland continues. "One of my many side jobs over the years has been as a taste tester for restaurants and shops. They ask me to give feedback when they're thinking of adding a new product."

I gape at him. "What kinds of things have you tried?"

"Mustards, chocolate, sauces for bitterballen—those are like deep-fried meatballs—all kinds of stuff. You'd think the chocolate would be my favorite, but it's actually not. I tried too many and it gave me stomach cramps."

"I never thought of taste as a skill that could get you a job."

"Eh, it doesn't pay very well. But I've met some cool people and have gotten to eat a lot of interesting foods."

"What else do you do, then? You don't seem to keep regular hours."

"I don't have traditional jobs. I taste-test when I can, and I get commissions for art from four different shops. They have certain art prints that sell well, and since each is hand done in Holland rather than mass produced, they can sell them for a higher cost. And I also design tattoos."

Tattoos? Now that I think of it, I guess someone does need to design those, but I always thought they came out of a big generic book, or that the tattoo artist did the designs. I say as much to Ryland and he nods.

"Yes, but every once in a while Dan will have a client who's looking for something really unique and then she'll call me."

"Is this the Dan I met before?"

"Yeah, she's an old friend from school. She's very talented, but we've worked together on some of the more complex designs." He smiles, the sun shining through his red hair. "In some ways, it's actually the biggest compliment I could get—to have someone believe in my work enough that they'll let her permanently ink it on their body. My art will be around as long as they are."

"Unless they have it lasered off. I hear that's pretty common nowadays."

"You could get freelance work keeping people humble."

"No way, full-time or nothing. I need the money for med school."

He chuckles. "Well, no one is lasering off *my* work."

I haven't been paying attention to our surroundings, but I look up to see flower stalls, one after another. "Are we at the Bloemenmarkt?"

His eyes light up. "You really have been researching, haven't you? Yes, this is it." He points at one of the stalls. From the sidewalk it just looks like a flower shop, but I know that each stall is actually permanently floating on the canal. Inside are masses of tulip bulbs, cut flowers, and houseplants, with plenty of touristy stuff mixed in. I pause to take in the ceiling, which is completely filled with hanging bouquets of dried flowers. *Oh*, I wish Ellie were standing next to me right now. She'd be breathless from the beauty. I snap picture after picture for her, though I wish I could bring the store back to America instead.

"Are you a secret botanist?"

I laugh. "No, just taking photos for a friend."

"Then here"—he gently plucks the phone from my hand—"I bet they'll like the photos better if you're in them."

Actually, I think, *she'd like them better if* you *were in them*. But I smile and pose with Diederik for a few despite his growing antsiness. Flowers aren't exactly exciting to a three-year-old.

"Hold on, one more." Suddenly, Ryland is beside me. He wraps his arm around my shoulder and tilts his head to mine so that his hair brushes against my cheek. "So you don't forget me."

Looks like Ellie is going to get a present after all.

chapter 11

I go into the institute Saturday afternoon to work on Katina's new project and spend the evening laying out the conference poster on my computer. Once it's printed, it'll be three by four feet, but it's surprisingly tricky to include all the text and graphs while still using a font big enough for people to read it from a distance. That night I also take Ryland's phone away and block Evi after she texts him ten times in a row. Maybe that was harsh, but really, ten times? Take a hint.

By Sunday, I have to admit I'm a little restless to do something other than stare at screens. Out of boredom, I pull out some yarn and knitting needles I brought over from home. I've knit Maddie so many baby blankets that Wren doesn't have closet space for them, but maybe I could make Diederik something while I'm here.

"Just when I thought you couldn't be wilder, you prove me wrong." Ryland stands in my open bedroom doorway.

"Be careful. These are pointy." I hold up one of the knitting needles and mime stabbing him with it.

"Thanks for the warning. Clearly you've got a riveting day

ahead, but if you're looking for something else to do, then you should tag along while I drop off some commissions and get dinner. You can meet Espen."

"That sounds like something other than work."

"Dropping off my commissions is absolutely work. And as for eating . . . well, we all have to eat, don't we? My friends keep asking to see you again. What if we both met them this evening?"

I narrow my eyes at him.

"I'll have you know it's been a full *five* days since I last saw them. I've earned a visit, and if you come with me then you can make sure I don't get sucked into more plans."

"I doubt your friends want me lurking around and ruining their plans. I bet they only want to see me so they can tell me off."

"They won't tell you off. If anything, I think they're scared of you."

"Why?"

"Because I told them you're scary."

I laugh. I don't think that's true, but I won't fight it. I hesitate for a moment. I don't mind staying in, but I don't have a built-in excuse since I've been so productive lately. And maybe it *is* a good idea to come so dinner doesn't turn into some all-night outing.

I nod. "Okay, I'll come. But under two conditions. We come back when I want to, at a *reasonable* time."

He nods.

"And we don't bike again."

"Fine, but you'll need to build up your endurance if you want to make it here for the rest of the summer."

Ryland goes up to get the commissions and leaves his phone on the table. At this point, I don't hesitate to pick it up and scroll through his texts. I mean, it is my job. It's the usual players: Dan, Twitch, and one from Lillie. Another text comes in, this time from a name I don't recognize: Hazel. I roll my eyes. *Another* girl? Where does he even meet all these girls? And this one is especially clingy.

I still can't believe you're not here. You're so selfish. We need to make plans so I have something to look forward to.

Whoo-boy. Even Evi started out more subtle than this. Another text comes in immediately after.

Call me when you get this. I miss you.

I cough out a laugh. Looks like I'll be using the block button again this weekend.

"Ready?" Ryland holds up his bag of commissions.

"Yeah." I hand his phone to him. "But you should block this new girl and save us both some time. She'll be on the doorstep soon otherwise."

"Who is it?" He takes the phone and laughs. "Are you talking about Hazel? Because she's definitely not going to come to the door."

"You say that now, but then I'm the one dealing with them when they come."

"You don't need to worry about her."

He starts typing and I sigh. A tingle of annoyance runs up my spine at the way he's dismissing me. "Ryland, what's the point of this arrangement if you won't listen to me? She's clearly emotional and desperate to see you."

"Well, you're not wrong there, pining does seem to be part of her DNA. But I'd argue she got that from her mom's side."

"What are you talking about?"

His eyes flash with amusement. "Hazel is my half sister."

I gasp. "Your sister?"

"Remember when I told you how I usually spend the summers with my dad and his family? Well, that includes Hazel." He holds up his phone to show me a picture of himself sitting on a porch swing with a dark-haired girl who looks just slightly younger than him. He smiles down fondly at the photo. "She's the best."

"Oh! Well, I guess you really can't block her, then." I laugh. "I'm sorry, she just sounded a little . . . desperate."

"She's bored. Dad has always babied her and been extra protective—maybe because he never got a chance to do that with me—so he's picky about who she hangs out with. She's close with the neighbors, but usually the two of us hang out a lot when I'm there." His eyebrows furrow. "I need to get back there to see her."

He texts again and then pockets his phone, shaking his head in mock irritation. "I can't believe you almost blocked my sister."

"That's on you. We should have included a list of off-limits people on the agreement."

"We'll include an addendum tonight," he says with a wink. "Hope you still have your red pen."

～

It's about a fifteen-minute walk to the gift shop. The first ten minutes are beautiful, but then the dark clouds come rolling in.

"Come on, it's going to pour soon!" Ryland takes off down the road. I can't predict the weather here, but I'm willing to trust the locals. The stone sidewalk is slippery under my feet, but we manage to make it to the doorway with only a splattering of rain. He opens the door and ushers me inside. "Don't forget I warned you."

An alarm flashes in my mind. "What do you mean you warned me? You didn't warn me about anything."

He chuckles. "Oh, right, it slipped my mind." And then he walks into the store.

I'm seriously wishing I'd stayed home with my knitting, but it's too late now. The shop is narrow and deep, with a short flight of stairs that takes me to a small balcony. Up there is a section of wooden clogs in a rainbow of colors and designs. There's Delft pottery, with its detailed blue-and-white patterns, and a whole variety of tiny houseplants that Ellie would love.

On the lower level is a wall full of postcards and art prints. Some of them are clearly mass-produced watercolor prints of canals and windmills in tulip fields. They're pretty, but my eye goes a little farther back on the shelves. These are block-printed scenes of Amsterdam in jewel tones, the greens, purples, and blues layering over each other. In many of them, there's also a small cat hidden someplace in the scene. I smile and pick one up, already knowing that I'll find Ryland's name on the back. This one is a five-by-seven and costs €20. Not too shabby, assuming he gets some of that money.

I walk toward the back, ready to question Ryland about his

false warning, but then I see what he's probably referring to. On my left is a wall of condoms. Much like the shoes, they come in every color, size, and decorative pattern. I burst out laughing. I'm actually pretty used to the sight of condoms all around me. After Wren got pregnant, Mom took to buying large boxes for me and leaving them in the bathrooms, the kitchen, and even my book bag. Maybe I should bring back a few jumbo zebra-striped ones for her. I take a selfie in front of them to send to Ellie. She'll think it's hysterical.

Ryland waves me over and I lift my chin in defiance. If he thought he was going to freak me out over condoms, then he doesn't know me very well. But then I hear laughing, and one of the most unusual people I've ever seen comes out from behind a door. The white man is older, maybe in his sixties, and his hair is buzz cut . . . and colored to look like a beach ball. He has on a rainbow sequin shirt with clashing tartan plaid pants, purple Dr. Martens, and—I can barely encode it—a ruff collar like he just stepped out of a sixteenth-century painting.

My jaw drops and Ryland grins before I can plaster on a serene expression. *Dammit.* He's totally gloating.

"Sage, I want you to meet Espen."

The man claps his hands together. "So, this is the new girl who's taking over your house?" He puts his hand out to shake mine. "So nice to meet you. Ryland says you're quite the task-master."

I sputter. "I don't know about that."

"No, no, never apologize. I love a taskmaster. Particularly for this one." He hooks his thumb in Ryland's direction. "His art is spectacular, isn't it? But he fools around constantly. I've been trying to make him get serious since I met him two years ago. I haven't had a bit of luck with it, but then, I don't look like *you*."

I run a hand over my hair, feeling self-conscious. I don't look like anything special and I'm perfectly fine with that. Short brown hair, black or gray clothes, nothing flashy. I like the Steve Jobs idea of wearing the same clothes every day so you don't have to think about a daily outfit. I'm very good at not thinking about clothes.

He holds his hands out to me and then makes a tsking sound. "So beautiful and yet so drab." He gestures to Ryland. "Where are your colorful T-shirts? Have you not been sharing with her?"

He shrugs, looking mischievous. "I tried. She doesn't seem to want to wear them."

"But they're gorgeous, so creative!" He points at me. "You should have more fun. Nobody should get to dictate what we wear."

"My thoughts exactly," I reply pointedly.

He laughs. "Oh, I like this one. Yes, she will do very well for you."

My cheeks flush and I shake my head. "It's not—"

"Of course, my dear." He pats me on the back and walks up to the front of the store.

I want to fight more and tell him that there's nothing happening between Ryland and me. That it's actually the opposite because I'm *stopping* him from dating. But I realize the more I fight, the more he'll grin, and I don't want to give him any ammunition.

Ryland and I slowly follow Espen toward the entrance. "I warned you," Ryland whispers.

"You really did not."

He only winks again.

Despite the annoyances of this conversation, this might be my best opportunity to pick up a few more gifts for back home. I point at the wooden shoes. "Do you mind?"

"Not at all."

I find the tiniest wooden shoes for Maddie and more pairs for Ellie, Dev, and Huan. I pick up a pretty Delft plate for Mom, and a little windmill for myself. I hesitate and then pick up one of Ryland's pieces. Would it be weird if I bought one? They're objectively beautiful. I hesitate for a second and then grab two.

When he sees, he pulls them out of my hand. "No, you don't have to do that. I didn't bring you here to make money."

I tug them back. "I know you didn't. If you had I wouldn't be buying anything. But I need gifts for back home."

"Then I'll make them for you." He takes them back again.

I narrow my eyes and jerk them back a little harder this time. "No, I'll buy them. You should be spending your time on *your* art. Right? Not making stock pieces for me."

He's aggravated, but he doesn't fight me again. I check out and it costs a lot of money, but I figure I've been spending almost nothing here, and if I don't bring back presents then people will be grumpy.

"You might not have good taste in clothes, but you do have excellent taste in art and friends," Espen says as he hands me my bag.

I smirk at Ryland, but also think about Ellie, Dev, and Huan waiting back home. "Yes. I think you're right."

"Well, that was different," I tell Ryland when we're back on the sidewalk. Luckily, the storm has blown through and hints of blue are breaking through the dark clouds.

"He's unconventional, but I can't argue with his success. He's got three more gift shops like this around the city, he rents bikes, and he just bought his first restaurant. I'm lucky to have his support."

Before I can reply, there's a yell and we turn to find Ryland's whole group walking toward us.

"I didn't think it was possible!" Dan calls. Maiya waves and leans her head on Dan's shoulder.

"I'm starving," says Twitch. "What are we eating?"

"We should take her for rijsttafel."

"Yes, you have to eat that at least once when you're here," Maiya tells me.

I look between them, not recognizing the name. "It means 'rice table' in English," Ryland explains. "It's Indonesian. Does that sound okay?"

"Sure." I'm not a picky eater, so I'm happy to go along with whatever they want.

We follow Dan and Maiya. I have my defenses up, waiting for them to ask what the deal is with Ryland and me, but no one brings it up. They don't even acknowledge that I'm an outsider, which I appreciate.

The restaurant they choose is smaller and nicer than I'm expecting. The host seats us in the far back at a long table with a white tablecloth and orchids along a partition wall. Ryland leans in toward me and points to the menu. "I hope you like it. They'll bring out a huge bowl of rice for the table, along with lots of small dishes of beef, chicken, prawns, vegetables, all kinds of things."

"Does it live up to your superpowered taste buds?"

He grins. And leans in just a little bit closer. "Yes. My super-powered tongue likes it very much."

My stomach swoops and I lean back. What the hell is my body doing? My stomach does *not* swoop when boys lean close and say suggestive things. I do not swoon or sway. I'm always in complete control of my stomach, and every other part of my body, for that matter.

"So, um, how did you all meet?" I say loudly, breaking into their conversations.

They all stop talking and look at me, but they don't seem annoyed. "Ryland and I went to school together, since day one," Dan says. "We've been friends for years. And I met Maiya when she came in to get a tattoo. She has the first jasmine flower I ever did."

Maiya kisses the top of Dan's hand.

"You'll have to excuse them," Twitch says. "They're very in love and like to show it constantly. Even around those of us who are heartbroken."

"It's been nine months." Maiya shakes her head at him. "It's time to move on."

"The heart wants what the heart wants."

"*Anyway,*" Dan says. "Ryland says you're going to college in America this fall?"

"Yes, at Johns Hopkins. I can't wait."

"And what are you studying?"

"Biology. I'm premed."

"She's very dedicated," Ryland says.

"At least one of us at the table will make some money, then," Dan replies. "The rest of us are destined to be poor."

"Hey, don't include me in that group," Twitch complains. "I'm going pro on the esports circuit."

Maiya shakes her head again. I get the impression this isn't his first time making this claim. "Sage, are you liking Amsterdam? And how is it living with Ryland? I have to imagine he's a mess."

"Hey!"

"Amsterdam is beautiful. I'm so glad I'm spending the summer here." I glance around the table. "Ryland . . . he's a work in progress. We'll see."

Everybody laughs and Ryland falls back with his hand over his heart. "A work in progress? And after I took you to KattenKabinet."

"Oh no, he took you to the cat museum?" Dan cries. "Ryland, there are so many better places to take someone in Amsterdam."

"I beg to differ. There's literally nothing better in the city than a canal house filled with cat art."

"Don't let him convince you, Sage. He's obsessed."

The food arrives then and takes over the conversation. There must be at least fifteen small bowls and plates covering our table, and Ryland insists I take a few bites of each. It's incredible. The group starts telling stories about school and teasing Ryland for coming home each summer with an American accent and the latest pair of Nikes. The time flies by.

Twitch elbows Ryland after we pay the bill. "I'm going with my family to Rotterdam next weekend and you should come. It'll be way more fun if you're with me. What do you think? Don't say no."

Ryland's eyes go wide and Twitch nods eagerly.

I clear my throat. "He won't say no, but I will. That's the weekend before the competition pieces are due—Ryland will need the time to work."

Twitch's mouth drops open. "Seriously?" He gestures at Ryland like he's waiting for him to shut me down.

"Like Sage said." Ryland shrugs. "Ever since I put her in charge of my schedule, I've been able to get so much more done. But I promise we'll do something after the competition." He claps Twitch on the back as we head out of the restaurant. I'm thankful that Ryland didn't resist me. It's one thing for me to say no to a girl he isn't close to, but it's another thing to say no to invitations from his friends.

"So, weekend trips are out, but how about a drink before we go home?" Maiya asks.

"I can't," Twitch says. "I told the guys I'd be online to play by nine. Next time, though."

Ryland gestures to me. "I believe Sage is in charge of our schedule tonight."

I hesitate. I just said no to Twitch a few seconds ago, but this doesn't feel the same. It's a beautiful night and I don't have a pile of work waiting for me at home. What's another hour when we've already spent the entire evening out?

"Yeah, okay. Let's do it."

Ryland blinks in surprise. I have to admit it's nice to shake up my reputation for once.

We end up going to a little hole-in-the-wall bar that's so narrow you can almost touch both walls if you stretch your arms out to the sides.

"Do you know what you want?" Ryland calls to me. It's so loud we have to yell to hear each other.

I shake my head. "You choose."

A few minutes later, he pushes through the crowd and sets a bottle down in front of me. "It's framboise. I think you'll like it—it's sweet."

He's jammed right next to me, his mouth close to my ear so I can hear him, and shivers run through me that I wish I could blame on the alcohol. The meaningful looks Dan and Maiya are sharing aren't lost on me either. Maybe this was a bad idea—it's feeling a lot more like a double date than I had imagined. But then Ryland asks Dan about a tattoo client and that launches them into a hysterical story about strange tattoo requests. I finish my drink faster than I'm expecting and Dan gets me a second.

You are the dancing queen!

A cheer goes up in the bar and Dan and Maiya spin toward each other. They start yelling out the words to the classic ABBA song and the other patrons join in, including Ryland, who only knows half the words. I take another drink and laugh at the crazy scene.

"I didn't know the Dutch liked ABBA so much," I call to him.

"ABBA is internationally beloved. Especially when you're drunk!" He gestures around the bar. He's definitely right. Whole tables are swaying to the song. I have to admit, this is kind of fun.

All right, it's a lot of fun.

Or at least it is until a bar fight breaks out between two forty-year-old balding men when the playlist switches to U2's "With or Without You."

"Time to go," Ryland calls to the group. We push through the crowd once they break up the fight. I can sense Ryland right at my back. I take a deep breath when we're out on the open sidewalk again and the cool evening air hits my face.

"Thanks for coming out," Maiya says, and hugs me.

"It was fun."

Dan hugs me next and then leans over to hug Ryland. "I see it," she whispers to him so softly that I'm sure she doesn't think I can hear.

I look at her sharply. See it? See *what*? Is she seeing something good or bad? But Ryland doesn't respond, and the girls melt back into the crowds before I can get another hint.

chapter 12

I wasn't sure it was possible at the beginning, but Diederik and I have fallen into an easier routine. We eat breakfast and play in the house, do crafts, have lunch, and then spend the afternoons going on walks or visiting the nearby park. It's easy to kill part of each afternoon pushing Diederik on the swing until my arms are numb or letting him throw balls across the park to his heart's content. I'm still not confident enough to ride with him on a bicycle, but—to his credit—Ryland has been a help and I feel more confident going out with Diederik now.

However, today is not one of the easy days.

Three years ago was Dad's last day with us. I hoped it might be slightly easier to get through the hours this year since Diederik keeps me busy and I'm not at home to see all the reminders, but the pain has been overwhelming me since the moment I woke up.

We make it through the afternoon, but now Diederik is fussing, probably sensing my gloom, and I can't keep him happy. I try to pick him up, but he wiggles and I'm not strong enough to hold him. I put him on the floor and offer several toys, including his favorite train.

"No!"

"Do I hear yelling?" Berend asks as soon as he walks in the door after work. He picks up Diederik. "Now, now, what's this sad face for?" Diederik thrashes in his arms, but Berend only smiles more.

My phone buzzes and I pull it out to find a text from Wren.

Wow, your box just arrived. I love all the stuff you sent.
Thanks for thinking of me and Maddie.

I'm always thinking of you both.
Glad you liked it. ☺

I wait for another text, wondering if Wren is going to say anything about today. For a moment nothing comes and I assume that she's going to avoid the topic like she usually does, but then I get another text.

Are you holding up okay? Mom seems a little better this
year, but I think I might be worse. I wish he'd gotten to
meet Maddie.

I suck in a deep breath and look away from my phone. The time since has gone so fast and so slow all at once, in that weird way that only time can work. Part of me feels like Dad was with us just yesterday, but I'm also scared that I'm starting to forget him. Do I still remember what his voice sounded like? I have a memory of it, but maybe the years have warped it? They've warped so much.

I'm okay, I text back. Missing everyone a lot, especially Dad.

Diederik yells and I snap my attention to him.

"Let's go on a ride, okay?" Berend says. He swings him onto his back and wraps Diederik's arms around his neck. "Hold on tight!"

Berend gallops around the room like a horse, neighing and bouncing him on his back. Diederik squeals with delight, yelling so loud it makes my ears hurt and giggling for more. After Berend is red in the face from it, he flops Diederik onto the end of the couch and tickles his stomach. Their laughter and joy is palpable.

"Ik hou van jou," Diederik says, and pulls his father into a big hug.

"I love you too."

I drop my gaze to the floor. That deep ache I try so hard not to acknowledge yawns wide inside me. Dad played just like Berend. I recognize the twinkle of joy in his eyes. His wide smile and infectious laugh. Like when Dad would pretend to be a bear to scare Wren and me. We'd yell and run and hide in the closet, and Dad's heavy bear footfalls would make us giggle and cling to each other. Ever so slowly, he'd open the door and we'd scream and then—

It would just be Daddy. Happy, funny, smiling Daddy—not a mean bear at all—and he'd pull us into a hug and call us his cubs, and kiss our heads.

His two little cubs.

"Sage?"

I look up to find Ryland in front of me, his brows furrowed in concern. I didn't realize he'd come into the room.

"I'm fine." I brush away the tears, embarrassed. I'm usually so good at putting the memories out of my mind, but I haven't been around a father in so long. Not since my own was still alive.

After dinner, I immediately retreat to my room, but I can tell it's a bad idea to spend tonight alone with my thoughts. The heavy weight of grief is falling on me again, and if I'm here I won't be able to fend it off. What I need is to work. When I'm working, I don't have to actively think about Dad, but he's still with me. I always feel closest to him then.

Ryland is deep into his own work when I come up the stairs. I pull out my things, but it's hard to settle knowing that any second he might interrupt to ask me why I was crying downstairs. I peek up at him.

"Okay over there?" he asks without looking up. "Or am I going to get in trouble for speaking?"

"No, you won't get in trouble. I'm not the silence police."

"You are clearly the silence police. In fact, I'm making that shirt later tonight."

"Please stop making me shirts I'm not going to wear."

He humphs. "I'm making shirts *I'm* going to wear. And that you should be wearing. Speaking of which, this one is ready for you."

He stands and walks over to me with a folded shirt.

"I chose gray since it ties into Earl Grey and is the closest to matching your style. But don't think I'm going to stop using bright colors in the future."

I unfold the shirt. The words *Pillows & Billows* are in a loopy font with a teacup below. In the cup you can see the small billows of cream wafting up toward the surface. My memory of that night wafts to the surface of my mind as well.

"Now this one I might wear. Thank you." We're silent for a moment and then I blurt, "Berend is a really good dad."

Ryland frowns, clearly surprised with the change in topic. "Yeah. He's probably the most patient guy I know."

I nod. I should shut up now. I don't want to talk about this. But the throb in my chest begs to differ. Maybe I don't *want* to talk about it, but I need to. The words are practically strangling me, they're so ready to pour out.

"And the way he plays with Diederik, as if he's the greatest gift in his life. It's wonderful."

"Totally."

Ryland slowly lowers himself onto the couch. I can feel him trying to tease apart this conversation, but I keep my eyes on the shirt, gently rubbing a thumb over the soft cotton.

"It's different from how I grew up," he says finally. "My dad is cool, but he's not like that with me. We've lived apart most of my life—I mean, I have to take an international flight just to see him—so every summer we had to relearn how to be around each other. I think that's why he's so eager for me to come back to America." He shrugs. "How about you?"

My chest tightens. We don't talk about Dad at home, but for once I want to tell one of the stories that rattles around in my brain and screams to be remembered.

"He was the best." My voice is only a whisper. "The silliest goofball dad ever. King of the dad jokes."

"Was?"

I can only nod.

A shadow falls over Ryland's face. "I'm sorry."

"Cancer. Freshman year of high school." I meet his gaze. "You know, Dad was always trying to make us laugh. Right up until the very end. It should have been us doing that—and we tried—but he was better at it than the rest of us. I don't even know where he found all those jokes."

"Do you remember any of them?"

I scan my memory, although it's treacherous territory right now. One comes back to me. It was always one of my favorites.

"What's the best thing about Switzerland?"

He smirks. "What?"

"I don't know, but their flag is a big plus."

Ryland snorts and we both chuckle, but I still have to wipe tears from my eyes. Rather than look pitying or change the subject, he stands and messes around in the corner of the attic. I'm relieved for the chance to get control of my emotions. I do *not* cry in front of people. A few minutes later, he returns with two cups of tea. He hands me mine in a big blue mug and then pours creamer slowly into it.

"Billows make everything better," I say.

"I'll never drink my tea the same." We both take a sip in silence. "Thanks for telling me. He sounds like a great guy."

"He was."

This conversation has become way too emotional. Time to change the subject.

"I don't know how I'm going to top your museum trip," I say, "but I'm going to have to come up with something fun to do with

Diederik tomorrow. We're both getting bored of the same park and crafts."

"Have you taken him to Vondelpark?" he asks.

"No. Should I?"

"Oh yeah, that definitely needs to be on your list before you go back home. It's gorgeous and it has a great area for kids."

"Perfect, it's decided. Diederik and I will brave it tomorrow."

"What about if I came with you?"

"You're supposed to be *working*."

"I am working. In fact, I already have four pieces done and I need to get supplies to keep going. I could come for an hour and then stop for them on the way home."

I put down my cup and cross my arms. I hate looking like a hypocrite by agreeing to these outings. "You *really* have to get the supplies? This isn't just an excuse to skip out?"

"Of course not. Consider this part of your 'payment' for your invaluable guarding skills. I've gotten more work done in the last two weeks than I did in the two months before it."

"I'm glad, although there hasn't been as much for me to do lately. Are you hiding away the texts and invites now?"

He laughs. "I think you scared some of them, but I just got another text from Sanne tonight. And also Jillian. She's coming back early from the backpacking trip in Nice."

My head snaps up. "Oh, really?"

I didn't know they were still in contact. I feel the tiniest flare of jealousy in the pit of my stomach at the news. I push it aside, hating it. There's nothing to be jealous about. All I care about is that he gets his pieces finished in time for the competition. Then he can do whatever he wants with whomever he wants.

"Yeah, her previous ex has become her most recent ex again." He shrugs. To his credit, he doesn't gloat the way I'm sure a lot of guys would.

"Are you going to hang out with her when she gets back?"

"You wouldn't let me even if I wanted to, right?" He winks. "But no. Fool me once and all that. I don't have time to get involved. Speaking of which—" He stands and points to his table. "I should get back to it. My cats miss me."

I stand as well and walk over. Sure enough, he's got at least seven different cat sketches spread out over the surface of the table. "What is it with you and cats? Seriously."

"What do you mean *what's with me and cats*? Cats are adorable. They're fun to draw and print. And people buy them in droves. What's not to like?"

I cock my head and regard him. "But it's not just because people buy them. People love dogs too. And cheese. And naked women. I don't see you drawing any of those."

"Didn't I show you my series of nudes covered in cheese? They're really stunning, actually." He puts his hands out in front of him like he's picturing them. "I named one of them *Cheddar Makes Her Better*. Provocative stuff. Big sellers with the Germans."

I roll my eyes and try not to laugh. If I encourage him, he'll spitball fifteen more titles and we'll be here all night.

When he sees I'm not going to give in, he sighs. "I like cats because they can be stubborn and standoffish. They don't constantly crave your attention. They aren't panting in your face, dying to be petted like—you know—cheese."

I snort with laughter before I can stop myself.

"Sometimes you have to work to get them to like you. You have to build their trust—know what they want and when they want it." His voice drops. "But then, once they decide they love you, it's all worth it." His expression sears into mine and heat floods through my veins. "Just like with people."

"People?" I say faintly.

"Mm-hmm." He takes the tiniest step closer to me. "I like lots of people. All kinds. But my favorite people are the ones who act like cats."

I shift my weight away from him. "You know, some cats never get won over by humans."

"That's true." He smiles mischievously. "But some do."

chapter 13

I'm nervous for this Vondelpark trip the next day. I can feel things shifting between Ryland and me. I don't know what got into me last night, telling him about Dad the way I did. Crying in front of him. I never do that. I've only opened up about it to one other person, outside of my family, and that was Ellie. I should have called her last night instead of talking to Ryland. She would have listened and understood and I'm sure she would have perked me up with stories about her new fairy-garden-making class or what Dev and Huan are up to. Now I'm scared I've given Ryland the wrong message about us and implied more about our relationship than I meant.

But when Ryland arrives for the outing, he acts just the same as always. There are no lingering looks or meaningful cat references. I take a deep breath and remind myself that he's the one who said he wanted to stop dating and focus on his art. With so many gorgeous girls literally at his doorstep, dating me must be the last thing on his mind.

I freeze mid-step and squeeze the toy in my hand. *Sage, what?*

Why am I even thinking about us dating? I shake the idea from my head.

We take the tram to the park and as soon as I step onto the grounds, I relax. Everywhere I turn there are people biking, some whizzing by and others pedaling more leisurely. Other people are having picnics, or reading on a bench, or taking selfies in front of a nearby pond. I'm really glad Ryland suggested we come here, and I can't help feeling guilty when I think of the days I kept Diederik up in the apartment because I was too nervous to go out.

"It's been a long time since I've been here," Ryland says.

I've let go of Diederik's hand so he can run in front of us, as long as he doesn't get too far away. Which means that either Ryland or I are yelling after him every minute.

Ryland stretches his arms out and looks up into the sky. "We should come here more and take advantage when the weather is nice. Though that's hard to predict."

"Diederik, too far! Come back!" The little boy turns around and reluctantly stops and waits for us. I sigh. "Eh, I think you'd have more fun with your friends and no little brother."

"I'm having plenty of fun. You make me laugh."

"Do I? I'm many things, but funny isn't one of them."

"Sure you are. You have a very dry sense of humor, but I like that. I need it. I have a very . . . wet humor." He pauses. "That doesn't sound right."

I smirk. "Maybe *humid* would be better."

"Right. That's better. I have humid humor. See, this is why we need to hang out. People hate when it's too dry or too humid—but together we balance each other."

"Actually, a lot of people really like the dry heat. That's why they all move to Arizona. It's the humidity people can't stand."

He looks mock-outraged for a second before turning serious. "Well, I guess all those people can't be wrong. I certainly prefer it dry."

Something about his expression makes my mouth turn as dry as my humor. How did ridiculous weather metaphors turn into something else? Or am I just making this up in my head?

"But, more important, we need to talk about the miracle happening next to me." He points at me. "You're wearing my shirt!"

I look down self-consciously. After much hesitation, I pulled on his Pillows & Billows shirt this morning. I don't have a lot of clean clothes left, and—if I'm being honest—it is kind of cute. And at least it's a neutral gray.

"I had nothing else to wear."

"You love it." He laughs and skips a few paces ahead of me. "It's your new favorite shirt. You just wish I would've put it in hot pink."

"I will never wear hot pink."

"Before you leave Amsterdam, I'll get you wearing it."

"Doubtful."

Ryland points ahead. To our left, surrounded by a short decorative metal fence, is a children's area. I can see a shallow pool for splashing, a large sandbox area, and playground equipment. It's fairly crowded, but I guess that makes sense since it's tourist season on a beautiful day at the most popular park in Amsterdam.

"What do you say?" Ryland asks with a smile.

"The crowds look a little intense to me, but I'm not going to be the one to break Diederik's heart."

"All right, let's do it!" Ryland takes off running and grabs Diederik's hand to bring him along. The two are adorable, like small and big versions of the same person with their bright clothes and red hair.

I find them at the slides in a shaded forest area. Ryland is waiting for Diederik to come down.

"I'm getting thirsty. Do you want something?" he asks. "A drink or an ice cream?"

I have a water bottle in my bag, but it's lukewarm and doesn't sound very good. "Yeah, if you don't mind."

"Sure." He points at Diederik, who has already slid down and taken off in another direction. "Watch out, there are a ton of kids around."

I keep my eye on Diederik as he runs over to splash in the water, then tromps through the sand and back to the playground. He climbs up the structure, runs past a few other children on a suspension bridge, and zooms down a slide, before going around the back to do it again. He's so fast that it's hard to keep track of him, especially with the other kids darting past, screaming and laughing. My heart squeezes when I lose sight of him for a moment, but I force myself to calm down. Whoever designed this children's area knew what they were doing by fencing it in. Even if he darts away, I can't lose him here.

I circle around the structure, but he's not there anymore. Awesome. I turn back to the splashing pool and sandbox, but I don't see him there either. More alert now, I jog once around all the playground equipment to make sure he isn't hiding before heading to the swings. I hadn't realized just how huge this place was. Could he have gotten all the way to the other side already? But no, I would be able to see him running across the lawn.

"Diederik!" I yell at the top of my lungs, and dash back toward the forested playground, straining to see a flash of his red hair. He probably ran back into the trees and is hiding. But when I get there, I don't see him. And that's not the only thing that's missing. The *fence*. The freaking metal fence that's supposed to keep the kids inside and safe doesn't extend into the tree line. Horror fills me.

I take off running even though I don't know where I'm going. I'm like a wild animal, dodging and jumping around people, screaming his name. I can't see his hair color or bright green shirt anywhere. Others turn in my direction, but I don't stop to explain. I have to find him. He can't be lost. The children's area is large, but his legs are short. He couldn't have gotten too far, right?

Someone grabs my arm and spins me. "Sage! What's going on?" Ryland stands in front of me with two drinks, his eyes wide and his face pale.

Tears pool in my eyes. "It's Diederik. I was watching him—I promise I was—but now I can't find him and there's a gap in the fence and I think he's gone." I spin around again and yell his name.

Ryland scans the distance and points to a small path through the trees that I hadn't noticed. "I'll search this way, you check behind us one more time." He puts the drinks on the ground. "We'll find him. Don't freak out."

I nod and dart off. I run a loop around the area as fast as I can. One time I see red hair and run flat out toward the child, but when I get closer I see that the boy is too old to be Diederik. My brain is overwhelmed with fear. *Please don't let anything happen to him! Please!* When I'm sure he's not here, I follow the path after Ryland. It leads through the forested area to one of the wide concrete sidewalks where dozens of people are walking and biking. My tears come faster. If Diederik made it to this path, he could be anywhere. Someone could have taken him, he—

"Sage!"

I spin and see Ryland on the other side of the sidewalk, holding Diederik. Ryland still looks scared, but Diederik seems fine, maybe a little pissed that he's being held.

I rush over and pull him from Ryland's arms. *"Diederik."* I squeeze him into a tight hug and kiss the top of his head. "I was so worried about you. You can't go off like that. I couldn't see you, I didn't know where you were!"

I wipe my eyes and squeeze him tighter. I don't want to let him go. All of our days together fly through my mind. Fighting over eating, the monotonous playing, the screaming and tantrums. When I arrived, babysitting Diederik was an annoying but required task in order to do the research I love. A means to an end. But now . . .

I set him on the ground and kneel in front of him, then take his face in both my hands. His cheeks are soft and chubby and his eyes are wide. This little face has wormed its way right into the depths of my heart. I kiss him on the forehead and pull him back into a hug.

"I was so scared. You have to stay where I can see you. I can't let anything happen to you."

He probably doesn't know exactly what I'm saying, but his chubby arms squeeze my neck tightly. "I'm here."

"Yes. You're here." I squeeze him one more time and release him before he starts wiggling. My heart is finally beating a little slower. I look around and realize we're standing in a huge garden. Countless hexagons of roses surround us and someone is playing "Strawberry Fields Forever" in the distance.

I turn to Ryland while still squeezing one of Diederik's hands in my own. "*Thank you.*"

I wrap my free arm around Ryland's neck and hug him as tightly as I hugged Diederik. It takes him a second, but then his arms come around me and he pulls me into him.

"Just because the unreliable American nanny spaced out doesn't mean I'm losing my little brother," he says in a teasing voice. His breath is warm in my hair.

"Thank you."

I loosen my grip, realizing how long we've been holding each other like this. He releases me and I look down at Diederik.

"We're all done," I say. "My heart can't take any more. Time to go home."

"No!" Diederik's face gets red and I can see a tantrum coming. Ryland scoops him back into his arms. "How about ice cream?" he cries, and runs off before Diederik can get angry.

I take a deep breath, so thankful Ryland was here to help. And knowing I will *not* be coming back again.

chapter
14

"Ouch!"

I suck my finger where I just nipped it with scissors. That's the second time I've done that since Diederik and I got home from Vondelpark. Aren't these called safety scissors for a reason?

True to his word, Ryland parted ways with us after ice cream to pick up his supplies, and Diederik and I came back to the comfort of crafts and locked doors. Supposedly, we've been cutting out shapes to make a "solar system" . . . but all we've really made is a mess. I flip through our paper reserves, which are quickly dwindling. Maybe I should text Ryland and ask him to pick up more for us while he's out? But he's probably already on his way home by now. Maybe he and I could go back out later to get them and—

"My stars!" Diederik shouts, and I jump up, then gasp in horror before I can stop myself. While I was preoccupied thinking about Ryland, Diederik managed to cover a three-foot area of the floor in the tiniest pieces of yellow paper I've ever seen.

Dr. Reese walks through the door just then and puts her keys in the basket by the door. She takes one look at the kitchen floor and her mouth drops into an O.

"Wow, having fun?"

"Mama!"

Diederik flies to her side and I scurry to the closet to get the broom. "Sorry, Dr. Reese," I call over my shoulder. "I'm cleaning it up!"

"Thanks, Sage."

I start sweeping and mentally kick myself. I've been *way* too preoccupied with thoughts of Ryland this afternoon—wondering when he'll be home, what shirt he'll make next (I'm betting it has to do with that dry/humid conversation), or if he'll say anything about our hug in the park. Just the thought floods me with memories of his arms wrapped around me. I've never been a hugger, but that hug tempts me to reevaluate my position.

What is wrong with me? Even if Ryland has been flirting with me, that shouldn't matter. I've had boys flirt with me before. I've had them ask me out. Hell, Dev—Ellie's now *very* serious boyfriend—thought he had a crush on me before he realized it was wildly misplaced. None of that has ever distracted me.

But I'm officially distracted by Ryland.

This is *bad*. I look over my shoulder at Dr. Reese, who is now crouched down by Diederik. I cannot screw up my relationship with her. Not after how much work I've put into her research and everything that's at stake for my future. I can't let down Mom or Wren . . . or Dad.

I've got to get Ryland out of my mind.

Dr. Reese walks into the kitchen and groans when she opens

the fridge. Desperate for a distraction, I deposit the paper shards in the trash (well, as many as I could sweep up. Some will be stuck to the floor in perpetuity) and come to her side.

"Is everything okay?"

She sighs and stands. "Oh, yeah. I thought I'd make stamppot—it's one of Berend's favorites—but we don't have enough potatoes." She runs a hand through her hair. "I'll run out and pick some up."

"Why don't you let me go?"

"Really?" She cocks her head to the side. "Do you even know where the store is?"

No, but I'm sure the map app on my phone does. I practically lunge for my house key, I'm so frantic to get out of the house and clear my thoughts. I need to shake this off before Ryland comes home and reads my expression.

"This is the perfect excuse for me to explore more." I peer into the mostly empty fridge and see the sad excuse for produce left on the shelves. "Anything else?"

"Well, actually, you could get some leeks. And some bread and fruit as well?"

"Of course."

She walks to a closet and pulls out a few blue bags. "And take these. Otherwise, you'll have to buy the grocery bags there."

I feel better as soon as I'm out on the street. My phone shows that there's an Albert Heijn grocery store fairly close, although I'll need to cross two canals to get there. I push thoughts of Ryland aside and suck in a deep breath, letting Amsterdam fill my lungs. I walk slowly down the uneven cobbled sidewalk, up one side of the curved bridge and down the other, admiring the overflowing flower boxes and the glint of the water. A boat full of young people glides by on the canal below me. They look so relaxed, as if they're barely paying attention to which way the boat is going, but that stresses me out. Who can live like that—with no plan?

This grocery store is much smaller than the ones I'm used to at home. It definitely isn't the kind of place where you can buy your eggs, motor oil, and a folding lawn chair in one trip. I grab the items that Dr. Reese wants and then linger in the aisles. Maybe if I kill a bit more time I'll miss Ryland's arrival and I can give myself even more time to get my emotions in check.

Honestly, this is all my fault. I'm only feeling this way because of what happened at the park. If I'd been thinking straight, then I never would have let Ryland come with us today. He should have stayed home to work instead.

Of course, my always-logical mind reminds me, if I'd gone alone then I'd potentially be talking to the police about a missing child instead of debating over which leeks look the best. I sigh and pause in the dessert aisle as my eyes fall on a big bag of stroopwafels. Those would be good with a cup of tea. I grab a bag and don't allow myself to think about the boy I drink tea with every night.

I head back. The bags are heavier than I was expecting and I have to stop to readjust my grip. When I look back up, Ryland is in the distance. And he's not alone.

I blink. He's walking—some might even say *sauntering*—over a canal with a very pretty auburn-haired girl at his side. They're smiling at each other and then she says something to make him laugh. He throws his head back in amusement and my stomach clenches. He's . . . out with a girl? I don't recognize her, so she's not someone who has come by the house before. Could that be Lillie? Or the elusive Jillian now back from the ill-fated trip to Nice?

I know I need to stop staring at Ryland like an obsessed fan who just ran into her Hollywood crush on the street, but I can't believe this. I really thought he was putting dating aside and dedicating himself to his work. I take a step forward in shock. He doesn't even have bags of art supplies with him. So, he was lying when he said he needed to leave the park to go to the art store? Was that his excuse to get away so he could meet this girl without me ruining it?

Because that's *absolutely* what I'm about to do.

I march over to them while trying to cultivate the perfect facial expression to express that I'm both disappointed and indifferent.

"Really, Ryland?"

His head snaps up and his eyes go wide. He looks around the street as if I've appeared from thin air. "Hey, what are you doing out?"

I narrow my eyes at him and lift the grocery bags. He's not going to distract me with questions. I turn to the girl. "Hi, I'm sorry to break this up, but Ryland shouldn't be here with you. He's not supposed to be dating."

Her eyebrows pull together in confusion. "I'm sorry . . . what?"

"He's not allowed to date. Now, I'm sure you're a perfectly nice person and clearly you're very pretty, and Ryland can certainly be charming when he wants to be—"

"Sage—"

I turn my back to him and continue. "But Ryland previously asked me to—"

"*Sage.*" Ryland's face comes around my shoulder. "This isn't a date."

"Oh, really?" My emotions get the better of me and my words grow louder and faster. "Then where are those supplies you supposedly needed? And why didn't you tell me you were going to be out this evening with someone? I can't believe you lied to me." I glare at him. "You know, Ryland, I never wanted any of this. *You* were the one who pleaded with me. *You* were the one who said you wanted the help. If you were done with our arrangement, then you should have just told me instead of lying."

"Wow, okay. Are you two together?" the girl asks.

"We most certainly are not," I snap.

Her eyes flit back and forth between Ryland and me in alarm, as if she expects me to produce a glass of wine and throw it in Ryland's face at any moment.

He sighs deeply. "Sorry about this, Rachel. It's just a big misunderstanding. Sage, will you listen for a second instead of throwing accusations at me?"

"Um, I don't think I should be here for this. It was good to see you, Ryland." The girl—Rachel—gives him a quick hug. "Have a good night." Her tone implies *Good luck with this one.*

As soon as she leaves, I do the same. I fulfilled my duty and now I'm done.

Ryland hurries to my side. "Are you seriously this upset? I didn't even get a chance to introduce you to her."

My stomach twists at the idea. Any joy I thought I'd get from watching him squirm dissipates into the air around me. Because this thing between us doesn't feel like a business negotiation anymore. It doesn't feel impartial. My jaw is sore from clenching it so hard and my chest is tight and all I want to do is drop these grocery bags and run in the opposite direction from him before he realizes every single emotion rolling around in me right now. I *hate* that Ryland now has the power to make me feel like this.

"I'm not upset," I reply. Two can play at this lying game. I roll my shoulders back and look him square in the eye. "Our arrangement is off."

He jumps in front of me so I can't stalk off the way I'm trying to. Somehow, he's still smiling. Does he take nothing seriously?

"Sage, listen to me. I am *not* dating Rachel. God, she's been with Ivan for three years now. She was finishing her shift at the art supply store when I walked in and she had some advice on the competition, so she walked home with me."

"You don't have any supplies with you."

He laughs, not a shred of shame in his voice. "I dropped them off at the house first. Actually, I asked her to come in so you could meet her and hear about the competition. One of the judges, Rois, came into the store and started chatting with her." He gestures down the street toward the apartment. "Come up to the attic and you'll see the supplies. I can even produce a receipt with the date on it, though I hadn't realized I'd be audited after shopping trips." He grins. "Where's your red pen? I think we need to add this stipulation to the agreement."

I want to hold tight to my suspicion, but already it's transforming into mortification. He didn't lie. But rather than walk up and ask him what was happening like a rational person, I jumped to conclusions and made a fool of myself. I want to melt into the canal and float away forever into the ocean. And the way Ryland is gazing at me *really* doesn't help. His head is cocked to the side with a small knowing smile, as if pondering my adorableness for acting this way.

I am not adorable. Ever.

I wave him away. "Just forget it. We're not adding a stipulation."

"Because we don't need one or because you're going to burn our agreement to ash?"

"I won't burn the agreement. Yet."

I stride down the street and Ryland silently takes a bag from me and walks at my side. I can't speak. The whole scene rolls through my mind, and my body is hot and itchy with horror. I can't believe I just embarrassed myself like that, acting like I'm some lovesick girl desperate to be with Ryland.

Like I'm jealous.

When we reach the building, Ryland holds the door open for me and then takes the second bag so that I don't have to carry anything up the steps. I'm unreasonably annoyed that he's being so nice.

"We're okay, right?" he asks quietly. "I didn't torpedo everything by walking home with Rachel?"

My chest caves in from another wave of embarrassment. "No, you're allowed to walk with people. Obviously. I shouldn't have yelled."

Ryland stops climbing and turns so he's standing one step

above me. The stairs are narrow and I have to stop too. I can't help noticing how close we are.

"Yes, you should have. That's our deal—you help me protect my time. I appreciate that you're holding up your end of the deal, even if nothing was happening." He smirks. "Although I think you freaked out Rachel. I *told* you you were scary."

I know he's teasing me to dispel the tension, but I can't bring myself to smile.

"Let's drop this food off and go up to the attic," he continues. "I can tell you what Rachel said and you can see the supplies I got. Red pen optional."

My stomach lurches at how much I want to go upstairs with him. None of this should be happening. Not my jealousy—which there's no point denying—and not his palpable amusement over the fact that I was jealous.

"I can't."

"Really? If you want to work instead then I promise I won't talk. I thought I'd earned back your trust on that one."

"You did. It's just . . ." I search for an excuse. "I'm just tired. And I'm not feeling well. I should probably lie down."

"Oh." At least that wipes the grin off his face. He steps away and we walk up the rest of the steps. "But you'll come up tomorrow night, right?"

"Mm-hmm," I mumble. His worried expression nearly cracks through my resolve, but this thing with him has gone too far already. There aren't going to be any more attic nights.

chapter

15

I barely talk to Ryland the next day. Ironically, I have Diederik and his lack of sleep to thank for that, because he's in such a bad mood that there's no time for flirting amid all the screaming and food throwing. Dinner with Berend and Dr. Reese is quiet, and afterward I go back to my bedroom rather than the attic. I shut my door firmly and settle onto the bed. My thoughts drift toward the top floor—wondering if Ryland's realized I'm not coming again and whether he'll ask about it—but I clamp down on my brain. No. He doesn't get to take over my thoughts. *I'm* in charge.

After a while, my mental warfare succeeds and I get to work. It's tedious, but I'm finally able to finish the reference list for a meta-analysis. I send an email to Katina and Dr. Reese, letting them know, and feel very proud that I finished before my deadline. Around midnight, I allow myself to get out of the bed and stretch. See, this was perfect. I was super productive all by myself. I didn't need a couch, or tea with cream, or the sound of Ryland carving his linoleum blocks. If I can just get a little space from him, then these ridiculous feelings will fade back into nothingness.

I change into my pajamas—a loose shirt and shorts—and pad over to the bathroom to get ready for bed. Diederik is asleep in the room across from the bathroom, and Dr. Reese and Berend are just down the hall. I don't want to wake anyone up, particularly after that rough day with Diederik.

I quickly wash my face and begin to brush my teeth. Wait, did I actually attach the file to that email? I don't remember doing it. Sigh. Maybe I wasn't *quite* as focused tonight as I thought. I hurry back to my room while I brush. It's a little hard using the mouse and brushing my teeth at the same time without slobbering toothpaste bits onto my keyboard, but I manage it. I hurry back over to the bathroom and almost run straight into Ryland. He's at the sink, also brushing his teeth. He smiles around his toothbrush and keeps brushing.

I take a step back into the hall and look down at myself. These are not appropriate clothes for other people to see me in. These shorts are basically glorified underwear. And I don't have a bra on. I casually put an arm over my chest.

He keeps brushing his teeth.

I tap my foot and listen for any sounds coming from the other bedrooms. Ryland bends down to spit and I step forward to take over the sink, but then he stands back up and keeps brushing with a smile. Is he always such a thorough brusher? What is he, a secret dentist or something? All right, this is stupid, he needs to get out of the way.

Just then he bends down and spits again, before rinsing his mouth and taking a drink from the faucet. I can't stop my eyes from running over every inch of him when his head is down. A strand of his hair falls down into his face, getting soaked, and I have an irrational urge to reach out and put it behind his ear. That might not be the only urge I'm feeling right now.

He stands and smiles. "All yours." He puts out a hand to the sink, but rather than leave the bathroom, he just steps deeper into it.

There isn't space for two people to be in this bathroom without being right up next to each other. I want to say this, but my mouth is full of spit and I'm not about to talk and have it dribble down my chin.

I glare at him and spit into the sink. I'm uncomfortably aware that Ryland is inches away and my shorts are riding up even more as I bend over. I straighten up as quickly as I can even though my mouth is still gritty with toothpaste. I'll come back and rinse more thoroughly when he's gone.

"Had a good night?" he whispers.

"Yes. Very good." I narrow my eyes. "Do you always brush your teeth for ten straight minutes?"

"Not usually." He cocks his head to the side and his damn hair falls in his eyes. He definitely knows he's doing that.

"So, you were just screwing with me?"

"Can you blame me? Do you have *any* idea how fun it is? The way your eyes close into slits and your cheeks get pink. It's more fun than most dates I've been on."

Did he move closer or did I? I don't remember either of us moving, but there's even less space between us now.

"Why didn't you come up to the attic tonight?" he whispers.

"No reason."

"Am I becoming too distracting for you?"

I grit my teeth. "No. Not at all. I just wanted to be by myself tonight. I like being by myself."

"Yes. Clearly." He looks down at the few inches of space separating our bodies.

Our eyes lock and I get the distinct feeling that he knows every impulse rushing through me right now.

"Sage?"

I yelp and jump back. I swing around to find Diederik standing in the hallway, his small fists filled with paper sweetener packets. Ryland and I share an incredulous look.

"What are you doing? You're supposed to be asleep," I whisper.

"Snack?" he asks at a regular volume, and Ryland and I both flinch. I glance down the hall, waiting for Dr. Reese or Berend to crack open their door and find all of us hanging out together. I don't want to explain that.

"Shhh, we need to use a quiet voice, sweetheart." I pull a sweetener packet out of his fist. "Why do you have these?"

He shrugs.

"Did you take those from the kitchen?" Ryland asks. He leans over my shoulder so I can smell his shampoo. I turn my head away.

Diederik shrugs again and starts to rip one open.

"No!" I take it before he makes a huge mess on the floor.

Ryland takes the rest. He squeezes around me and out into the hall. "Time for bed." He picks up Diederik and slings him onto his hip. "Good night, Sage," he whispers over his shoulder. "Sweet dreams."

Yeah, right. My dreams are as sweet as the strawberries rotting in the back of the fridge. I dream I'm in med school. I walk into an examination room to see a patient, but instead I find Dad there. He's alive and holding Maddie and he asks me when I'm going to have a baby. Instead of being happy to see him, I argue with him that the only reason he's alive is because of my work. He's disappointed with me and disappears, leaving Maddie behind, but now she's much older. I know it's her, but I also don't recognize her. And then she disappears, and I burn myself with a huge cup of tea.

I'm not well rested when I wake the next morning, but I *am* decided. I'm not going to hang out with Ryland anymore. I can still be nice to him. We can chat about the weather and eat dinner together with his parents. I'll even run interference for him if someone comes to the apartment. But I can't spend any more afternoons with him and Diederik. And I *really* can't spend quiet evenings in the attic.

Now there's just the small issue of telling him.

Usually, I have *no* problem telling people my feelings. Wren and Ellie might argue I'm too happy to give my true thoughts. But this time . . . I can't find the courage. Maybe because I'm not sure how he'll react. Will he argue and tell me he has feelings for me? Or will he reassure me that he has no interest in dating me?

And which option would be worse?

The fact that I can't easily answer that question tells me I'm already in too deep.

I'm given a reprieve from the conversation when Ryland skips lunch to finish one of his pieces. Instead, I throw myself into my day with Diederik. He really loves this rhyming picture book about trains, so I've built the entire day around it: we make train tracks using Popsicle sticks, match colors and letters on construction paper train cars, and I even make a train from crackers for a snack. I take a picture of that one to text to Wren, Ellie, and Mom. It's objectively impressive.

Around two o'clock, my phone rings, and I'm surprised to see Katina's name. We exchanged numbers when I first arrived here, but we never call each other.

"Katina?"

"Hey, Sage. Do you have a minute?"

"Sure. Is everything all right?"

There's a pause. "Well, I finally got a chance to look at the abstraction data you put together for us at the beginning of the summer, but something isn't right with it. It looks like we're missing data for some of the participants. And I think the social support variable was coded wrong."

My heart speeds up. There's missing data? Wrong data? This was one of the first things I did when I arrived—I know I was tired and overwhelmed, but did I really mess up their data set? This is bad. Just then, I jump at a crash. Diederik's flipped over a huge bucket of blocks, but I'll have to clean it up later.

"Do you want me to pull up the data over here and take a look? I should still have a copy of it on my laptop."

"Yeah, that would be good. Or . . . there's probably no way you could come to the lab, right? I think we'd figure this out faster if we were together." Her voice sounds a bit panicked. "I'm behind and promised Dr. Reese that I'd get these analyses done this afternoon so she can share them with the hospital administrator."

"Um . . ." I look around the room in desperation. "Yes, I can come. I just, uh, need to—"

"You can't bring Diederik with you, though. That'll only make it worse."

"No, I'll . . ."

Ryland.

I suck in a breath. "I might have someone who can watch him. I'll call you back."

I run for the staircase and then think better of it and sweep back to get Diederik. I don't need him getting into trouble because I left him for a few minutes.

"Ryland?" I call as I climb the steps into the attic with Diederik squirming on my hip. "Are you up here?"

I expect to find him, head down and focused, but the attic is dark and empty. I frown. Did he leave the house without telling me? Not that he's required to check in with me before leaving, but I'm still surprised.

I come back down and then hesitate before knocking on his bedroom door. It feels weirdly private, particularly after the way we've been acting around each other, but there's no time to lose. I need to help fix this mess as soon as possible before I ruin the reputation I've been building for myself.

The door swings open. Ryland's evidently in the middle of getting ready. His dress shirt is unbuttoned, and it takes every ounce of common sense in me to pull my eyes away from his chest and focus on his face. Wait, he's wearing a button-up? I thought he only owned T-shirts? Granted, this shirt is a horrible clash of purple with green polka dots, but it's still fancy for him.

"Hey." He looks between Diederik and me. "Is everything okay?"

"Actually, no." I put down Diederik and he immediately wanders into Ryland's room. He would probably destroy it if it wasn't already demolished. "Katina, from your mom's lab, just called me. It looks like I maybe"—I swallow hard—"screwed up their data. I was supposed to be pulling information from patient medical records, but I think I might have skipped some variables and mixed up the coding." Dread fills me as I say it aloud. I can distinctly remember doing that work on my bed during the first weeks here. It was tedious, and I was so exhausted. I thought I'd been paying attention, but maybe not as much as I should have been.

"Oh no." He looks back at Diederik, who is now pretending to swim in the pile of laundry on his floor. "Did you need me to watch him so you can go in?"

"Could you? I'm really sorry, I know I said I'd help you work instead of giving you more things to do, but I think I should really be there. They're under a time crunch." He's finished buttoning his shirt, so I run my eyes over his outfit. "Unless I'm interrupting something? You look like you're getting ready to go out."

He smooths down his shirt. "Oh . . . uh, no. I mean, I was going to go meet someone, but it's not a big deal. I'll cancel."

I bite my cheek to stop from asking who he's meeting.

He shakes his head. "It's not a date. Just a chef—for a taste test."

"Oh, then never mind. I can't take work from you. I'll just bring Diederik with me or figure out something else."

"Go. Really, it's fine." He waves me away when I hesitate. "I can tell every second you stay here is strangling your soul a little bit more."

He's not wrong. "You're sure? Thank you! I so appreciate it!" I turn to run down the stairs.

"Good luck!" he calls behind me.

chapter
16

I'm a disaster the entire ride to the lab and take the steps two at a time when I arrive. When I get to the offices, Katina is sitting at the main table.

"Hey, I'm here. Have you figured anything out?" I sit next to her. On the screen is the data set I created. She's flipping between that file and one of the patient medical records.

"Well, for one thing, you've coded the start of treatment date as the end of treatment date." She points to the record.

I lean in, horrified, to see that she's exactly correct.

"And here"—she scrolls down and points to the record—"you inputted each of the patient's chemotherapy treatments, but I don't see the hormone therapies listed." She sits back and turns to me. Her usually cheery expression is a dour mask. "I've been trying to piece everything together, but I've only looked at about six patients so far. Do you think you did this for all of them?"

Fear floods through me. Did I? I don't remember. I could have sworn I entered this all correctly. I know Dr. Reese trained me on how to search for and code each variable . . . but maybe I wasn't my usual thorough self when I was doing this work.

"Do you mind if I look?"

Katina sits back and I pull her laptop in front of me. I scroll through the data set again, then look at a few more patient records. I'm sick to my stomach. It's clear that I wasn't paying enough attention and made the same mistakes throughout the whole data set. That's 120 patients.

I take a deep breath and turn to Katina. "I think it's all like this."

She drops her head into her hands. "Shit. Dr. Reese is going to be back any minute and she'll have my head when she realizes. She's been wanting these analyses for weeks, but I've been so busy with another project. When she finds out I didn't even check the data until today . . ."

I slump into my chair, feeling absolutely horrible. "I'm so sorry. I can't believe I did this."

"I should have checked the data as soon as you emailed it. You're just always so reliable that I thought it would be fine. It's my fault."

I shake my head. "No, this is obviously my fault." I pull the laptop closer. "I'll start fixing it now. Should I just try to correct the mistakes in the data or—"

"I think the whole process needs to be started from scratch. But . . . I'm not sure you should be the one working on this." She holds up a hand. "It's okay, data abstraction can be really hard. Mistakes happen a lot. I'll do it this time."

"You don't have time."

She gives a weak smile. "Welcome to your future. I'll make it work. Somehow."

"No." I put my hands on either side of her laptop so she can't take it back. "Please let me fix this. I want to prove I can do it."

"This isn't about proving yourself. It's about getting the work done."

"I know, and I'll do that. I'll dedicate myself to it, okay?"

"Sage . . ." She sighs. "Honestly, it's not up to me. We're going to have to tell Dr. Reese about this when she gets back and then she can decide."

The idea of having to admit what happened to Dr. Reese makes me want to run out of the building and jump in the nearest canal. That sounds significantly more pleasant than seeing her disappointment. One of my biggest goals this summer was to show Dr. Reese how reliable I am so that she'd agree to keep working remotely with me while I'm in college, and now I might have screwed that all up.

The door clicks open behind me and I turn to find Dr. Reese. She jumps when she sees me. "Sage?" She looks around the room. "What's going on? Is Diederik here?"

"No, Ryland is staying with him so I could come here." I exchange a look with Katina and stand.

"Ryland? I don't understand, we didn't talk about you coming in this afternoon. Katina, what's all this about?"

"There's been—"

I cut her off. "I made mistakes when I was doing the data abstraction at the beginning of the summer. I'm really sorry. When

I heard, I asked Ryland if he could watch Diederik for the rest of the afternoon so I could come and help fix it. If you're willing to let me."

Dr. Reese frowns and comes to the table. "Show me."

Katina explains what happened while I stand silently, waiting for judgment. Not that their judgment could be harsher than my own judgment of myself. I've never made mistakes like this in my life. Yes, I was exhausted from watching Diederik, but that's no excuse. If I can't pull off this task, how am I ever going to be trusted with more important jobs like actual data collection?

"Sage, I have to say I'm surprised." Dr. Reese inspects me. "I expected more from you."

I wilt. "I'm sorry about the mistake. I'd like to correct it."

"Hmm." She purses her lips. "Do the data abstraction for the first ten patients now and then bring in the data to me. Do you remember the training?"

"I do."

She stands and waves me toward the laptop. I exchange a nervous look with Katina and then sit down to begin. Forty-five minutes later, I'm finished. That's a slow pace, but I am not going to repeat my past mistakes this time, so I checked and rechecked. I pick up the laptop and gingerly knock on Dr. Reese's door. She waves me in.

"Here's the data you asked for." I hand her the laptop and lower myself into a chair.

She scrolls through it, her eyes darting around the screen. Tension claws up my rib cage. I really hope she hasn't lost her faith in me.

After a few minutes, she nods and sits back. "The data looks fine this time. I don't see any problems."

"Yeah?" I suck in a breath. "Would it be okay for me to work on the rest, then?"

"Do you actually want to? It's not a fun task. Which is why we gave it to you."

"I know. But I don't like failing at anything. I'd like to redeem myself." I square my shoulders. "And I want to apologize again. I know you were hoping to present the results at a meeting and now you won't be able to. I'm sorry that I let you down."

She regards me a moment and then smiles. "I appreciate that. Listen, one thing you'll find in college and far beyond is that people make mistakes. It's human nature and is only exacerbated in academia. What's important isn't the mistake, but how you handle it. And I think you're handling it in a really responsible way. You found a way to make sure Diederik was taken care of so that you could come and help. And the fact that you're owning it and trying to correct the mistake, rather than making excuses, says a lot about your character, Sage."

Relief and warmth flood through me. Thank god. I thought maybe I had messed up my chances for good. "I'm so glad you gave me the opportunity. This day aside, the experience has been even better than I imagined."

"Are you excited for Berlin?"

"I'm *so* excited. The poster is almost done, so I'll send that to you soon. I can't wait to hear the keynote by Dr. Singh, and I think one of the faculty members from Johns Hopkins will be there. I'm really hoping for an opportunity to introduce myself."

She raises her eyebrows. "Oh, I'll make sure to introduce you. I want everyone to know that I was the one to find this superstar in the making." She laughs. "Now get back to work. We still have another two hours before we need to go home."

chapter 17

When Dr. Reese and I get home from the institute, Ryland is sitting on the ground with Diederik. They're painting on a huge piece of paper rolled out on the floor. I would never have the guts to get out ten different colors of paint and give Diederik full rein to go wild, but Ryland seems totally relaxed.

"Mama!" Diederik cries, and runs to her. His hands are covered in paint. She grabs him before he can accidentally finger-paint her, then nods at Ryland. "Thank you for watching him. But maybe . . ."

"Yeah, I'll get him washed up." He looks at me. "See, I still got some art in today."

"I love to see the multitasking."

He steps closer to me. "Did everything work out?" he whispers. "Or did they try to behead you?"

I cut a glance over to Dr. Reese. "No, I get to keep my head for now. Thank you so much for helping me today. I really appreciate it."

"Of course."

My resolve to keep my distance from Ryland wavers. Ever since he and I started working together upstairs, I've been able to focus so much more. I bet I could really knock out this data abstraction if I were up there rather than doing it from my bed. But continuing to go up there will bring other complications that I don't want to deal with. I'll have to make do without the attic.

The next afternoon I'm trying to convince Diederik to eat a carrot stick for his snack when there's a knock on the door. Could this be another girl for Ryland? He hasn't had anyone coming over for him lately—not since the Rachel incident.

I open the door. "Oh, Dan, Maiya. What's up?" I'm relieved to see familiar and friendly faces. They both look as cool as usual, especially Maiya, with her new pink highlights. "Are you here for Ryland? He's upstairs."

"You don't need to get him. We told him we'd stop by this afternoon to drop this off." She hands me an envelope. "That's his share from the last tattoo design. Can you make sure he gets it?"

"Of course. Do you want to come in?"

"No, we need to get back to the shop. But is Ryland okay?" Maiya asks. "We couldn't tell from his text."

I cock my head. "As far as I know. Is there a reason he shouldn't be?"

They exchange a look. "Well, he missed his big meeting. I'm sure he must be upset about it."

"About the taste testing? He mentioned it, but he made it seem like it wasn't a big deal."

"Taste testing? No, not that. With the competition judge?

Actually, maybe we should come in."

I put on Miffy, Diederik's favorite cartoon, to keep him occupied. The girls sit down in unison. They're like two halves of the same person. "Ryland was supposed to have a consultation with Rois Baatz yesterday," Dan explains. "He's one of his idols so we wondered, you know, if he missed it because of you."

"Because of *me*? He didn't tell me anything about it. I did have something come up yesterday and I asked him if he could watch Diederik for a few hours, but he told me it was fine. I would never knowingly do something to hurt his chances with this competition."

Dan puts her hands up in defense. "I know you wouldn't. I could tell after having dinner with you that you had his best interests at heart."

I stare, stunned that he missed a consultation like this and said nothing to me. How could he sabotage himself like this?

"Listen, this whole thing with you and Ryland"—she shakes her head—"I've known him for a long time. And yes, he's distractible."

"And popular," Maiya adds.

"But if he doesn't want to date someone, then he'll find a way to break it off. He certainly did that with me." She looks at Maiya tenderly. "Which I'm very thankful for."

"Okay?" I think I know what they're insinuating, but I'm not ready to face it.

"We're just saying that we haven't seen Ryland in weeks now. No one has . . . because he's spending so much time with *you*." Dan's voice cuts into me. "And now he's missing meetings to watch Diederik for you. Meetings that could move him closer to his dreams."

Maiya squeezes Dan's hand. Her voice is softer when she says, "We like you, Sage. Really. But we love Ryland. We can't stand by if there's a possibility of him being hurt."

"I . . . right. Of course." I nod even though I'm still processing their words and implications. Part of me wants to deny that anything is happening between Ryland and me, but I know that would be a lie. It's not right to continue whatever this is with him if it means I'm leading him on. "Yes, I'll talk to him tonight."

"Good." Maiya stands and pulls Dan up with her. "We just want him to be happy."

"I do too."

Dan smiles. "We know. And that's why we're talking to you now rather than badmouthing you with our friends tonight."

I'm a jittery mess the rest of the day. I let Diederik watch more Miffy and then play games on the iPad because I can't think straight enough to engage with him. All I can think about is Dan and Maiya's comments. I've got to shut down this situation with Ryland. I still can't believe he missed a meeting with Rois Baatz for me. What the hell was he thinking? Hasn't he been listening when I told him to put himself and his dreams before anyone else? Instead of helping him, I've become another girl who distracts him. It makes me feel sick to think about.

I don't even bother taking work upstairs to the attic this evening. I won't be spending much time there. When I get to the doorway, I find Ryland bent over his desk, sketching. He barely looks up.

"Hey," I say.

"You're back. Is this a night where talking is allowed? Because I actually need to focus on this sketch."

"You missed your meeting with Rois Baatz."

He snaps his attention up to me. "How do you know about that?"

"Dan and Maiya came by this afternoon to give you this." I put his envelope on the desk. "They told me."

He grimaces. "It's fine. Don't worry about it."

"What do you mean don't worry about it? He's one of the competition judges and you just threw that meeting away. What were you thinking?"

"That I wanted to help you. You didn't see your expression yesterday. It was clear you needed to get to the institute. Anyway, I've already finished my competition pieces—there's no telling whether the consultation would have led to anything."

I gape at him. There's no telling? How can he be so blasé about meeting one of his idols?

I roll back my shoulders and swallow hard. I've got to say this. "Dan also . . . insinuated that you did it because of me. Because you have . . . feelings for me." He doesn't break eye contact, but he doesn't speak either. "That this whole agreement has been a ruse and you only asked me to help you stop dating because that would mean you'd have the excuse to spend more time with me. And maybe make me drop my guard around you."

"Did it work?" he murmurs.

"I . . ." I'm completely thrown off. I was *sure* he'd deny it. "What? It's true?"

"Of course it's true." He smiles ruefully. "Honestly, I can't believe you went along with it for as long as you did. I thought you'd see right through me."

"But . . . why?"

He stands and walks over to me. "Isn't it obvious? I've been half in love with you since I found you taking pictures of my stuff that first night. You're so cute when you're annoyed. And the way you read—your mouth moving, biting your bottom lip when you get to something confusing. I'm a goner." He takes a deep breath and his throat bobs. "I figured, if we could spend time together— without the possibility of dating hanging between us—I might be able to win you over." He reaches for me. "Is there any way to convince you?"

"Ryland, no," I whisper, and take a step back. His honesty is giving me whiplash. "This has to stop. We *cannot* date." I try for my usual strong voice, but it comes out uncertain. It's hard to sound strong when his gaze is melting through my layers of defenses and turning my insides to goo. "I explicitly promised that I'd *stop* you from dating. Maybe the reasoning was a ruse, but the logic was not. You need time and energy to devote to your work and I won't distract you from your dreams. Or, at least, I won't do it anymore. I still can't believe you blew off your meeting."

"Have you even noticed how much work I've been doing?" He gestures back at his desk. "That I've been home, in this attic, every night since we started working together up here? You're not a distraction, Sage. You're the reason I can focus."

He takes another small step toward me, and my vision goes wavy with his nearness. My hands ache to touch him, but I force myself to think about the practicalities and not what his hair would feel like if I ran my fingers through it right now.

"Well, there are other reasons why this can never happen. That's why I came up here—to stop this." I scramble for my rationale. I know I had one even if I can't remember it now. I swallow and try to stand firm. "I'm leaving at the end of the summer. And your mother will never approve if we started dating. We could never tell her, or I'd lose my job."

He closes the remaining distance between us. "I'm very good at keeping secrets," he whispers seductively.

"But most importantly," I nearly yell in the desperate hope of distracting myself from the heat rushing through me, "I'm not looking for a relationship. This is exactly the situation I've been trying to avoid—I just want to be single and focus on my research while I'm here."

"Are you sure about that? Because I could swear you want something else."

My chest tightens. "I can't be in a relationship."

"Then don't be in a relationship. We won't be in one. We'll just . . . I don't know . . . be together. No commitment. Just be with me now. Date me now." His voice is low and hoarse. "I know you want to."

"I don't want anything from you," I whisper even as I lean closer.

"There's only one way to know that for sure." We're millimeters apart now. "Kiss me. And if you truly feel nothing, then we'll both know immediately, and I'll never bring it up again."

I try to ignore the sparks that sear me at his words. "Ryland, I'm telling you I don't want to be with you and you're saying I should prove it by *kissing* you? That makes no sense!"

"Nothing about this makes sense. That's what makes it so fantastic." His fingers slide down my arm and curl into mine. There's a pause before he speaks again. "It's the best thing about love."

Shivers race down my spine. Reason and thought flee my brain and I can't contain myself for a nanosecond longer. I lean in and kiss him. I'm all sensation. His lips burning through me, his breath in my mouth, his fingers in my hair. Now that I've started kissing him, I may never stop.

He gathers me to him, one arm wrapped around my lower back and the other on the base of my neck. My eyes roll back in my head. God, he feels so good. I kiss him deeper. I run my hands through his hair and smile into his mouth. His hair is so soft. I've been wanting to do that forever.

We bump into his table and there's a clatter. Ryland pulls away just enough so we can look each other in the eye.

"You've made your point. Clearly, you feel nothing for me."

His eyes flash with amusement and I think about biting his lower lip to get back at him. So I do. He leans away in surprise, then laughs and pulls me close again. "Oh, I like this side of you."

"What are we doing?" I whisper. I can't pretend to fight this anymore.

"I know you haven't done this much, but that was something called kissi—"

I whack his arm. "Stop, I'm serious." I extract myself from his arms and sit down on the couch. "If your mom finds out, she's going to be so pissed. That first night when she introduced us, she told me unequivocally that I couldn't date you."

He sits down next to me. "I know, she told me the same thing. What do you want to do? You know how I feel, but if you truly don't want to do this, then we won't. I'll work at my table and you'll work over here and I'll pretend that I'm not reliving that kiss over and over. I won't even make you more T-shirts. Well, maybe just a few. I have some really good ideas. Some of them about kissing and more about cats, but definitely not about cats kissing. That's too much even for me."

He's impossible. I lean over and kiss him again.

"Sage, you're killing me. Do you want to try to make this work or not?"

"Are you *really* good at keeping secrets?"

A grin spreads across his face. "I'm insanely good at keeping things from my mother." He leans in and lightly kisses my jawline. "Berend is completely clueless and we'll make sure Mom never knows a thing. We'll be perfectly well-behaved." His lips move to the corner of my mouth. "Except when we're alone."

"No one has to know," I whisper. Then I turn and kiss him.

chapter
18

As soon as I get back to my bedroom that night, I call Ellie. It's midnight and I'm going to be dragging tomorrow, but I won't be able to sleep until I've told someone about this, and Ellie is the only one who will understand.

She picks up on the first ring. "Hey, what's going on? You never call in the evening."

"Is it a bad time?"

"No, of course not. I always want the latest update. Is everything okay?"

"Yeah, but something just happened and I need to talk about it."

"Does this *something* involve the boy? I still can't get over that picture of him, by the way."

"Yeah, it might be about him."

She gives a tiny squeal. "Okay, spill."

"So . . . we kind of kissed tonight."

"*What?!*" she shrieks. "Hold on, hold on."

And then the call ends.

I stare down at my phone in shock. Did Ellie just *hang up* on me? When I'm talking about kissing? I thought she'd be begging me to tell her more. A second later my phone buzzes, but this time it's a FaceTime call. I take it, and rather than seeing just Ellie on the other end, I see her, Dev, *and* Huan. Their faces are squished cheek to cheek and their eyes are wide with shock.

"Sorry, but this is big enough news that we all need to be on the call."

"What are you all doing together?" I calculate the time in my head. If it's midnight here, then it's six p.m. on the East Coast.

They exchange glances. "We were about to leave for a movie," Dev says. "But the movie can go screw itself when there's news like this to hear."

"I'm so glad I didn't skip tonight," Huan says. "I'm half convinced Ellie misheard you."

"Say it again." Ellie's practically vibrating with excitement. "Slowly!"

I sputter. "I'm not saying it again." Ryland's bedroom is just down the hall, and I won't be able to take the embarrassment if he knows I immediately called my friends to dissect the details of our kiss.

"Sage, do you have any idea how monumental this is? You should be happy I'm not inviting you to a Zoom call so I can record this for posterity. You and Ryland *kissed*? Like a platonic little kiss on the cheek?"

I shake my head, my cheeks growing hot. Ellie and Dev look at each other with glee.

"Holy hell, I never thought I'd see this day!" Huan hoots with excitement. "Our evening just got way more fun."

"I'm *so* mad that I'm in another country and can't talk to you in person!" Ellie says. "We have to know everything."

"All right, everyone calm down, it's not that exciting."

Dev snorts. "This is like finding out that Elon Musk churns his own butter."

"Wait," Huan says. "Are you talking actual butter or is that a euphemism for—"

"It's just," I interrupt, "we get along really well. You wouldn't think so at first because we have such different interests, but he makes me laugh. And he's really passionate about his art and I like that. I like how consumed he can be with it. It reminds me of myself."

"Did you kiss him or did he kiss you?" Ellie asks.

I roll my eyes. Clearly, they aren't going to drop it until they've heard more about the kissing. "I kissed him."

They all exchange another shocked and excited look. "But you always said you weren't interested in dating," Ellie says.

"I know, I know. I told him that I needed to prioritize my research and didn't want a relationship. And then he said that if I didn't feel anything toward him then I could prove it by kissing him, and so I did, and he . . . um . . . kind of proved me wrong."

The three of them burst into laughter. They're so loud I have to turn down the volume on my phone before I wake up the whole house.

"Oh, this is the best thing I've heard in a long time," Huan says. "Wait until I tell Frank."

"He sounds *perfect*," says Ellie. "Anyone who can make Sage admit she's wrong is definitely her equal."

"Very true," Dev agrees.

I pace back and forth in front of my bed. I can't stop grinning even though I'm trying very hard to be annoyed.

"I just . . . what should I do? This is a horrible idea."

"Why is it a horrible idea? He clearly likes you and you like kissing him." Ellie cannot wipe the smile off her face. "This sounds like the best idea."

"Well, for one thing, his mom forbade us from dating."

"Seriously? Doesn't she know anything?" Dev shakes his head. "If you've read *Romeo and Juliet*, then you know the fastest way to get people together is to tell them they aren't allowed."

"Ugh, I've become a cliché!" I groan and flop onto the bed. "What am I doing? I don't want to upset Dr. Reese or lose my connection with her. But Ryland and I freaking *live* together. I couldn't stay away from him even if I tried. And I don't want to try."

"I know how much this research means to you," Dev says. I can tell he's trying very hard to be serious and empathetic, but his amusement shines in his eyes. "Is there any way you could talk to her and see if she would understand?"

I shake my head. "No, she made her feelings very clear."

"It doesn't need to be something serious, right? Can't you guys just act normal until you're outside the house?" Ellie asks. It's clearly killing her that I'm debating breaking it off. Although, for all my big talk, I don't think I have the strength to. "She wouldn't need to know you were anything but friends."

"Friends who do a little kissing on the side," Huan adds with a smirk.

I smile. Maybe a lot of kissing, but who's counting.

"All I'm saying," Ellie continues, "is that, as far as I can tell, this is the first time you've *ever* felt this way about somebody else. Don't give up on it so easily. You're the smartest person I know—no offense, guys—I'm sure you can figure out a solution."

Maybe she's right. If Ryland and I are careful and set rules for ourselves, then no one needs to be the wiser. I can babysit and Ryland can do his art. We'll eat dinner together normally and spend evenings in the attic like we have all summer. Maybe it's not impossible to pull this off.

I nod slowly. "Okay. Yeah, I can figure it out."

"Yes!" Ellie punches her fist in the air. "You can absolutely figure it out. I'm so excited and I need to know every detail." She leans toward the screen. "I won't tell the boys if you don't want me to."

"Hey now, you can't leave us out!" Huan cries.

"Don't believe her, Sage," Dev says. "She'll tell me everything the moment she gets off the phone with you. She won't be able to help it." Ellie elbows him and he kisses her on the cheek.

"I'll keep that in mind," I reply. "Thanks for talking me down, even if your excitement is fairly mortifying."

They wave and Ellie blows me a kiss. I hang up and lie back on my bed. Ellie's right. I've never felt this way before and it's only going to last a few more weeks. I have to find a way to make this work.

I have a hard time sleeping and wake up extra early the next morning. I can't relax in my bed now, knowing that Ryland is asleep mere feet away in his own bedroom. This is such an insane situation to be in. I've always been *so* good about controlling my emotions, but all of that disintegrates when I think of him.

A light knock sounds at the door and I jump. I climb out of bed and cautiously crack the door open. Ryland is leaning in the doorway only inches from me and I'm reminded of the evening he came to my room after Dr. Reese forbade us from dating.

He gives me an alluring smile. "Good morning," he whispers.

My stomach flips over. If I thought one evening of kissing was going to get him out of my system, I was dead wrong.

"Good morning. But you shouldn't be here."

"This is my house."

"And this is my *bedroom*."

His smile deepens. "Oh yes, I can see that. And there's your bed." His eyes trail down my body. "And I see you're still wearing those shorts."

I fill with heat. I *knew* he'd noticed the shorts.

"Ryland, I was just thinking about this. We have to be smart. We have to act like nothing has changed."

"I completely agree. We can't let my mom know anything." He takes a step into the room and I block him from going any farther.

"I don't think so. That's a definite change."

He pouts.

"Listen, we'll talk about it later. Figure out a plan. But for now, we need to be back in our bedrooms."

"Counterproposal. What about both of us in one bedroom?"

I poke him playfully on the arm and he muffles his laughter. "I'm just kidding," he whispers. He checks the hall and then lightly kisses me. "I have to drop off my competition pieces with the judges early this morning and then I'll be working on commissions in the attic. Come see me after everyone leaves."

I nod and close the door behind me, then lean against it. How can this be so exhilarating and so scary at the same time?

chapter
19

I manage to behave normally until Dr. Reese and Berend are gone for the day. I distract myself from thoughts of Ryland by texting Wren about the daily "lesson plans" I've been putting together for Diederik. I emailed them a few days ago since I figured all my work to make themed activities shouldn't go to waste. I wasn't sure what her reaction would be, but she sounds pretty positive.

You're really dedicating yourself to babysitting. I'm surprised . . . and a little impressed, if I'm being honest.

I'm glad to have an exchange with her that's mostly free of judgment or bitterness, but reading her text gives me a twinge of guilt. I really love Diederik, but lately my mind hasn't been solely focused on the *younger* boy in the house.

I wait ten minutes after Dr. Reese and Berend are gone just to make sure they're not going to backtrack and burst through the door for their forgotten purse or wallet before taking Diederik's hand and bringing him up to the attic. True to his word, Ryland is sitting there sketching with headphones on.

"Hey, you two." He gives me a devious grin and tingles roll through me. He's impossible to be around now.

"Should we talk up here or is he going to destroy everything?"

"I think we can make it work."

Ryland rummages around in a closet space and pulls out a very old-looking board game that I don't recognize. He opens it up and lays it on the ground. Diederik runs over, immediately intrigued.

"That'll buy us at least three minutes," he says with a wink.

"Four, if we're lucky."

"So, you clearly have a plan, which does not surprise me. What are you thinking?"

"I'm thinking that we have to act just as normally around here as usual. No early morning kissing, no flirting at the dining room table, no spending every second together. I don't think anyone's suspicious right now, so if we just keep acting the same, then we should be fine."

"But if we're acting the exact same as before, when do I get to do this?" He kisses me gently and a zip of electricity goes down my spine.

"We'll have the evenings together."

He raises an eyebrow. "Won't you want to work during the evenings?"

"I'm sure we can do a little bit of both."

"I do like that idea."

"And maybe I tell Dr. Reese that I want to explore the city more. Once I get this latest data abstraction work done, I could start going out during the evenings sometimes. All by myself, of course." I smile mischievously. I glance over at Diederik to make sure he's okay, but luckily he's completely engrossed in the game.

"And I can go out with friends, completely independently. I wouldn't even know you were going out."

"Exactly. We'll go out at different times and come back at different times, and no one will ever have to know."

"You're cunning and I love it. I do have one small request, though," he whispers.

"Okay . . ."

"We only have one weekend left before you go to your conference. So, we'll follow all your rules, and I'll behave just the way you want me to, but"—he leans in so he's only a hair's breadth from kissing me—"this weekend you're mine."

My stomach flips.

"We can tell my mother whatever you want, but come into the city with me and we'll spend the whole time together. I want to have you all to myself where we don't have to hide or sneak around."

He kisses me then, and I have to hold on to his arms so my legs don't give out. Wow, I am in over my head.

"Deal?"

"Deal." I kiss him again. Actually, maybe a little bit of kissing during the days wouldn't be horrible. . . .

"Je kust Ryland!"

We jump apart and swivel to where Diederik is sitting. Ryland shares my same horror-struck expression.

"Tell me he just said he pooped his pants," I whisper.

"No such luck."

I hurry over and kneel down in front of him. "No, no. We weren't kissing. Not really, we were just—" I look to Ryland for help.

"We're friends." He kneels down next to me. "Friends kiss and hug sometimes. Just like you and I do." He kisses Diederik on the cheek.

"Yes, friends." I kiss Diederik on the other cheek. "Ryland and I are friends."

Ryland switches to Dutch and says something else. My heart pounds in my chest. Ryland stands and beckons me to a corner away from Diederik, who goes back to messing with the board game.

"What are we going to do?" I whisper. "What will we say if he blurts out something to your mom?"

He shakes his head. "It's okay, don't freak out. For one thing, Diederik says wild things all the time, so my parents won't pay attention to him. And if they do, I'll just explain that you helped me with something and I gave you a kiss on the cheek." He squeezes my hand and looks intently at me. "We'll tell her it's my fault. She'll believe that. I won't let anything happen to your internship."

I nod, grateful, but it's hard to push the fears from my mind. We haven't even been together for twenty-four hours and already we have a witness. Keeping this secret feels impossible. Ryland rubs his thumb over my hand, and I force myself to take a breath.

"For the record," I reply, "this is all your fault."

"Nice try, but I'd argue it's at least fifty-fifty. Maybe sixty-forty. Those shorts really upped the ante."

I elbow him. "All right, I think Diederik and I need to leave before we get into more trouble."

"I'll come down at lunchtime. I was thinking I could spend the afternoon with you both."

"Didn't we just establish that we can't be spending more time together? And you should be working."

"I turned in my competition pieces, so I'm a free man. And just in time." He winks at me. "Plus, it doesn't count if Diederik is with us. Mom and Berend won't mind it since I'm helping you get around the city. And giving Diederik a nice day out." He turns to the little boy. "How about an afternoon at the zoo?"

Diederik squeals and runs up to me. "Ja, zoo!"

I swing him up into my arms and give him a little squeeze.

"And I have something exciting for you before you go," Ryland continues. "I worked on it last night after you went to bed." He unbuttons the messy plaid shirt he wears while painting, his eyes gleaming. He puts his hands out wide to show off the T-shirt underneath. "What do you think?"

I squint at the design. It's a book covered with leaves. Honestly, it's not the most exciting design he's shown me, despite the bold green material it's printed on.

"Um, it's nice."

He looks offended. "*Nice?* Don't you know what this is?"

"I think I can recognize a book."

"Can you?" He points to the leaves. "That's sage. The herb. *This* is a book of Sage."

I blink and my mouth drops open a little bit. I step closer. I can see now that my name is written on the spine and the little leaves that wind all around it.

"See, *this* is the reaction I was looking for. What's a more perfect encapsulation of you than you as a book? Here." He hands me two shirts. They're just like his, but one is printed on black material and the other is hot pink. "I figured I'd try to get you to wear a color, but I made a black version as a backup."

"Wow, thank you." Diederik takes one from my hands and drapes it over his face. "This is really sweet. Though I think that pink one is staying safely at the bottom of my drawer."

"Yeah, I know. But you're welcome anyway. Now go put the black one on!"

I lift the other shirt over my face. "Peekaboo!" I say to Diederik to make him laugh. "I promise I'll wear it, but I don't think we need to go out in public wearing matching shirts today."

"Why not?"

"Because it's weird."

"Who cares about being weird? You're weird, I'm weird, the whole world is weird. If somebody asks, we'll just tell them this is the newest underground band."

I chuckle and play peekaboo again.

"It actually is a pretty good band name. I'm going to see if I can copyright it. Don't go stealing the idea."

"Ryland, you're not even in a band."

"That's not the point. Choosing a name is the first step in creating a band. The most important step, actually."

I pull the shirt off Diederik's head with a flourish. "Can you believe this one?" I ask him, and gesture to Ryland before putting the toddler back on the ground. "So, you're saying the name is more important than playing an instrument or being able to sing?"

"Oh please, do you listen to music? When you're standing in front of the crowd in your hot-pink *Book of Sage* T-shirt, screaming your heart out over my latest EDM hit, you'll realize I was right all along."

I can't help but laugh when he gets on one of these kicks. "Fine. But I'm still not wearing matching shirts."

I have to admit that I haven't been to many zoos in my life. It just wasn't something that interested me much, so after the early childhood trips, our family stopped going. I'm not sure what to expect, but it's beautiful, starting with the ornate green and gold entrance gates. The zoo is in the middle of Plantage, a quiet area in the eastern part of Amsterdam. Unsurprisingly, families are everywhere. There are tons of moms and kids, babies in strollers or being carried on backs.

I turn to Ryland. "Where first?"

He shrugs. "I say we let the little one decide."

"Elephants!" Diederik cries immediately.

"Elephants it is."

I keep a tight grip on Diederik's hand as we walk. There are lots of people here and I'm not going through another playground incident.

Ryland's shoulder brushes against mine. "It's fun being out with you today. And being able to do this." He slips his hand into mine.

I smile up at him. "Are you sure we can do that? Diederik might notice."

"That's why this is perfect. We're all holding hands together.

It's completely normal. I need to hold your hand to make sure you don't run off."

I laugh, but I wonder how deep his words go. Whether he can feel my low-grade worry about all of this. But then his thumb rubs against mine and my tension fades. His touch has a way of doing that.

"Do you know what I love just *slightly* more than holding your hand?"

"The fact that there are cats at this zoo?"

He arches an eyebrow. "Oh. That's a good guess. I hadn't considered that. But these cats don't really count—I'm a house cat person."

"What, then?"

"Seeing you wear the shirts I make for you."

I look down self-consciously. At the last minute, I decided to put on my black *Book of Sage* shirt. What's the point of denying how cute it is? Or how cute he is?

"Shirts you made for me *and* about me, don't forget."

"How could I? Most of my life is for you and about you lately."

Distantly, I can feel Diederik pulling on my hand as he tries to tug me along, but my brain only has room for Ryland. His gaze and his words that heat me from the inside out.

"Ryland . . ."

"I know what you're going to say. It's too much. I need to focus on myself. My life shouldn't be about someone else."

I clamp my mouth shut. That was *exactly* what I was going to say. I know we've spent a lot of time together, but does he really know me that well?

"Just because you can quote me doesn't make me wrong."

"True. But it doesn't make me wrong either. I finished all of my competition pieces in two and a half weeks because of you. And I'm really proud of what I created. You're a great influence on me."

"I'm glad." My voice is quiet.

"But you're not stealing my band name. I'm serious about that."

After we see the elephants, we visit the lions, then the penguins and the monkey house. We aren't exactly taking the most efficient path through the zoo, which would usually drive me crazy, but it's nice to wander without a real purpose for once. And all this walking will make Diederik exhausted when we get back to the house, which means an easier bedtime, a fact that Dr. Reese and Berend will particularly love.

The wind starts to whip up and suddenly it's raining. Diederik squeals and I pull him to me to shelter him, which does absolutely nothing. We all run under a big tree.

"How are we going to get home without getting totally drenched?" I ask.

"Actually, I have an idea. We're going to get wet, but it'll be worth it." Ryland takes off running and Diederik and I follow behind. I'm trying to dart around the puddles, but Diederik giggles and jumps directly in one.

"Ah!" I yell when more water hits me.

He jumps again, then stomps around making the biggest splashes he can. For a moment I think of stopping him, but we're both already soaking. So I jump with him.

"Jump, Sage!" he cries, and breaks out in peals of laughter.

The rain is running down my hair and face in rivulets so I can hardly see. I laugh and tug him along. "I see an even bigger puddle!"

"*Puddles!*"

"One, two, three!"

We jump into the next puddle together, water flying everywhere. His face is radiating in sopping-wet joy and my heart squeezes to see him so happy. Another huge splash hits me and I look over to find Ryland next to us.

"Having fun?" he asks with a smirk.

I hold up a finger to him and whisper in Diederik's ear. He giggles.

"What are you two—"

Splash! Diederik and I land in unison, completely drenching Ryland's lower half. We get into a jumping and splashing battle then, two against one, but no one can beat a toddler in a puddle-jumping match. Particularly not Diederik.

"Okay, I surrender, I surrender!" Ryland finally exclaims, and holds his hands up. I'm trying really hard not to focus on how his shirt is clinging to his chest right now. And from the look he's giving me, I think he's doing the same.

"Are we ready for my idea now?" he asks, and beckons us forward. Not far ahead is a glass building capped with a dome.

"Is that a planetarium?"

He nods. "Dry, quiet." His gaze fixes on me. "Dark."

Oh, he's tricky.

We go inside and I do my best to dry off Diederik and myself in the bathroom. We buy tickets and are ushered into a circular room. It turns out Diederik has never been to anything like this before and he's so excited that he can't sit still. He's wiggling and dancing in front of his seat and I worry this is going to be a disaster. I can't get him to settle through the introduction, but once they dim the lights, Diederik is absolutely enthralled. He leans back and gawks at the sky.

At any other time, I would do the same. However, I can feel Ryland on the other side of me and it pulls me from the screen. I look over and find his eyes on me.

"See, you're not the only smart one," he whispers, and tangles our fingers together.

"Can we stay here all day?"

"I don't think Diederik would mind."

"I wouldn't either." I point at the domed ceiling. "This looks absolutely fascinating. I always wanted to know more about space travel. I can't wait to watch it." I lean back like I'm settling in for the show.

He chuckles and then pulls me to him, kissing me while everyone else's attention is focused above. A jolt of electricity burns through me. My first kiss under the stars.

That evening I'm back up in the attic with Ryland. Since I've now proven myself capable of doing the data abstraction, Katina gave me another hundred participants to go through. I am not messing this up again, so I'm being extra careful to check and recheck each data point. Things feel so different than they did at the beginning of the summer, though. I remember how mentally exhausted I was then. I was just *done*. Now I'm energized about the research again, and knowing that Ryland is steps away is comforting.

I'm not sure how long I hunch over my computer, scrolling through patient records, before finally sitting back and groaning.

"Ugh, I hate when I do that," I mutter.

"What's that?"

I look over my shoulder and groan again. I shouldn't have moved my neck. "Sit in one position so long that my neck and back cramp up. I need to set a reminder to stop working and walk around every once in a while."

"You know, most people have to set timers to *make* themselves work, not to stop themselves." He stands. "Let me help you with your back."

He sits down behind me on the couch and lays his hands on my shoulders. I face the wall and close my eyes. His touch is relaxing and electrifying all at once. I sit in complete stillness as his thumbs work their way down my spine, one vertebra at a time, rubbing in slow circles. My entire body vibrates. I try to breathe normally so he won't know just how much this is affecting me. His hands drop lower . . . and lower . . . until they halt at my lower back right above my pants.

He lifts my shirt and I hold my breath. Ryland's fingertips touch my bare skin and I shiver with pleasure before I can control myself. He shifts even closer.

"Feeling better?" he whispers. His lips graze the back of my neck, sending flurries of fire up my spine.

I try to say something calm, rational, but all that comes out is the smallest moan.

"Good." He kisses my neck again, featherlight, his thumbs

still rubbing melodically. My entire body is aflame. I can't stand another second of his lips grazing my skin. I need much more than that.

I twist to face him, practically in his lap, and wrap my arms around his neck. I pull him to me, his mouth already open against mine. His tongue flicks against my own, pressing me tighter to him. His hands are already under my shirt and they slide up my back, under my bra clasp. His fingers are hot on my skin.

I kiss him harder, simultaneously terrified and desperate for him to go further.

Instead, he pulls away slightly.

"Aren't you supposed to be working?" His voice is thick.

"I don't care." I push him back onto the couch arm. I don't care about data or conferences or Dr. Reese. All I want is his mouth on mine and his hands everywhere else.

The opposite happens. He sits up with difficulty and extracts himself from under me. When I realize what he's doing, I pull away in embarrassment. Did I push too far? Did he not want—

"Don't even let your mind go there. I'd like nothing better than to stay on this couch with you until we're too old to stand. But I also don't want you to run off, and I know how your brain works."

I shake my head.

"You're still looking for reasons to get rid of me. I know you are even if you won't admit it. So, if you need to work, then that's what you're going to do." He kisses me again and my entire body sways into him like I'm drunk. His gaze fixes on me. "I'm not going to let you regret me, Sage."

The conviction behind his words startles me. I stare up at him, dumbfounded. "Are you serious right now?"

"For once, I'm being the rational one." His eyes are liquid. "And you have *no* idea how hard that is."

I sit in shock for another minute, but he walks back to his table and leans over his latest commissioned work. I straighten my shirt and pull my laptop back onto my legs even though my body is still humming from him. I sneak a glance. His hair has fallen over his eyes. I bet it'll be tinged with blue paint when he stands back up.

His gaze meets mine through his hair and my entire body ignites like a firework. Whoo-boy. I'm in So. Much. Trouble.

chapter

20

Saturday morning, I find Dr. Reese sitting at the kitchen table, drinking a cup of coffee and reading something on her laptop. Diederik and Berend are playing with toys in the living room.

"Morning, Sage. How did you sleep?"

In all honesty, I slept very poorly because I couldn't stop thinking about today. But, of course, I don't say that.

"I slept well. How about you?"

"The same. Do you have big plans today?" She winks at me as if we both know that I never have big plans. For once, she's wrong.

"Actually, I was thinking I would spend the day exploring the city." I grab a cup of coffee.

"Oh really?"

"Well, my mom and friends back home keep nagging me about it. They say I'm going to be sorry if I don't take advantage while I'm here."

"They're right. I appreciate your dedication to the lab, but I'm glad you're getting out today. Do you need any recommendations? Berend and I are happy to share our favorite spots."

"Oh, thank you, but I actually spent last night planning it out."

My chest burns from the easy lies I'm telling. For once, I have no itinerary. I'm going to do something very different—go with the flow.

"Of course you did. Just like you. And you'll be okay on your own?"

"Yes, I'll be totally fine. Thanks."

"It's too bad you didn't mention it earlier. I bet Ryland would have had recommendations. He already left to meet up with friends, though."

You don't say.

I wait to see if she'll add anything else, but she gives me a wave and turns back to her computer. I grab my house key and wallet and force myself to take slow steps out of the apartment and down the stairs. I laugh as soon as I'm on the street. Who the hell am I? Blowing off an entire day when I could be working? Sneaking out and lying to meet a boy? I know I should be ashamed or worried, but all I feel are waves of excitement rushing through me.

An entire day alone with Ryland.

I meet him at a corner café a few streets down. This one is bright white, filled with butterfly prints, and is absurdly cozy. He's at a back table with a small sketchbook in front of him. He looks more slumped than usual and there's a crease between his eyebrows that I haven't seen before. But he lights up when he sees me.

"Thank god you're here. I know we decided to leave at different times, but I was getting worried you were going to stand me up." He leans across the table to kiss me. "Mm, it's fun to do that in public."

I have to stop myself from looking around for Dr. Reese and Berend even though I know it's ridiculous to imagine them casually popping in here of all places. "How are you?" I ask, thinking about his strained expression a second ago.

"Me? I'm great. I finally get a day alone with you."

"All right, tour guide, where are we going? I'm all yours for the day."

He dips his head. "Just for the day?"

How is it possible for him to have me swooning when no one else has been able to do it? Honestly, I thought that was a made-up reaction. I have some serious apologizing to do to Ellie when I get back home.

"I want to see your Amsterdam. The things you love the most."

"So more cats?"

"How many cat sites can a city have? You can't possibly fill eight hours with only cats, can you?"

"Sadly, no, but I could try." He taps his chin. "There is one thing I'd like to show you, though."

It's a pretty long tram ride to the west of the city. I've studied the map a bit while I've been living here, but I can't think of any attractions in this area and Ryland is having way too much fun not telling me anything.

When we get off the tram, Ryland walks me to a suburban apartment complex with lots of brick buildings and parking lots.

"This is your favorite place in Amsterdam?" I ask.

"It's high up there. This is a street art museum."

"Is it? It's very . . . mundane."

He laughs. "Not literally right here. It's different from any museum you've ever gone to—this is one of the best street art museums in the world."

"Show me the way."

We hold hands and he takes me through the area. Mario and Homer Simpson make appearances, along with butterflies, nooses, and monsters. Some of the pieces are huge—murals and portraits that take up the entire side of a building. Other pieces are small— a paving stone that's been painted to look like a notebook or an electrical box with a smile. But all of it is graphic, colorful, and in your face. I can see Ryland in this art, even though he isn't a street artist. He has this same energy.

I point to an enormous mural of a woman with flowers cascading down her back as hair. "Is that what you'd like to do someday?"

He stares up at the mural, and there's a faraway look in his eyes. He's somber and contemplative in a way he never is. After a moment, he nods. "Yeah. This and more. I want to do everything. I want people to commission my murals and block prints and T-shirt designs. I want to see my work in galleries and museums. I want to make a career out of this, even though everyone tells me it's impossible." He looks at me. "Do you ever feel like your dreams are too big?"

I shake my head. "Not *too* big. Maybe they look that way from the outside, but they're realistic to me because I know I can achieve them. Asking any less of myself would be . . . an insult."

He squeezes my hand. "I love your confidence."

"I don't think your dreams are too big either," I tell him. "Other people make a living as artists—you can too. I can't imagine you doing anything else."

"I can't either. It's what I've wanted since I was little." We wander down the street hand in hand. "Like, you know how Diederik is all over the place, playing and running around and making messes?"

"Uh, yeah. It's come to my attention."

He smiles. "Well, I was the opposite growing up. If my mom gave me a pad of paper and colored pencils, I would spend hours drawing. She used to put art tutorial videos on and I would watch and rewind them all afternoon. For all her worrying about my art, I know she's also thankful for it. There's no way she could've made it through med school and her residency if I wasn't such a quiet, absorbed child."

It makes me sad to think about tiny Ryland alone for hours, drawing and imagining other worlds. I'm grateful for my own parents, who both loved spending time with Wren and me growing up.

We stop in front of another mural—this one of a couple embracing—and stare up at it. "Thanks for showing me this," I say quietly.

"I love it here, so I wanted to share it with you." He smiles. "Are you hungry?"

I nod. "Yeah. I was too anxious to eat anything this morning."

"Same. I know just the thing."

We take the tram back into the city center and he drags me over to what looks like a small wooden food stand decorated with flags of the Netherlands. I swallow nervously.

"Is that . . . fish?"

"Herring. A beloved national treasure. You have to try it."

I remember reading about herring briefly when I studied up on Amsterdam, but I did not put it on my list of things to eat.

"How about I watch you take a bite, and we'll check it off the bucket list."

"Oh no, I don't think so. Everyone needs to have herring while they're here." He turns to the employee and speaks quickly in Dutch. The man hands him a flimsy paper container with fillets of herring, cut into bites, along with chopped onion and pickles. A little Netherlands flag toothpick is stuck in the center.

"Is it raw?"

"I mean . . . yes, but you'll love it. I'd recommend dipping it in the onion, though. It really enhances the flavor."

I study him, but he seems serious. I eye the fish dubiously.

"Hold on a second—" He shoves his hand in his pocket and pulls out his phone. "I need to take a picture."

I glare at him even though I know Ellie, Wren, and Mom will absolutely love to see this. Then I stab a piece of the fish with my toothpick, take a deep breath, and bite into it. The fish is tart and salty. It's honestly not too bad, but it's not going to be my next snack either.

"What do you think? Good, right?"

"It's, um, better than I expected. Though you won't want to kiss me after eating this."

"Ah, finally something you're wrong about."

He pulls me into him and kisses me deeply. I'm vaguely aware that we're standing in the middle of a sidewalk and people have to stream around us, but I don't care. They can take a few extra steps.

Eventually we pull away and Ryland finishes the herring in a few quick bites. "You're probably still hungry, I assume?" he asks.

"Starving."

"Okay, next stop."

I dig my heels into the ground when I see where he's brought me next. The words *Coffee Shop* stand out in big bold letters on the front of the tiny café, but I know that doesn't mean we're about to order espressos.

His eyes twinkle. "Is there a problem?"

I can tell he's trying to work me up. Coffee shops in Amsterdam sell weed legally. I've seen packs of wild-looking tourists on the sidewalks here and I know one of the biggest draws is the weed . . . along with the red-light district. Ryland is probably hoping I'm going to freak out and refuse to go in, just so he can tease me about it. But I'm not going to give him the pleasure.

I smile serenely. "No problem at all. I've been wanting to check one of these out." I march in confidently and he hurries after me. The inside is cute. It's very small, like many places in Amsterdam, with a variety of posters hanging on the white walls. There are several small wooden tables and stools lined up at the front window, but only a few are taken by customers. To my left is a counter where it looks like you can buy weed. I choose a table randomly and sit down. Ryland sits across from me, smiling but eyeing me like he's waiting for me to bolt for the door.

I skim a menu on the table: *Big Bud Cheese, Candy Kush, Royal Amnesia*. I blink and then realize I'm reading a list of different types of weed. A laugh bubbles out of me, imagining being able to walk into a corner shop in America and easily buy weed off a menu.

Ryland raises an eyebrow at me. "Are you serious about this? Because you have to be at least eighteen to buy."

"I'm just shy of that."

"You don't have to do it if you're just trying to prove a point. I truly don't care."

"Well, I don't want to take anything that could affect how I feel today. We aren't going to have many days like this together."

He plucks the menu from my hand. "Very true. How about we order some ham and cheese toasties instead? They're pretty tasty."

I nod and he goes up to the counter. I'm relieved that he doesn't care whether I smoke.

I take a few covert looks around me. I may not be about to smoke weed, but I'm definitely going to be inhaling some second-hand thanks to the other customers. Since I won't be doing this again, I pull out a phone and take a selfie. I need proof of this moment, if only so I can see the looks on Ellie's, Dev's, and Huan's faces when they realize where I've been today.

"Whoa, whoa, whoa, are you taking a selfie without me?" Ryland's face appears next to mine on the screen. He kisses my cheek just as I take the picture.

"Have you smoked before?" I ask him.

"Oh sure, it's not a big deal. All my friends do it, but not every day."

A worker brings out two sandwiches and waters and we both dig in. It tastes delicious, but I can't help looking around in disbelief at the fact that I'm sitting here with a boy I'm desperate to kiss, eating grilled cheeses only steps away from loads of weed. I snort into my sandwich.

"What?" Ryland asks. He wipes his mouth. "Do I have cheese on my face?"

"No, I was just . . ." I gesture around us. "I can't believe I'm here. Doing all this with you."

"Yeah? And are you happy you're doing it?"

I look down at my sandwich and back up at him. "Happier than I've been in a long time."

We spend the afternoon wandering blissfully through the Amsterdam neighborhoods. Ryland points out some of the historic sites and we fill the time telling stories about the past. I tell him about high school in America and living in England last fall and even some of the more difficult memories about Dad. I haven't told anybody about those last days, but somehow it's easy to speak with him by my side, squeezing my hand when I need it. He tells me about his childhood going back and forth between the Netherlands, America, and Dr. Reese's sabbaticals at other universities.

He cuts off his latest story and pulls out his phone. "Dan and everyone keep texting me. They want to have dinner." He shakes his head. "Today is supposed to be just for us, though. I'll tell them no."

"Actually, that sounds nice. If you want to."

"Yeah? You're sure? They'll be happy to hang out with you again before you leave for the Berlin trip next week."

The reminder of my trip hangs over me. I can't wait to fly out next Friday for the weekend conference, but that also means I only have two more weeks left in Europe—this upcoming week and the last week in July after the conference. It isn't nearly enough time. I can still hear Ryland's words from that first night clearly: *No commitment. Just be with me now. Date me now.* But did he really mean that? His words lately seem to suggest the exact opposite. But how could it ever be more? It can't be. And I know if I point that out, it will only ruin the time we have left together.

We meet his friends at Foodhallen, which is an indoor food market built in an old train station. It's a large industrial space with tall ceilings and train tracks still running through the brick floors. The group is sitting at a high-top table in the center of the hall, and they cheer and wave us over when they see us.

"Look at you two holding hands!" Dan says. "I guess he finally won you over."

Ryland kisses me on the cheek. "It was tough, but I think it was the T-shirts."

"Like this one?" Twitch asks. He's wearing Ryland's *Puss in Clogs* shirt. "Girls love this shirt."

"Cats win people over every time." He gives me a superior look.

We stop talking so we can order food from the various restaurants within the hall. Ryland gets us two orders of bitterballen because he says I can't possibly leave the Netherlands without having them at least once.

"So, tell us the whole story of how you got together," Maiya says once we're settled.

Ryland and I exchange glances. I've heard quite a few couples tell their "stories" before, including Ellie and Dev, but it's surreal that I have a story now. Seeing their expectant faces makes all this feel real in a way that it didn't before. It was just Ryland and me messing around in his attic, but now we're public with his friends. And if we break up, they'll know that too. My chest feels tight at the realization.

"You start," I tell him.

"Well, after Dan and Maiya came over, Sage was angry at me. She interrupted my very productive work session to yell at me—"

"I did not yell."

"Don't feel bad, we've all yelled at him before," Dan adds, and everyone laughs.

"You definitely raised your voice with me." Ryland smirks. "But I wasn't mad. You're sexiest when you're angry."

Twitch coughs into his hand. "Please, not you two as well. I can barely stand Dan and Maiya together anymore."

"*Anyway*, then we kissed and here we are," I say quickly. "The weather was nice today, wasn't it?"

They laugh and get the hint.

"Ryland, any news on the competition yet?" Twitch asks.

He shrugs and dips his bitterballen in mustard.

"Oh." Twitch slouches over his drink. "I'm sorry."

I look between them. "What do you mean?" I swivel in my seat to study Ryland. "You already heard?"

"They called early this morning. I couldn't go back to sleep after that, so I picked up the pieces from them before meeting you."

"I could have gone with you."

He gives me the smallest smile. "No, you couldn't. That would have been weird to explain to Mom. Anyway, I wanted to do it alone."

I think back to his expression this morning when I found him in the café and his somber mood at the street art museum earlier. No wonder he was asking me whether his dreams are too big. I slip my hand into his.

"I'm so sorry. I wish you would have told me sooner."

"I didn't want to ruin the day. There will be other things. There always are." He shrugs and smiles at the table. "Another round?"

"Sorry," Dan says, and the others nod in sympathy.

My throat grows tight. "Your work is amazing. And I'm not just saying that to be nice."

"I know. You never say things just to be nice."

I roll my eyes and look around the table. "This is total bullshit. His work is amazing, right?"

They all nod fervently, but he shakes his head again. "They just went a different direction. Really, it's fine." He pulls his hand from mine and squeezes my knee.

I want to keep talking about it until we can find some logical reason for why he wasn't chosen. Were there certain criteria he missed? Did he turn everything in by the deadline? Or . . . did he hurt his chances when he skipped the consultation with Rois Baatz for me? I feel nauseous at the possibility, so I put that out of my mind.

This is why I like science. Science has objectivity. Impartiality. But that's not true for art. I don't know what makes art good or bad. Or if it can even *be* good or bad. All I know is that I'd like to find those judges and punch them in the throat. Do they have any idea all the work that went into those pieces? The late hours and dedication? Ryland deserves so much more.

The sun is setting when we leave Foodhallen, which means it's late. The sun doesn't set here until close to ten at night.

"We should probably head home before your mom starts to worry I've been abducted or something."

"There's one last thing we need to do today." We walk through the streets until we get to a wide canal. He points to a canal boat drifting through the water. "You should experience one of those."

"We don't have to do anything else today. I totally get it if you'd like to go back home."

"No." He turns to me. "The last thing I want to do is sit in that attic right now. Let's stay out a little longer, okay?"

I nod, more than happy to do whatever will make him feel better.

The canal boat is clearly made for tourists. It's jam-packed with people, all sitting at booths under a domed glass roof. We take our seats and I glance out into the night.

"Wouldn't this have been better during the day so we could see everything?"

"But it wouldn't have been nearly as romantic. And the city is beautiful at night." He puts an arm around me and I lean against his chest as I stare out the window.

He's not wrong. I hadn't noticed before, but each of the bridges we pass under is strung with white lights. Streetlights brighten the tree-lined lanes that run parallel to the canals, and it's clear the city is still awake and bustling. We pass people all along the canals, some sitting on benches and others walking down the sidewalks.

And, to my surprise, I can see right into many of the homes along the canal.

"They don't mind people looking in?" I ask, pointing to a window. A couple is in their living room slow dancing. It's very pure, but also feels like a personal moment.

He shrugs. I can tell he's fighting it, but he's been subdued since the conversation about the art competition. "Some of us aren't bothered by it. We don't like the curtains. We'd rather let the light in."

It's an interesting way to live. I feel like I've always hated people looking into my life. I keep the curtains closed, not just in my bedroom but in every other part of my life too. It's scary to have someone look into your depths and see everything that's private about you. I trust almost no one to do that. But I think Ryland might be the exception.

We're quiet on the way back to the apartment. Only when we're a block away does he turn to me.

"You go in first. I'll walk around the block a few times and then come in."

I don't want to get pulled into a conversation with Dr. Reese and Berend, so I head straight to my room when I get inside. I sit on my bed, feeling miserable on Ryland's behalf. I wonder if there's anything he could do with those pieces now? Maybe there's another competition or a gallery where they could be displayed? I turn on my laptop and start Googling. I don't get very far before a knock sounds on my door. I shake my head. Ryland's playing with fire coming to see me so soon.

I open the door, a smile on my face, only to find Dr. Reese waiting for me.

"Sage, I thought I heard you. Can you come out to the living room? I have something I want to talk about."

Immediately, anxiety pushes every other thought from my mind. Dr. Reese *never* calls me out of my room like this. And why do we need to talk at eleven at night? Ryland is already sitting on the couch when I arrive, his shoulders hunched and his hands knotted together. His gaze flicks to mine and I can see the fear.

What kind of chat are we about to have?

"You two were both out late."

We look at each other again and then away. "Late dinner with friends," Ryland says.

"I was walking along the canals. They're beautiful at night."

"They are." She looks between the two of us. "Is everything okay? You both seem a little on edge."

I nod robotically. This feels like she's slowly leading us into a trap. "Just tired. What's going on?"

"Actually, Berend and I were talking tonight about how well this whole summer has gone. To be honest, I had my concerns at the beginning, but you and Diederik have really hit it off. I can tell he feels comfortable with you, Sage. And Ryland, I saw your newest pieces up in the attic when I went looking for you tonight. Those are really gorgeous. I'm proud of you."

Ryland shrinks just a bit more and my heart breaks. She doesn't know about the competition.

"Anyway," Dr. Reese continues, "Berend and I think you both deserve a day out. What about a little family day trip tomorrow to Zaanse Schans? It's a short drive by car and you'll get to learn about historical Dutch culture, Sage. What do you think? They have working windmills."

I almost collapse to the floor with relief. She doesn't know about us. She's not angry. "I'd love to go," I blurt out.

"Great. And don't worry, you won't be on the clock," she says with a laugh. "This will just be a fun day for you to explore. Ryland, are you up for it too?"

"Sure, sounds fun." He looks over at me. "I can get to know Sage a little bit better before she leaves."

She smiles. "Yes, exactly. A nice day together before the summer's over."

I look down at my hands, wishing I could pretend the summer would never end.

chapter 21

We all pile into the car the next morning and it's a tight fit.

"Sage, do you mind sitting in the middle next to Diederik? I'd really rather not move that car seat if I don't have to," Dr. Reese asks.

"Oh, sure, of course."

I move as far as I can into the seat and then Ryland scoots in next to me. We're crammed next to each other with zero wiggle room. I smile at him quickly before facing forward. We aren't exactly going to be able to keep up this facade if I'm staring dreamily into his eyes. I put my hand at my side between us and his lies on top of mine, hidden by our legs. A shiver shoots up my spine.

We make our way out of Amsterdam, driving fairly slow because we have to keep braking for pedestrians and cyclists. But Zaanse Schans is only twenty minutes from the house, so soon Berend is turning into the parking lot. He sighs contently.

"It's good to be back. It's been a long time."

We all climb out of the car and follow him. Sheep lounge in the rich green fields that surround us. Dr. Reese points across the field and I suck in a breath. Four brown-and-green wooden windmills sit in the distance, their sails slowly spinning.

"Is this your first time seeing windmills?" she asks.

I nod. "They're beautiful." I knew that the Netherlands was known for their windmills, but it's one thing seeing them stamped onto plates and shirts and another thing to see them within walking distance of me. A wave of gratitude hits me that I was able to come here this summer.

We cross a tiny arched bridge over a canal that looks more like a wide stream and make our way into a village of buildings. They're painted green with decorative white trim and each looks slightly different, like they're siblings instead of identical twins.

"These are all part of the open air museum," Dr. Reese explains, pointing to them. "Each displays a particular part of traditional Dutch culture. Like this one is the weaver, and farther down there's one dedicated to carving wooden shoes."

"And don't forget the cheese," Berend adds. "They have all kinds of free samples."

"He's going to make himself sick eating them all," Ryland says.

"And it'll be completely worth it."

"Where should we go first?" Dr. Reese asks.

They all look at me expectantly. Well, except for Diederik, who is surreptitiously picking his nose.

"Um . . . I'll follow you."

We walk through a re-created grocery store and candy shop, then watch women in traditional outfits weave sails for the windmills. Wherever I walk, Ryland is right there, walking just slightly behind me. I can sense his presence like the sun on my back and I find myself lingering to get closer to him. We don't speak, other than a few bland words about the attractions. But then, as soon as Berend and Dr. Reese are focused away from us, he'll lean in to kiss me on the back of the neck or brush his fingers against my own. It's clearly a game—and a dangerous one at that—but I don't want to stop him. It's too much fun.

Next, we visit the cheese shop, where Berend does eat his weight in cheese, before heading to the clog shop. We crowd around a man who demonstrates the original way they used to take blocks of wood and carve them into clogs before showing us how a machine can do it in a few minutes now.

"Enjoying the trip so far?" Ryland whispers in my ear.

I have to take a breath from the goose bumps. "You're making it a little difficult to concentrate on this excellent clog-making talk."

"I could say the same for you."

I lift an eyebrow at him, but then catch Berend waving at us. We leave the demonstration behind for the shop—which is clog heaven, with wooden shoes lining the walls and the entire ceiling—before heading out.

"Diederik was about to lose his temper in there, so I figured we needed to leave before he started tossing clogs at people's heads," Dr. Reese says.

I laugh at the very real possibility.

"I'm thinking we get some food before we walk over to the windmills, but—" Berend points to a clog on the sidewalk that is so large you can climb into it. In fact, people are doing just that.

"We have to get your picture inside the clog, Sage. Every tourist who comes here does it."

I shake my head. I can't think of a tackier tourist attraction than this. "Oh, I don't—"

"How about I get in it with you? So you don't feel alone?" Ryland asks me with a barely concealed smirk.

"That's not necessary."

"I insist." He gestures toward the clog, where there's an actual line of people waiting to get pictures.

"I can't believe you're making me do this," I whisper to him.

"Are you kidding me? This better be your phone home screen by the time we get back to the attic tonight. This is too good."

The people in front of us leave and I gingerly step inside the huge clog. Ryland steps in next to me and puts his arm casually around my shoulder.

"Smile!" Berend calls.

That's not hard to do.

He gives us a thumbs-up sign. "Looks great!" he says. "I'll text the pictures to you. Now let's get some food."

We stop at a little take-out window to get sandwiches, fries, and drinks and find an empty outdoor table that lines the sidewalk. To my surprise, Diederik comes around the table to sit in my lap. "Hey there," I say, and move so he has room. I feel guilty that he left Dr. Reese to sit with me, but she seems happy and possibly a little relieved to have a few minutes to eat in peace. "Are you having a good time?" I ask him.

He nods and picks up my apple. I stifle a squeal of excitement and exchange a look with Dr. Reese. Is he actually going to take a bite of apple? That would be *huge*. Maybe I've really made a difference with him.

He smiles up at me, all adorable plump cheeks and red hair . . . and then chucks my apple into the narrow canal that runs on the other side of the walkway.

"Duck food!" he cries.

Ryland snorts into his drink and starts coughing.

"Diederik, no!" Dr. Reese calls. "Sage, I'm so sorry!"

I really want to keep a straight face, but one look at Ryland and I start laughing. I'm such a sucker.

"It's okay. I should have known better," I tell her.

She chuckles as well, though just a bit. "I guess we did let our guards down."

Berend stands and takes Diederik from my lap. "The troublemaker and I will go get you a replacement apple."

Dr. Reese shakes her head and turns her attention to her older son. "Ryland, I'd love to hear more about that art I saw up in the attic. I can't believe you were keeping that hidden up there!"

"It's nothing," he replies quietly, and takes a bite of his sandwich.

My amusement from a second ago disappears and I drop a hand to touch Ryland's knee under the table. I can sense the pain radiating off him even if his mother can't.

"Nothing!" She makes a tsking sound. "It's the best work I've seen from you yet. Are you trying to sell them?"

"They're already sold, actually. Espen is buying them to sell at his tourist shops."

"What?" I exclaim before I can stop myself. "You sold them?"

"What else was I going to do with them?" he says in a quieter voice. "He's giving me a good price."

My mouth drops open, but then I realize I'm acting like I have a vested interest in the pieces. Dr. Reese watches us curiously.

"Ryland created them during the nights I worked in the attic," I explain quickly. "That's how I know about them."

She nods. "Yes, of course. Well, congratulations on selling them, Ryland." She beams at him. "We should be celebrating today."

He shakes his head.

"No, listen, you've really impressed me this summer. You stuck to your word, and look at the success you've had now." Berend and Diederik arrive back just then. Dr. Reese sits Diederik on her lap and Berend hands me a new apple. "You know, Jacqueline had a family emergency come up, so she's pulled out of the conference. I hate to waste her ticket, and you've been working so hard . . . what if we transferred her ticket to you? Would you have any interest in coming to Berlin?"

Ryland's eyes go wide. "To . . . go to the conference?"

She laughs. "No, of course not. So you could, I don't know, see the city? You won't see much of us. Sage and I will be at the conference during the days and will likely be out for dinners with colleagues in the evenings, but I think you're old enough to take care of yourself. I've heard Berlin has an impressive art scene—I thought you could find some new inspiration."

I almost drop my new apple on the ground in surprise. I know I need to tamp down my excitement since we're supposed to be practically strangers, but it's hard to control the elation rushing through me. And that's nothing compared to Ryland's palpable joy.

"That sounds amazing!" he cries. "Are you sure? The expense?"

She waves away his concerns. "Consider it an early birthday present and a congratulations wrapped into one."

"Thank you!" He stands and walks around the table to hug his mom and Berend. "Actually, I'm finished eating. Do you mind if I take Sage to see the windmills? You can catch up with us."

"Well, I guess." Dr. Reese looks at me. "If you want to, Sage?"

"Yeah, I'm anxious to see them." I hold up my apple. "I can eat it on the way."

Ryland and I weave through the crowds at a casual pace. We don't touch or look at each other. Finally, after making sure we're far enough away that we can't see his parents, Ryland whoops and lifts me in his arms.

"Berlin!" he whispers, and swings me in a circle.

I laugh and squeeze him.

"I can't believe I get to come to Berlin with you!"

"Well, Berlin with your *mom* and two other grad students. We won't exactly be making out on the plane."

"That's true. And you'll be gone during the days, but maybe in the evenings when you come back we can walk around the city together? Mom would probably approve of that so you aren't exploring a new city alone at night."

I grin. "It's a plan."

He points down the flat path in front of us. In the distance, past the green museum buildings, I can see the same four enormous windmills from earlier. "You really should see them," he says. "In fact, there's one I have to show you. You're going to love it."

He grabs my hand and tugs me down the walkway toward the windmills, which arch around a large body of water. They were impressive and iconic from far away, but I didn't anticipate how large and powerful they would be up close. Three of them are turned toward the wind and their sails rotate quickly. I slow down to look closer, but Ryland keeps walking.

"This isn't the one I want to show you. Hurry, before they catch up to us."

I follow his lead, craning my neck to take in the whole structure before being pulled away. A bit farther down he slows and pulls me toward a building attached to the windmill. He points to a sign by the door.

"I promised I'd find you more."

The sign says *De Kat* next to a painting of a small black cat. I swing around to look at him.

"*No.*"

"Yes! I told you—nothing but cat attractions when we're together."

I laugh and shake my head. "Are you sure you didn't come here early and switch out the signs just to screw with me?"

"Come see. It gets even better, if you can believe it."

We buy our tickets and walk inside. I wasn't sure if we'd be able to see the inner workings, but it's open to explore. The entire structure is made of enormous pieces of timber. As the sails rotate, it turns huge wheels inside to grind . . . well, I'm not quite sure what. I squint and lean closer.

"De Kat is a *paint* mill," he says, and pulls me closer to look. "They grind minerals that can be made into oil paints and watercolors. It's said to be the last working paint mill in the world."

I look up at him in shock. "But that's too perfect for you. It can't be real."

He grins. "Yes, I am too perfect, but I've come to accept that about myself. You will too, in time."

I groan, but I can't stop smiling. I'm standing in a real-life windmill named *The Cat* in Holland next to a cat-obsessed artist boy who I'm quickly falling for. I could *never* have predicted this when I was waiting for my luggage at the airport in June. Usually that would bother me, but this time I'm happy for the surprise.

chapter
22

Ryland and I manage to sneak out of the house a few times during the next week, but I'm cautious not to do too much. I don't want to risk getting caught with the conference so close, and I also want to spend the evenings triple-checking that I'm completely prepared for the weekend. Soon we're gathering our bags and heading to the airport. I'm surprised when my phone buzzes with a text from Wren.

Good luck this weekend! I hope the conference goes as well as you dreamed.

I blink and do the math in my head. It's only seven here, which means it's one a.m. back home.

What are you doing up?!

Maddie hasn't been sleeping well lately. And I wanted to

text at the beginning of your day before you got too caught
up and missed it.

Another text bubble pops up to show she's writing more.

Dad would be so proud of you. I know he'll be with you
this weekend.

I inhale and squeeze the phone tightly. I've been thinking
about Dad, wondering what silly jokes he'd be making about the
trip or what advice he'd give me. He would be happy for me, absolutely. But I can't quite believe that Wren would send me this. I
wasn't sure she'd even know when the conference was, let alone
care enough to text me about it in the middle of the night.

Thanks.
I'm proud too.

I swallow hard.

Same.
Now get to bed!

Things were rocky at the beginning of the summer, but maybe
they're starting to change between us. I hope so.

I am positively vibrating with excitement the entire way to
our gate. This Amsterdam trip has been more than I could've

anticipated in so many different ways, but *this* was always what I was most looking forward to. It was always the end goal. And, somehow, I've actually made it. Ryland and I pulled off the secrecy, and I'm going to present research at one of the largest international oncology conferences in the world. I can barely believe it.

At the gate, we meet Katina and Ezeudo. "Are you excited?" she asks, and gives me a little side hug.

"So excited. I can't wait for the conference."

Ezeudo laughs. "I wish I was that enthusiastic. It'll be good to see some friends, but conferences are exhausting."

"*Incredibly* exhausting," Katina replies. "I usually come home and crash for two days, and that's assuming I don't get sick too."

They will not dampen my excitement.

"You all remember my son, Ryland?" Dr. Reese asks. They nod and wave. Ryland stands an acceptable distance from me, looking polite and mildly uninterested in the entire situation. He's a pretty good actor. It's hard to be so close to him and pretend like I barely know or care who he is. As happy as I am that he gets to come to Berlin, it might be a bit miserable as well. How are we going to make it the entire weekend pretending to be indifferent acquaintances?

"Sage," Dr. Reese says, "I'm thinking you and Katina should sit together and I'll sit with Ryland? Does that sound okay?"

My stomach sinks just a bit and I try not to show it. "Whatever you'd like."

Katina's gaze flicks to me and then she interrupts. "Actually, Dr. Reese, if you don't mind, I was hoping I could sit with you. I had a thought on a new study and I wanted to run it by you before we got to the conference."

"You did? Well . . ." She hesitates. "Sage, Ryland, are you okay sitting together?"

"No problem," I say. Ryland nods.

Dr. Reese smiles. "Thanks, you two. Okay, I'm going to run to the restroom before they start boarding."

Ryland sits down and I turn to Katina when Dr. Reese is a safe distance away. "You just did that on purpose, didn't you?"

"He's very cute."

My cheeks warm. "Am I that obvious?"

"No. But I have little sisters, so it's easy to recognize the signs."

"Well, you should probably know that Dr. Reese has forbidden us from doing anything close to dating."

She sneaks a glance at Ryland, who is doing a decent job of looking absorbed in his phone. "And how's that going?"

I bite my lip, scared to say it out loud. "Very poorly. Or maybe very well, depending on how you interpret it."

She laughs. "Oh dear, I remember those times. Well, I'll try to keep Dr. Reese distracted on the plane." She puts a hand on my arm. "But Sage, be careful."

I nod and then go sit next to Ryland. "Lucky break," he whispers. He has his earbuds in and is looking at his cell phone. He bobs his head to a beat I can't hear.

"Are you actually listening to music?"

"No," he says without looking up. "But I'm very good at pretending."

I have to push down a laugh. "Well played. Keep it up."

We end up squished into two very tight seats next to a business-man. Ezeudo is sitting directly behind us and Dr. Reese and Katina are behind him, so we're fairly safe for a bit. Ryland lays his hand on mine under the tray table, and I take a calming breath. It's been painful trying not to touch him this entire time. "Do you have a plan for what you're going to do in Berlin this weekend?" I ask.

"I have a few ideas."

"You understand that I'll be at the conference all day, right? And if I get invited to lunch or dinner by other researchers then I really need to go."

He squeezes my hand. "Of course you need to go. That's the whole point of the trip. You should do what you need to do."

"Okay. Thanks." I hesitate. "Do you think you're going to spend your time looking for new art inspirations like your mom talked about?"

"Definitely. How could I not with a brand-new city to explore? There's nothing like traveling to give me new ideas. It's one of the reasons I was always happy to go back to America each year."

"Good. I was just a little nervous. You haven't wanted to talk about the art competition, and it made me think you might be burned out."

He frowns. "There isn't much to say about the competition. I mean, I'm disappointed, but I can't change the outcome."

Now that we're finally talking about it, I can't help myself. "Couldn't you try to get those pieces into a gallery or something rather than selling them to tourists? They're too beautiful to be sold at a gift shop."

He shakes his head. "There are a lot of galleries, but if you don't know the owners or you haven't made a name for yourself then it can be hard to have work displayed there. At least this way I'm making some money to pay for supplies. And Mom is clearly excited or she wouldn't have let me come on the trip. If I'm making money, then I'm successful in her eyes." I can hear the edge of resentment underlying his words.

I give him a small smile. Now is not the time to push. "Well, whatever the reason for it, I'm glad you're here with me."

Dr. Reese, Ryland, and I take a taxi to the hotel in central Berlin. The city is beautiful, but *so* different from Amsterdam. Although Amsterdam is a major European city, it's very walkable, with lots of quiet neighborhoods and peaceful canals. Berlin, in contrast, is a sprawling city of metal and glass and skyscrapers. It's hard and modern, but you can feel the history—both good and bad— seeping through everywhere. The hotel is also large and modern, filled with reclaimed wood and brick walls. Our entire conference will be at this hotel, so I don't think I'll be seeing too much of Berlin while I'm here.

My stomach jumps into my throat as soon as we walk into the lobby. There are a lot of people here, standing in line to check in or talking together in small groups. Many of them look too dressed up to be casual tourists. And a few of them already have lanyards hanging from their necks with their names and associated hospitals and universities written on tags.

I look down at myself with a grimace. I didn't realize I'd be making my first impression as soon as I walked into the hotel. I settled on black leggings and a long gray tunic for comfort on the plane, but now I wish I'd worn one of the two suits that I brought.

Dr. Reese checks us in and then waves over a man standing a few feet away. "Jon, it's good to see you again." She shakes his hand and gestures to me. "This is a young student from America I've taken under my wing, Sage Cunningham. And this is my son, Ryland."

The man's name tag reads *Dr. Jon Banet, Université de Paris.* Dr. Banet . . . I think I read one of his articles when I was in London.

"Hello." He shakes both of our hands. "So, you flew all the way from America just for the conference? I hope it lives up to your expectations." He has a charming French accent.

"I know it will. I've been excited about it all summer."

He smiles cordially. "I hope to see you at my talk then, tomorrow at two. It'll be one of the best things you attend here."

Dr. Reese laughs after he walks away. "He's as conceited as he is brilliant," she whispers. She must see how intimidated I am because she shakes her head. "Just stick with me, I'll introduce you to everyone."

It turns out Dr. Reese is sharing a hotel room with Ryland and I have one all to myself. It's a pretty basic room—white walls, a single bed, a small desk by the window—but it's an absolute thrill all the same. Despite having traveled quite a bit in the last year, I've never spent much time in hotel rooms. My family never went on big trips when I was young, and once Dad's medical expenses piled up we didn't have the money for it.

We're supposed to meet up with the graduate students again for dinner, so I text Ellie, Wren, and Mom to tell them I landed safely. Then I take my time unpacking my bags and hanging all my clothes up. Even though I'll only be here for two nights, I'll still feel more settled if I take the time to do it.

I wish I could do something with Ryland tonight, but there's no way to do that without having Dr. Reese in the mix as well. Instead, I skim all the articles I read this summer. At least five of these researchers are here and I'm hoping to get to meet them. Maybe I can even speak to them a bit about their research, enough to make an impression on them.

The next morning, I'm up at five, already filled with nerves. I take an extra-long shower and slowly get dressed, trying to kill time. I flip through my folder with the agenda for the day. The keynote doesn't start until eight thirty.

A little knock sounds at my door and my pulse quickens, wondering if Ryland found a way to sneak over. I open it to find him wearing his neon-green *Walking Interruption* shirt and a satchel.

"Hey! What are you doing here? Is your mom around?" I peek out into the hall, but it's empty.

"She's still in the room getting ready. Can I come in?"

I hesitate and step back to let him walk in, making sure there are no witnesses before securely shutting the door behind me.

He leans over and kisses my cheek. "I'm heading out, but I wanted to see you before I left."

"You're leaving this early? What's gotten into you?"

"Well, Mom made sure I was awake, what with the shower, and the lights, and the hair dryer . . ." He rolls his eyes.

I laugh. "It's good for you. Where are you going?"

"Everywhere." He smiles. "Berlin has amazing museums, but it also has an unbelievable street art culture. I want to try to see as much as possible. I have a feeling I'm going to be exhausted by tonight."

"Yeah, I will be too even though I'm not leaving this building."

He takes my hand. "I'm glad I got to come here. It's fun to see you like this." He gestures to my gray suit. "I have to admit, the gray *does* work on you."

"Of course it does."

"I'm proud of you, Sage. Just seeing you with all these renowned researchers and imagining that one day you'll be one of them. It's really cool."

I glance at the door to reassure myself that it's shut and locked. Then I reach up and kiss him. He drops his satchel to the ground and wraps his arms around me, pulling me close. His fingers glide into my perfectly brushed hair, but I don't care. Kissing him is the only thing that can make this trip better.

Knock, knock.

We jump apart and stare at each other in horror. "Is that your mom?" I whisper.

"I don't know. I thought she was still getting ready."

"Could be Katina. Go hide just in case."

There's another knock on the door.

Ryland grabs his satchel, dashes behind the bed, and lies down on the floor. I hurry over to the door. "Just a second," I call. I look over my shoulder to double-check that he's hidden and then open it.

"*Dr. Reese!*" I exclaim loudly.

"Uh, good morning." She looks confused at the volume of my voice. "I'm heading to breakfast. Do you want to come down with me?"

"Oh, um, well . . ." I look around frantically. "I just need to finish getting ready."

She looks me up and down and frowns. "All right. I'll wait for you, then. I hate eating by myself." She walks in and I scurry after her, getting in front of her before she can get too far into the room.

She sits down on the bed and I about scream, but she doesn't look over the other side.

"Look how organized you have everything. You're just like me. I hate being in disorganized spaces." She shakes her head. "Unfortunately, Ryland takes after his father on that account."

"Oh yeah?"

My heart rate and thoughts are flying as fast as the jet that brought us here. I could make an excuse and kick her out of my room, but then I'd still have to sneak Ryland out and someone could see us together. I glance around the room. Maybe I should just grab my stuff and leave Ryland here? He could wait until we're gone and then sneak out.

Dr. Reese shifts on the bed and I decide. "I'm starving, let's go!" I practically yell.

She jumps in surprise. "Didn't you need to get ready?"

"Oh, um, I just needed to get my hotel key and folder." I grab them from the dresser and usher her toward the door. "If we don't get down there soon all the tables will be taken."

She stands. "True, the whole conference will be there."

I sigh in relief and open the door for her. Once she's in the hallway I exclaim, "I forgot my phone. Just a second!" I close the door and run back across the room. Ryland jumps up and crosses the room in three steps, takes me by my shoulders, and kisses me.

"That was inspired," he whispers.

"I'm going to kill you. Do *not* get caught sneaking out of here."

"Or you could get sudden food poisoning and stay locked in here all day with me."

"You're the worst." I kiss him again. "I'll see you tonight."

chapter
23

My mind is still racing as Dr. Reese and I crowd onto the elevator with several other sleepy-looking conference attendees. That was *so* close. This whole thing almost blew up in my face. It's getting harder to hide everything.

I'm imagining if there's any possible way that someone could see Ryland leaving my room when the elevator opens and I'm hit with the tinkle of silverware and people chattering. I guess lots of researchers are early risers because the breakfast room is busy, but we manage to grab a table. An attendant comes over and drops off a basket of croissants and bread, a bowl of fruit, and a large plate of lunch meat. She also asks how we'd like our eggs cooked and whether we want coffee or tea.

The grad students arrive, looking even more exhausted and rumpled than everyone else.

"Coffee," Ezeudo says, and grabs the carafe.

Dr. Reese hands me the lunch-meat tongs. I look at the meat dubiously and then select a slice of ham. I'm not used to these European breakfasts.

"Have you all decided on your schedule?" Dr. Reese asks as she looks at the conference app on her phone.

Katina takes a drink of tea. "I wanted to hear about Dr. Bryan's latest immunotherapy research."

"After Dr. Keller's keynote, I'm headed to the talk on genome function," Ezeudo says.

"And you'll stay with me today, Sage?" Dr. Reese asks.

I nod, happy to stay at her side. I don't want to miss an important talk because I didn't know it was happening.

"It should be a good day." She beams at me. "Your very first conference! Exciting!"

The grad students are correct. Conferences are exhausting and overwhelming. The keynote has several hundred attendees, all lined up in rows like we're sitting in a lecture hall. Then we head to smaller breakout talks in conference rooms throughout the hotel. We don't have time to go to the Saturday-morning poster session, but after a quick boxed lunch, Dr. Reese and I speed through the afternoon poster session—mostly so I can see how the room is set up and where I'll be located tomorrow—before hurrying off to see her friend's talk on RNA translation. I keep a notebook out at all times to write down names, citations, and notes I can look back at.

And after each talk, people come over to Dr. Reese to say hi or to chat about her latest publications, and once or twice to bring up some criticisms. I always knew that she was a prolific and respected researcher. That's why I reached out to her about volunteering in her lab back as a junior. But I guess I didn't know *quite* how well-known she is. She's like a minor celebrity. People watch her walk by and whisper, and younger grad students speak to her with shaky voices.

Given all the attention, I would understand if she forgot I was standing next to her like a personal assistant. But she doesn't forget me. As soon as there's an opening, she introduces me to these research gods as if I am . . . an equal. As if she's lucky to have *me* working with her.

I text Ryland in the bathroom to tell him that I've been invited to dinner with Dr. Reese, the grad students, and one of her old friends from med school. I feel a bit bad ditching him, despite warning him that this exact thing might happen, but luckily he takes it in stride.

I'm too busy with the art here to worry about eating, he texts back.

We don't see each other that night because there's no way to see him without making an excuse to go hang out in Dr. Reese's hotel room, and that's just too awkward.

Another busy day tomorrow? he texts that night.

> Yeah. Even busier. But let's try to do something together if we can. Tomorrow night maybe? If we can get away?

It's a date.

I'm nervous when I wake up Sunday. Yesterday, I got to be a spectator. I listened to talks and took notes, and if I didn't know what to say it was fine because I wasn't expected to say anything.

But today is different. Dr. Reese has her talk in the morning and then this afternoon is my poster session. I know I shouldn't be intimidated—there are forty posters in my session alone and it's likely I'll stand there without visitors for the entire ninety minutes—but that doesn't make me feel better.

I half expect Ryland to come see me again, but he has the good sense to keep his distance when I need to focus.

Good luck. You've got this, he texts at breakfast.

I smile down into my lap and then put my phone away. This is the day I've been working for all summer.

I sit next to Katina in the front row of the breakout room for Dr. Reese's talk. As always, she's confident and eloquent, explaining her research in a way that's simple to understand while still conveying the underlying complexity. She's exactly who I want to be when I'm finished with medical school. I look up at her, smiling but barely listening as she wraps up her talk, just imagining the possibility that someday I might be standing where she is now.

"Finally, I'd like to thank my team who worked tirelessly on this important project. My students: Katina Volkov, Ezeudo Umar, and Jacqueline Lange, as well as my intern, Sage Cunningham, for pulling together reference lists and data entry. Thank you, all."

I blink in surprise. A few people around us are nodding and smiling. Katina elbows me happily.

When the talk is finished, a small line of people come up to the front to chat with Dr. Reese. I'm debating sneaking out to the restroom before it gets overrun when I hear my name.

"Sage! Come here, there's someone I want to introduce you to."

I hurry over and my stomach leaps into my throat as I read the name tag of the man in front of me. *Jim Lee, MD, PhD, Johns Hopkins University.* I immediately recognize him from all the hours I spent researching the university. He is the director of the cancer institute there and conducts cutting-edge research on immunotherapy for lung cancer. He's an absolute pioneer and icon in the field and I'm not sure I should be breathing the same air as him.

"Jim, this is my intern, Sage Cunningham. I'm glad you came up because I was hoping to get a chance to introduce you two. Sage is an incoming freshman at Johns Hopkins."

He leans back in surprise. "Are you really? I have to say, I've had a few students attend conferences with me, but I've never met an incoming freshman at one."

"Yes, um . . ." I try to pull myself together. "It's wonderful to meet you." I put out my hand and he shakes it. Another spark of nerves shoot through me. "I read your latest article in the *Journal of the National Cancer Institute.*"

He glances at Dr. Reese, as if looking for confirmation, and then back at me. "Do you often read journal articles during your summers?"

"More often than I read novels. And I'm particularly invested in research related to lung cancer." I try for a small smile even though I can hardly get the words out.

"She's very diligent," Dr. Reese adds.

"Yes, it seems that way. It's lucky for you that she's already working in your lab or someone else might poach her." He raises an eyebrow at her and then smiles at me. "Nice to meet you."

Dr. Reese and Dr. Lee turn back to their conversation, switching over to discuss her talk, but I stand at attention the entire time just in case they ask me anything. My hands shake slightly so I put them behind my back. Did his comment mean that he would be open to me working in his lab in the future? I would *love* to volunteer in two labs this coming year. I could continue with Dr. Reese remotely, perhaps even contributing to one of her upcoming articles, while also getting involved in a new on-campus lab. And not just any lab—if I were able to work with Dr. Lee, I might be able to contribute to the creation of a new treatment for lung cancer. That work could save lives—it would be the ultimate way to honor Dad. Of course, I highly doubt anyone as famous as Dr. Lee would want an undergrad getting involved in their work, but it's fun to dream.

Dr. Reese looks happy after he leaves. "How did I do?" she asks.

"Wonderful."

"Good." She takes a deep breath. "I always feel better after I'm done. You should grab lunch so you'll be ready for your session afterward."

I'm jittery as I pull my massive glossy poster from a tube, unroll it, and gingerly tack it to the bulletin board in the large conference hall. Around me are many other people doing the same thing, except they look much older and more confident. When I'm sure my poster is level, I grab my handouts and roll my shoulders back with a small smile on my face. Soon, attendees will start meandering through the room, glancing at the posters and stopping to ask questions if something catches their attention. In the grand scheme of things, it's not a big deal to present a poster at a conference. It's much less impressive than giving a talk, but this still feels *huge* to me. To be standing here among med students and post-docs, sharing research that I contributed to . . . it's what I've been working toward for a long time. Now I just hope I don't puke on the first person who comes up and asks me a question.

Soon it's clear this session is going to be a slow one. I'm in the last poster session for the conference, when everybody is tired and spent. It's the worst session to be put in. Mostly people just walk straight past, pretending to look interested or maybe pausing for a second to read the title before walking on. I'm half relieved and half disappointed every time they continue by without speaking. Maybe it's better this way. I'll still get to put this on my résumé, and I won't risk making a fool of myself.

Then I see Dr. Keller from the University of Zurich coming down the walkway toward me. She's a very prominent researcher in Switzerland and gave the opening keynote address yesterday morning. My stomach jumps into my throat. She also happens to be referenced no less than four times on this poster. She glances at each poster without interest before pausing at mine and then looking at me.

"You're studying Ras mutations?"

"Um, yes, I'm an intern in Dr. Reese's lab. I helped with this research last fall."

She nods and looks back at the poster. There's an awkward silence as she reads. She's as sharply dressed as she was yesterday, in a tailored black suit with a bright red blouse that matches the small flag pin on her lanyard.

"And you were looking at correlations with clinicopathological features?"

"Patient age, metastasis, and histological type."

She looks me square in the eye and says, "Tell me your results."

The information is clearly written on the poster, but I recognize her command for what it is—a test. I take a breath and launch into an explanation that I've gone over in my mind many times in the attic at night, pointing to my carefully crafted graphs as I do.

She nods, her eyes flicking between the graphs and me. When I'm finished, she pauses for a moment and then gives a curt nod. I think that's a good sign.

"Remind me again, you said you were one of Dr. Reese's postdocs? I thought I knew all of her students."

"No, an undergraduate student from the United States. Well, I will be in August. I've been interning with her over the fall and this summer."

She cocks her head to the side. "Very interesting. And your name is?"

"Sage Cunningham."

"Hmm. I'll remember that for when you're on the job market." She gives me a small wink before moving on.

I stand very still until she's far away. The girl next to me gives me a small thumbs-up. When I know that Dr. Keller can't see me, I bend over at the waist and suck in a huge breath. Oh my god, she liked the poster. Or at least she didn't criticize it to my face or tell me I was explaining things incorrectly. And she's going to remember me for the job market?! I mean, that's highly unlikely since I won't be looking for jobs for at least a decade, but *still*. She didn't have to say that! I bounce on the balls of my feet and exhilaration fills me.

I see her again in my mind's eye, her eyes sharp and piercing. Then another detail comes back to me and my throat gets thick, remembering my favorite joke from Dad. *What's the best thing about Switzerland? I don't know, but their flag is a big plus.*

The pin on her lanyard. It was the Swiss flag.

The rational part of my mind shuts down the connection immediately. It was a fluke. An absolute coincidence that means nothing.

But . . . I can't quite make myself believe that.

My heart wants to believe that maybe Dad is here right now, in his own way, watching me. That he's proud. Mom and Wren have seen a lot of signs since Dad passed, but I never have. Or maybe I just wouldn't let myself look for them.

But this one I can't ignore. I wipe at my eyes. *Thanks, Dad.*

chapter
24

The rest of the poster session flies by, as does the ending address. I can't wait until I can see Ryland and tell him how it all went. He messaged to ask and I sent back a string of smiley faces, but it's too much to put into a text. I want to see his face. Of course, that's going to be easier said than done with Dr. Reese by my side at all times.

Reluctantly, I agree to go to dinner with her and another friend. It's hard to keep my mind on the conversation, particularly since it has less to do with medicine and more to do with drama at the hospital the person works at, but I do my best. After they've paid, Dr. Reese turns to me.

"I told a few people I'd get drinks with them, but I don't think it's appropriate to invite you along for that."

"That's totally fine," I say with a smile. "I'll just head upstairs to my room. It's been a great day, but I'm tired."

"Of course."

I move to leave and she puts her hand on top of mine. "I'm really impressed with how you handled yourself this weekend,

Sage. I always knew I was smart to put my trust in you, and you didn't let me down."

Guilt seeps into me as I walk toward the elevators. She trusts me, and what have I been doing? Lying and sneaking around behind her back. I feel slightly nauseated at the thought, particularly because my fingers are already twitching to text Ryland and see if we still have time to go out tonight.

A small voice in my mind reminds me that—with the *tiny* exception of Ryland—I have done everything she's asked of me. I've worked incredibly hard this summer and last fall as well. I gave up countless opportunities to blow off work and spend time with my friends in England, or travel, or just *relax*. I've read every article, created every reference list, learned every new skill she's asked of me. I've taken this as seriously as someone ten years my senior. Can't I have tonight to explore Berlin with the boy who's quickly become one of the closest people in my life? The boy I'm leaving in just a week?

Yes, I can have this, I decide.

I will.

My fingers fly as I text him. I'm coming up. Are you at the hotel yet?

I rush into the elevator, body jangling with anticipation. Now that I've decided, I can't wait to see Ryland. We have so little time here and so much that we could see. And I want to tell him everything—about my poster session, the Swiss flag, meeting the other professors. I can't wait to see his expression when he hears.

The elevator door opens and he stands there with an expectant look on his face. "Well?"

I quickly glance down the hall to check that we're alone and then throw myself into his arms. "It was *amazing*. One of the best days of my entire life."

"That's so great." He beams at me. "What are you doing now? Do you have somewhere you need to be?"

"No. I'm all yours."

He smiles and kisses me. "The words I've been waiting for. Let's get out of here."

I quickly drop my stuff in my room and change into more comfortable clothes. It's a little tricky to get out of the hotel without being noticed, but we take separate elevators a few minutes apart and go out the patio entrance just in case Dr. Reese is in the lobby.

"Where should we go first?" I ask. I feel so alive walking next to him on this foreign street. So free and happy, like I'm flying instead of walking. I squeeze his hand and lean my head against his arm. The trip is so much better because he's here with me.

He kisses the top of my head. "I didn't get to everything today, but I made the rounds. We only have a little bit of time before the sun goes down and people start worrying, so let's start at one of the biggest sites—the Reichstag. Unless . . ." His eyes sparkle mischievously.

"Berlin can't *possibly* have cat attractions too."

"I've already found three cat cafés and I haven't done much research."

I laugh. "As fun as that sounds, maybe we should see the Reichstag instead. Since we only have a few hours here?"

"You could argue that we should be even more motivated to

visit a cat café given our lack of time. But fine, normal attractions it is."

The German metro system is clean and efficient, and soon we're stepping out of the metro station. Ryland pulls out his cell phone and looks at a map. "I think we have to walk this way."

We take off in that direction, happy to stroll and look at the scenery. Then I see a building in the distance. "Oh, there it is," I say, and point ahead of us at a massive building with a glass dome on top.

He looks at me in surprise. "I thought you'd never been to Berlin."

"Well, you know, I had to do a *little* research."

"Of course you did. Now I want to hear every detail about the conference."

I start at the beginning, telling him about all the sessions and the people that I met. I end with my interactions with Dr. Lee and Dr. Keller.

I hesitate for a second before adding, "I think Dad was there. Somehow, in some way. I think he was cheering me on." I look down at my shoes rather than at him when I say it. The connection felt so real when I was standing in the poster session, but now I feel silly, like a little girl making up stories. "I know that probably sounds dumb."

He jiggles my arm until I look at him. "It doesn't sound dumb at all. I'm sure he was with you, Sage. I'm sure he's incredibly proud of you and everything you've accomplished."

My throat gets thick from tears and I nod and look away again. I hope that's true.

Ryland puts an arm around me and we keep walking. After a minute, I feel strong enough to speak again. "I want to hear about your weekend too. What did you do?"

"I spent most of the day yesterday in East Berlin, visiting the neighborhoods and art galleries. And luckily I brought my sketchbook because I ended up staying at Museum Island for most of the afternoon to sketch." His eyes are bright with excitement. "The city is amazing. There's so much energy. Being away from Amsterdam is exactly what I needed."

"I'm so glad. And today?"

He sighs contentedly. "Today I went to the East Side Gallery. It's a section of the Berlin Wall that they kept up, but they've turned it into an enormous mile-long art installation. Artists come and draw huge murals on the wall. It's breathtaking."

We wander down the streets and under the Brandenburg Gate, stopping to take a photo together.

"You must be exhausted," he says.

I'm anything but tired. I actually twirl on the sidewalk, which is *so* unlike me. "Nope. I don't want to go back yet."

He smiles. "Me neither."

We get take-out kebabs on Unter den Linden and peek into a few of the stores that line the street. Finally, when the sun starts to set, we head back to the metro. My exhilaration from the day is still pumping through my veins. We half skip together down the sidewalk headed toward the hotel, giggling like little kids. Ryland points to a little take-out restaurant with bistro tables on the sidewalk.

"How about we stop and get dessert before we go back?"

I kiss him. "Yes. That's the perfect end to today."

We both order ice cream sundaes and sit across from each other. He takes a bite of his ice cream and gets whipped cream on his upper lip.

I laugh and reach out with my thumb to wipe it away. "You're cute, but you're messy."

"Not as cute as you."

Happiness floods through me. I'm not sure I've ever been so happy. The conference was as amazing as I always expected it to be, but the fact that I'm getting to share it with Ryland makes it exponentially better. I swipe my pinkie finger through my whipped cream and put a dollop on his lips. His eyes widen with surprise just as I lean over the table and kiss the cream away.

Behind me there's a cough and Ryland jerks back. I spin to find Dr. Reese and Katina on the sidewalk next to our table, along with two strangers who are clearly conference attendees. These must be the people Dr. Reese was going out with. Burning horror rushes through me so suddenly I'm lightheaded from it.

"*Ryland.*" Dr. Reese's voice is sharper than I've ever heard it before. "I thought you were staying in to sketch. And Sage, you said you were tired."

"I . . ."

My eyes flick to each of the faces. The two researchers look amused, like they're watching a juicy part of a reality show. Katina gazes at me with pity and Dr. Reese looks like she's about to spontaneously combust.

"I got a craving for ice cream," I whisper.

"I remember those cravings," one of the researchers whispers. The other man chuckles and Dr. Reese's cheeks redden.

"Mom, I—"

Dr. Reese puts up a hand to silence him. "Finish your ice cream and go back to the hotel. We'll talk about this later." Her glare cuts into my soul before she walks off. Katina gives my arm a quick squeeze as she passes, and I turn to Ryland in shock.

Did that just happen?

"Maybe it'll be okay?" Ryland whispers. "She's surprised, of course, but we aren't doing anything wrong. You did all the work you were asked to do. She can't be mad at you."

Reality comes crashing down on me. I look at my ice cream like I'm waking up from a dream. "What were we thinking, sitting out here where the entire world can see us?"

"How could we know she'd be walking in this direction right now? We're blocks from the hotel. It was just really bad luck."

"No, it wasn't bad luck. It was terrible decision-making."

I drop my head in my hands, new waves of panic and mortification swirling in me. Did Dr. Reese just see me *lick whipped cream off her son's mouth*? What the *hell* was I doing? What was I thinking? We shouldn't be out in public. We shouldn't be doing this at all.

"If I'd been thinking," I whisper, my voice shaky, "I would have known that we shouldn't be out in public. And certainly not right on the sidewalk, kissing. How could we be so reckless?"

"My mom is being completely unreasonable. When we get

back to the hotel, I'll talk to her. I'll explain everything."

"I don't want you to talk to her. It's already bad enough as it is."

"You don't know that it's bad. Just give her the night to sleep on it. I'm sure she'll be calm in the morning."

He reaches across the table for my hand, but I pull away. Of course he thinks it'll be fine. He's always so calm about everything, and it's not like Dr. Reese is going to disown him or anything. She's his mom. But what about all the work I've put into this lab over the last year? What about the possibility of future poster presentations, and articles, and letters of recommendation? I might have just screwed up *everything*. I can't even imagine what Mom and Wren will say.

"We should go back." I shove away from the table and hurl my almost-full ice cream cup into the garbage. "I need to pack. And think."

He frowns. "Think about what?"

I shake my head. I can't answer that question right now. I just need to be alone and try to sort out this ridiculous mess I've gotten myself into. "Are you ready?"

He's still for a moment. "Yeah, I'm ready."

The walk back to the hotel is short and silent, as is the elevator ride back up to our floor. He stops me before I can go into my room. "Sage, I think we should talk about this more. Maybe we should go through our stories, figure out what we're going to say to her."

I narrow my eyes. "This isn't a criminal investigation and I don't want to get my story straight with you. I'm going to tell her the truth when she asks me."

"I know, just—"

"I can't right now, Ryland. I'll talk to you tomorrow."

I unlock my door and walk in without waiting for a response. I'm too sick to my stomach to talk anyway.

chapter
25

I'm up most of the night, barely sleeping an hour at a time before I'm awake again, sick and pacing my small hotel room. Mom, Wren, and Ellie all text to hear more about the conference—Mom actually calls me too—but I can't talk to anyone until I know how Dr. Reese feels. I can't believe how foolish I was last night. We were so careful and then I got drunk on happiness and completely let my guard down.

The light knock comes at six a.m. I'm starting to recognize Dr. Reese's knock.

"I hope it isn't too early," she says when I open the door.

"No, I've been up for a while."

She walks in and sits in the desk chair by the bed. "Have a seat, Sage."

My fear ramps up into my throat, but I do as she says. "I'm sorry," I blurt out.

"I'm just so surprised." She rubs a hand over her face. "I almost couldn't believe it was you last night."

I drop my gaze to the floor.

"I made it very clear from the first day that you and Ryland could not date. I'm using grant funds to pay for your flight and admission into this conference. I've introduced you to all my colleagues as my intern. I've given you opportunities to present work and was planning to include your name on a publication." Her voice is sharp and I peek back up at her. "If you're seeing Ryland, then that puts me in an uncomfortable position. It looks like a strange form of nepotism where I'm giving you special treatment because you're dating my son. It could appear that I'm incorrectly using my grant funds to pay for international flights for family friends." She waves a hand. "That's not how I run my lab."

"I know, Dr. Reese. I'm sorry. I . . ." I don't know what to say. How can I explain what happened? I got caught up? I lost myself?

"I knew this was a possibility as soon as Ryland came home. Two young people living in such close proximity . . . well, I shouldn't be surprised." Her shoulders slump. "But I *am* surprised. And disappointed. Were you lying and sneaking around behind my back in Amsterdam? Or did this begin here?"

"It started a few weeks ago."

She sighs heavily. "Sage, if you were any other girl, I wouldn't be so upset. I know Ryland is a good kid and I can understand why you would like him . . . and why he would like you." She sighs again. She has bags under her eyes that I've never seen before. "It's just, you always reminded me so much of myself. Actually, you're even better than I was at your age. You seemed so focused and determined."

"I'm still focused and determined. I'm so grateful for all of these opportunities and I feel even more passionate about medicine than I did before the conference."

"I'm glad to hear that. But that doesn't change the fact that I don't feel comfortable having you date Ryland while also being associated with my lab. I don't want to be this person—and maybe you were going to end it anyway since you're going back to America next week—but I need to be clear: if you want to continue our professional relationship in any capacity, then you cannot date Ryland."

A sinking, heavy heat pulls on me at her words. I'm not surprised by them. I knew they were coming as soon as I saw her on the sidewalk last night—she already said the same thing at the beginning of the summer—but somehow I still hoped she wouldn't give me the ultimatum. My thoughts and emotions whirl together.

She puts a hand up. "You can think about it if you need to. And I'll also talk to Ryland and explain my reasoning so he doesn't blame you. He . . . didn't want to talk last night and was still asleep this morning when I left, but he'll understand eventually." She moves to stand and then settles back in. "Before I go, can I give you some advice?"

I nod mutely.

"I know what it's like to be torn between your goals and a boy. I wasn't quite as focused as you when I was your age. My junior year of undergrad, I fell for a boy. Completely head over heels, madly in love with him. We were together for almost two years of undergrad and into my first year of medical school. And then I got pregnant with Ryland." She pauses. "I don't regret Ryland, of course, but it took a huge toll on me and Ryland's father. We got married and tried to make a new marriage, a baby, and medical school work—but it just couldn't. Something had to give, and that was my relationship with my ex-husband." She leans back against the chair. "What I'm trying to say is that you should keep your life simple for now. You have time later to be in a relationship. To fall in love." She squeezes my hand. "Wait until you can do it justice. The relationship will be there later, when you're ready to balance it all. Like it was for me and Berend."

She stands and walks to the door. "We'll leave for the airport at nine thirty."

The nausea hits me before the door clicks shut. I wrap my arms around my waist and swallow down the churning bile. Holy hell. What am I going to do?

But even as I think that, I already know what my decision will be.

I've always known it.

Ryland is amazing. He's funny and kind and I really like him. Maybe even more than like him. But I can't let anything stand in the way of reaching my goals. Dr. Reese is incredibly well-known in the field. If she were willing, she could give me more research opportunities, include me on future posters, talks, or journal articles, write me a letter of recommendation for med school some-day . . . am I going to give that all up? Particularly when it's clear that Ryland and I are destined to break up after I leave Amsterdam anyway? People collaborate on research across continents—they do it all the time—but keeping a relationship together long distance is an entirely different thing.

I lie down on the bed. I don't need a relationship distracting me. This was exactly what I always feared—that if I started dating, then I'd get so caught up with the boy that I wouldn't be able to focus on my research. And here I am moping in my hotel room about a boy when I could be getting ready and networking at breakfast before we leave the country. Frustration fills me. There's only one thing to be done. And I need to do it now.

I quickly throw on some leggings and a black shirt and run a brush through my hair. Come to my room when you get this, I text him.

To my surprise, he's at my door in a matter of minutes.

"Hey." He walks in, hands in his pockets, looking much less cheery than I've ever seen him. "Mom said you already talked this morning?"

"Yeah, she came over early."

He nods and looks at the ground. "And how'd that go?"

"Ryland." I take a deep breath. "We can't date anymore."

He crumples just a little. "Please don't do this, Sage."

"I don't have a choice. Your mom made it very clear that I can't keep dating you."

"She said that?" He looks up at me, anger flashing in his eyes. "She's forbidding us from dating no matter what?"

"Not exactly that, but—"

"Oh." He rocks back on his heels. "Right. She said you have to choose. Me or the research?"

I don't speak.

"I know how important your work is to you and I don't want to take opportunities away from you. But you're important to me . . . and I was hoping I was becoming important to you too." He reaches for me, but I pull away. "This can't be the end of the discussion. There has to be some way to convince her."

"She's not going to be convinced. It's done. Her mind is made up."

"But you already got to go to this conference and present your poster. You met other researchers. You're almost finished babysitting. Does it really matter now if you stop working with her?"

"Yes. I don't know what other opportunities could come from this. Collaborations, introductions, recommendations to labs or schools. I don't want to burn this bridge."

"Dating me isn't the same as burning a bridge! It's not like she'd speak badly about you if we were together. And from what you were telling me, you already have a lot of opportunities. Wasn't Dr. Lee insinuating that he'd like you in his lab?"

I take a step back. My thoughts are getting all muddled. Everything made so much sense before Ryland started speaking. . . .

His gaze burns into my own. "My mom laid it all out there, so I'm going to do the same. I'm falling in love with you, Sage. Do you understand that? Maybe it's fast, but it doesn't feel fast to me. Or irresponsible or stupid. It feels inevitable. And I think you feel it too."

He closes the space between us and kisses me. I sway toward him even though I try to stop myself. It feels so right to be with him, like every flyaway emotion and thought is settling inside of me. Like peace.

But it's not enough.

I push away from him. "Ryland. We both knew this had to end at some point."

"Did we? Because I didn't have an expiration date on us."

"I'm starting college in America in a few weeks. I'm not giving that up for anything."

"Is that how little you think of me? That I'd *ever* ask you to do that?" He throws his hands up in the air. "I don't want you to give up your dreams for me. In fact, I'd be pissed if you suggested it. But that's the point, Sage. I hoped you'd want me to be in your life to support you. To help you. We all need help."

"But you live in Amsterdam! How are you going to help me from across the ocean?! I'm just being practical. It's better to end it now. Everything else aside, how could this have ever worked long-term?"

He walks across the room away from me, then turns around. His expression is raw with pain and it cracks something inside me.

"If you'd asked me, I would have come to America for you. My dad's been asking for me to move to the States forever, and he isn't all that far from your campus." His face closes like a shade covering an open window. "We could have made it work."

My breath catches. My brain can barely comprehend what he's saying. That he'd even *think* of giving up his life in Amsterdam for me . . . that I could possibly mean that much to him.

And it isn't lost on me that he's speaking in past tense now, as if this option is impossible. Which I guess it is.

"Ryland, I . . . I could never ask you to do that. It's too much."

He opens the door just a crack. "I can do my art from anywhere, Sage. In fact, this trip has proven that a change of scenery would be good for me. I can only block print so many cats on canals." He gives me a ghost of a smile. "I had hoped we could figure it out . . . if we both wanted it."

"It's not that I don't . . ." I trail off. Maybe it's better not to say anything. I'm close to tears as it is, imagining a different world where Ryland and I lived in the same city instead of different continents, where I could come to his apartment and study anatomy while he worked on his sketches. Where we were together. But then that same voice breaks into my mind, reminding me of what I'd be giving up and how much of a distraction it would be. That I'm better on my own.

"I know you're going to do great things," I whisper.

"And I'm sure you will too." He steps into the hall. "I just think we could have done even better things together."

After he's gone, I manage to get inside the bathroom and turn on the loud vent before I let the sobs come.

chapter
26

The flight back to Amsterdam is torturous. Ryland sits with Dr. Reese. He doesn't make eye contact with me. I fill the time by writing an email to Mom. I know it's a cop-out when she's expecting me to call, but I'm not ready to talk to her. I'm not sure I'm ready to talk to anyone.

As soon as we arrive back at the canal house, Berend hands Diederik off to me so he can go into the office for a few hours. It's such a welcome relief to have his squishy arms around my neck and hear him squeal my name. He and I fill the afternoon with trains and a trip to the local park, and before I know it, it's dinnertime and then I'm free for the evening.

Dr. Reese catches me in the hall as I'm retreating to my bedroom. "Sage, Katina has some new data abstraction that she needs done. Do you think you can work on that before you go?"

"Of course," I say immediately, glad that Dr. Reese still trusts me. Plus, I'm grateful for something to occupy my thoughts. Despite my best efforts, my mind keeps wandering back to the attic. Is Ryland up there? He didn't come down for dinner. Would it be completely cruel to go upstairs and see if there's some way to make this work as friends? Yes, it would. But I'm still tempted.

I hadn't realized how much I'd taken working with Ryland for granted. At the time, it felt like working anywhere else, but now I realize it wasn't. There was something both calming and invigorating about having another person working in the room with me. At the end of the night, I needed to be able to tell him I'd been productive. It pushed me harder.

But that time is over, so I settle onto my bed and focus on the data. This is what I wanted and I still have it.

An hour goes by without me thinking of Ryland. I'm so absorbed that I almost don't notice when my phone buzzes. Ellie's name appears on the screen and I wince. Mom isn't the only one I've been neglecting. I take a deep breath and answer.

"Hey." Ellie's voice is a lot less confident and happy than it usually is. "Is it a bad time to call?"

"No. Just working on research, but I can take a little break."

She exhales. "Oh, good. When I didn't hear from you, I worried that something bad happened at the conference."

"But I texted to tell you it went well."

"Yeah . . . but you didn't sound like yourself."

"On a *text*?"

"You always have a lot to say when it comes to research." She chuckles. "It's the only time you use exclamation points."

I smile, but sadness also fills me. She's right. Usually, I would be jumping up and down about the conference, but now all the stories are intermingled with Ryland. In fact, now that I think about it, he's the only one who really knows how it went . . . and now we aren't talking anymore.

"So . . ." She pauses again. "Do you want to tell me more about the conference? I'm happy to hear all the details if you're up for it. Or, of course, we can talk about my other favorite subject."

"Dev?" I ask to distract her.

"Dev did manage to make a very impressive pond out of epoxy during my fairy garden class this afternoon, but don't distract me. You know I want to talk about Ryland."

"Yeah . . . but *I* don't want to talk about Ryland."

There's another pause. "Well, that explains it, then. Shit, I'm sorry. I was worried you were going to say something like that."

"I didn't want to tell you." I lean back into my pillow and close my eyes. "I knew you'd be disappointed."

"No, listen, I'm not disappointed. I just want you to be happy— that's the only reason I was so excited before. But if he doesn't make you happy, then screw him. You don't need him."

My stomach twists with guilt. I'd be lying if I said Ryland didn't make me happy. That's all he's done all summer . . . well, along with driving me up a wall sometimes. I don't respond because she'll be able to hear the truth if I speak.

"Anyway," she continues, "you've got so much else to look forward to. You're almost home! It's almost college time!"

"Yes, definitely. Lots going on."

"And remember, a very smart person once told me that boys are only distractions," she says in a teasing voice.

I told her that at Emberton Manor last fall when she was struggling with boy drama. At the time, I said it with total confidence and conviction, but it hits differently now that the words have been turned back on me.

I let her fill the awkwardness of the conversation with stories about what she's been doing with Dev and Huan. We get off the call with promises to see each other as soon as I'm back.

"I'm bringing breakup ice cream and a horror movie," she says.

I groan. "Can't we just call it ice cream?"

"We could, but if we call it breakup ice cream then we get to eat double the amount."

"Well, I won't fight those rules."

After I hang up, I scroll through the data set I was putting together. To my annoyance, I find some errors. I thought I had this process figured out by now, but I guess not. I wasn't even thinking about Ryland while I was doing it, but somehow I made the mistakes anyway.

Tuesday goes by in a similar way. Ryland is a ghost again, the way he was at the beginning of the summer. I know it's for the best. The smartest thing I can do is get through these last days as quickly and painlessly as possible. Still, I feel his absence like a knife in the chest. And if I thought the days were miserable, the nights are a hundred times worse. At least during the day I have Diederik, but nights were our time together.

I filled tonight with the rest of the data abstraction. It's done now, at least. I open an email from Johns Hopkins with logistical details about the upcoming move-in days, but the words blur. My thoughts keep returning to Ryland's art competition. Maybe because it's safer to think about that than to think about him. I just hate that he sold those amazing prints to Espen to be gifts for tourists rather than trying to get them shown where they can really be admired. He deserves so much more than to be making the same stock prints for a gift shop. His work deserves to be seen by thousands of people—*millions* of people—and I wish there were some way I could make that happen for him.

It's obvious that I'm not going to be able to do anything else productive tonight, so I decide to get ready for bed. I push open the bathroom door to find Ryland there. He looks over at me, his face dripping water into the sink. He stands quickly and dries off with a towel.

"Sorry," I say. "I'll let you be."

"It's okay. I'm done."

For a second, I think that he's going to step deeper into the bathroom like he did earlier in the summer. Instead, he pushes around me to go into the hall.

"Did you have a good night?" I whisper before he can walk away. I don't know what I'm doing. I'm making it so much harder by trying to talk to him.

He shrugs. "You?"

"Yeah, I guess. It was . . . hard to concentrate."

He watches me for a moment and then his gaze drops to my lips. It's as if he's just set me on fire. It takes everything in me not to grab him by his shirt collar and kiss him until the sun comes up.

He swallows hard. "Have a good night."

A second later I hear his door close. I take a deep breath and lean against the sink. I'm being selfish and I know it, but I can't stop myself. I need to say something else to him. I need to fix this in some way.

I walk down the hall and stand outside his door, taking measured, quiet breaths so that he won't hear me until I know exactly what I want to say. But what *can* I say? I lean my forehead on his door. I don't need to say anything romantic. I just need him to know I still care about him.

Suddenly, I'm falling forward. I wave my arms wildly to get my balance and collide into something hard—his chest. Hands grasp my waist and I pull back, realizing that Ryland must have opened the door and I tumbled directly into him. My face heats in embarrassment. There's no explaining this one away.

"Sage?"

He's still holding on to me and his fingers are hot against my skin. I have to push away memories of us together in the attic. I right myself and take a step back. "I'm sorry, I was just . . ." It's hard to think straight. We're still so close. His bed is only steps away. If I wanted, I could step inside and close the door behind us. No one would need to know.

"What's going on?" he asks.

I shake my head and try to think of something coherent to say. "I, um, I was going to say that I think you should contact the competition judge again. The one who you missed the appointment with before?"

His expression sours. "No, he won't want to see me."

"How do you know that?"

"Because I already tried." His shoulders hunch. "I guess I didn't make that great of a first impression, blowing him off like that before."

My heart sinks to the ground. I ruined that opportunity for

him. I know it's not really my fault. I would never have asked him to do that if I'd known. But he put me above himself when he shouldn't have and now he's lost that chance.

But if he hadn't done that, then I might've lost mine.

He must realize what I'm thinking because he shakes his head. "Don't blame yourself. I made my choice."

"You shouldn't have done that."

"Maybe not. But I'll have other chances. I would have hated it if you left Amsterdam with nothing to show for it."

Our eyes lock and my breathing goes shallow. Is that what's happening? *Am* I about to leave Amsterdam with nothing real to show for it—except a padded résumé?

"Ryland," I whisper.

He clenches his jaw and takes a step back into his room as if it physically pains him. "You don't need to explain your decision again. I knew what I was getting into with you from the first minute we met. You never lied to me about your priorities. You never lied about anything. I just thought—" He shakes his head. "You didn't do anything wrong. But I think . . . it's best if we don't talk anymore."

Pain squeezes me tight. I can see it swirling in his eyes as well, and it feels like a knife slowly slicing the tendons from my bones to know I'm the one causing it.

I step back into the hall. "I'm sorry, Ryland."

"I know."

chapter

27

I still haven't called Mom. In my defense, I did write her a detailed email and replied to her texts, but I don't want to have any more calls. Unfortunately, I didn't think about Wren calling in her place.

When I see the number on my phone, I stare for a second. Wren and I have been doing a lot better lately, but that doesn't mean we call each other to chat. If she's calling me, it's probably not for a good reason.

I glance at Diederik, wondering if he might be a good excuse to ignore the call, but he's watching TV and doesn't even notice me.

"Hello?" I say.

"*Sage.*" Wren's voice is hard. "You picked up."

"Yeah."

"I hope you know why I'm calling. Mom is upset. And a little pissed."

I groan and sink deeper into the couch. "I wrote her an email."

"An email. After what was potentially one of the biggest days of your life? Why are you blowing her off? She's been waiting all summer to hear how this conference thing went and you write her an *email?*"

I roll my eyes. "It was a perfectly fine email. I wasn't trying to blow her off—I've just been tired."

"Fine. Did the conference go okay?"

"It was wonderful."

"Okay . . . and things are still good with Diederik?"

I glance over at him and smile fondly. "He's good. He's sweet, despite the messes. It's going to be hard to leave him."

"I never thought I'd hear you say that."

"Honestly, I never thought I would."

She laughs. "I'm not going to lie, I was nervous about this summer—for both you and him. But all those plans you sent me are really cool. I can't wait until Maddie is old enough that we can start doing those together."

"Well, it wasn't all perfectly created lunches and themed crafts. There were also messes and tantrums and tears—from both of us. And . . ." I hesitate and lower my voice. "I, um, lost him at the park once." I feel horrible admitting that, but it's also a relief to say it aloud to someone else. I haven't talked about it since it happened.

"Sage, oh my god!"

"I know. I was so scared. I was screaming and running everywhere. Thank god Ryland was there with us. He's the one who found him."

"Ryland's the older brother, right? Mom mentioned him when you first got there. Is he cool?"

"Yeah. He's really great."

It's impossible not to hear the angst in my voice, but—to her credit—Wren doesn't push it. "I'm glad you're doing well. I should go, though. I need to get some studying in while Maddie is napping, but *call Mom*."

"Wait!" I yell before she hangs up. "What are you studying?"

"I'm back in school for dental hygiene. I started last week. Didn't Mom tell you?"

I think back through her texts, but I don't remember anything about this. I would definitely remember if I found out Wren was back in school.

"That's amazing, Wren! Congratulations! How are you managing that with Maddie?"

"We found an empty nester down the street who is super excited to take care of her and isn't charging too much. Now that she's a year old and sleeping better, I think it'll be okay to leave her with someone a few hours a day. Though it's hard."

"Wow!" I desperately need good news and this more than fits the bill. "I'm so proud of you. That's really impressive, balancing all of that."

"Thanks." She pauses. "I just want to give Maddie the very best life I can."

"Of course. Honestly . . ." I think about Dr. Reese struggling to get through med school with Ryland. "Sometimes I don't see how anyone can do it. Balance it all, I mean. How can anyone devote themselves to school and still have room in life for parenting or dating or love?"

She scoffs. "There's no dating or love over here right now, *believe* me. Unless . . . we aren't talking about me anymore?"

I grimace. I wasn't watching my words closely enough.

"What's actually happening over there? Is Mom going to become a grandma for a second time?" she asks in a teasing voice.

I laugh. "No, things haven't progressed quite that far yet."

"Oh, but there are *things*."

"There . . . might be things."

"And these things are making you question your priorities?"

"No. I don't know. I haven't changed my priorities, but I'm starting to wonder if maybe I should."

She sighs in exasperation. "You know, this conversation would be a lot easier for me to follow if you'd just be open for once. I know you're used to being the one who always has her shit together, but it's okay to talk about stuff sometimes. We all need help."

I bite the inside of my cheek, her words reminding me of what Ryland said before. This is a huge reversal from our roles for the past few years. I was always the one helping Wren. Getting homework from her teachers, gathering every scrap of information on pregnancy milestones, telling off her old friends. I don't like being in this position. I don't like sharing personal things with other people, even my big sister. And I don't like asking for advice.

But maybe I need to just this once.

"Okay, fine. So, basically there's this boy and there's my research and I can't have them both. But I want them both."

"Why can't you have them both?"

"Um . . . because his mom is also the researcher I'm working for?"

She bursts out laughing. I can imagine her throwing her head back, her blond hair falling down her back. I haven't heard her laugh like that in a long time.

"*Oh my god*, Sage! You don't date at all in high school and as soon as you get out you choose the absolute worst person. I can't believe this. You always have to make things difficult."

"I don't mean to. And I already broke it off."

"And now you're wondering if you made the right decision."

"I'm a total mess about it, Wren." I can hear how small and pitiful I sound, but I can't help it.

"Oh, wow." Her voice grows somber. "So, you *really* like him."

"Yeah."

"Huh. Well, he must be something if he's got you questioning yourself."

"He just . . . somehow things got easier when he was around. Everything I was dealing with felt lighter."

She's quiet for a moment. "That's funny. Mom was just saying the same thing about Dad."

"She was? Why did that come up?"

"When I started back in classes, she was telling me about her MBA program. That's when she and Dad started dating, apparently."

I blink. It's so rare to hear her talk about Dad. "Yeah, I knew that."

"I guess they spent a lot of their early dates at the library. He'd come with her and read while she studied, and he'd get them coffees, and tell her jokes when she was getting stressed. Doesn't that sound just like him?"

My throat gets thick. "Yeah, it does." Wren doesn't say more, but I know what she's getting at. It's easy to see that with Mom and Dad. They always seemed meant to be. "I don't know," I say.

"It's hard for me to shake the idea that things would be simpler if I were single."

"Didn't you just say they were easier when you were with Ryland?"

I pause. "But it's different here. It's summer and I'm in a foreign country and I don't have as much pressure. It won't be like that in college."

But even as I say that, I remember how burned out and overwhelmed I was at the beginning of the summer. And how everything got better once I started spending time with him.

"I don't know, Sage. Obviously, you've got to figure this one out yourself. But I've known you for almost eighteen years, and never once have you even *entertained* the idea of being in a relationship. That has to mean something."

"Maybe. I'll think about it."

"You're coming home soon, so don't think too long." She laughs. "I can't believe I'm giving you advice. I'm not sure that's ever happened before."

"Don't get used to it."

"I won't. I love you."

"Love you too."

I end the call and sit in silence, staring at the opposite wall.

What do I want . . . other than everything? I want to collaborate on research that helps cancer patients and families. I want to make a tangible impact on the world. And I want Ryland. There's no point denying it. Knowing that he's in this apartment right now, living and breathing and thinking, and that I can't curl up in his arms, is like an open wound. I miss him so much.

But I guess the question is: Can I find a way to make this all work?

Ryland's words in Berlin come back to me. I've already formed connections with other researchers . . . maybe it's time I took the leap and pursued those. I haven't forgotten about Dr. Lee. Helping with his immunotherapy research would be unbelievable, though I'm not convinced he'll be open to taking on such a young student. *But* if I don't ask then I'll never know.

I Google Dr. Lee's lab and click on his contact information.

Dr. Lee,

I'm so glad I was able to meet you at the conference in Berlin over the weekend. Would it be possible to schedule a meeting to talk about volunteering in your lab this fall? I am really inspired by your work and would love to contribute.

I hope you have a good start to the semester.

Sage Cunningham

I take a deep breath, hit send, and open a new spreadsheet. Time to start working toward the future I want.

chapter
28

I've made a lot of plans in my day. Color-coded study plans, travel plans, even plans for when my big sister went into labor. They were all important, but this latest one might be one of the most important yet.

I pack some snacks and turn to Diederik. "Want to go on a bike ride?"

He squeals in delight and I push down a tremble of dread. I've got to suck it up and face my fears, including bicycling alone in Amsterdam.

It turns out that riding with Diederik isn't too bad. For one thing, he's ridiculously in love with it. No fussing or crying when he's riding through the city. And although I didn't exactly bulk up over the summer, I must have built some endurance, because my thighs are only *mildly* burning when we arrive at Espen's Emporium.

I prep an iPad with Diederik's favorite game and give it to him as soon as we walk into Espen's shop. I need him completely occupied so I can negotiate.

The shop is just the same as it was the last time I was here with Ryland. A quick glance shows me that Ryland's smaller block prints are in the same place in the store, though it looks like there are fewer of them than there were before. I don't see his competition prints, which means that either Espen hasn't put them out on the floor yet or they've already sold. I'm *really* hoping for the former.

Diederik's full concentration is focused on his airship game, so I maneuver him over to the person at the counter.

"I was hoping I could speak with Espen."

He glances toward the back door. "Um, he's not—"

Espen pokes his head out of the door and sees me. His outfit is just as over the top as the last time I saw him. He has on a neon-green tracksuit with a red feather boa around his neck, and his hair is colored to look like a dartboard with the bull's-eye at the crown of his head. It makes me nervous that he's going to walk outside and a drunk tourist will throw a bottle at his head, but to each their own. His eyebrows rise when he sees Diederik and me. He strides to the front of the store, though he looks less welcoming than before. "I didn't think you were in Amsterdam any longer."

I blink. I didn't know the owner of Espen's Emporium was tracking my schedule, but Ryland must have told him I was flying home soon. I wonder what else he said.

"Can I talk to you about Ryland's prints?"

He gestures toward the shelves. "There are still a few for sale if you'd like them."

I shake my head. "Not those. I mean the series of prints he made for the competition. He told me he sold them to you."

"He did." Espen's voice is quiet and he regards me warily.

"Well, I . . ." I grimace, realizing how badly this is going to come out. "I don't think he should have done that. It's not personal, but I don't think he should have sold them at all. They're precious to him and they deserve to be seen by more people. No offense."

Espen crosses his arms in front of his chest and stares at me. I glance down at Diederik, who's sitting at my feet. Espen won't tell me off in front of a toddler, will he?

"I'm glad you have some of the sense Ryland told me you had." He sighs. "You're right. The prints are too good to be sold here. But what could I do? He said he didn't want to look at them anymore. I did pay well for them, but it's a shame."

"He worked so hard on those pieces—he really thought those would get him to the next step . . ." I look at the ceiling. "I don't want to leave without helping somehow. Would you be willing to part with them if I could find a gallery that would take them?"

"Perhaps . . ." Espen is quiet for a moment before speaking. "But I have another idea. He wants to do murals, yes?"

I nod, thinking of our afternoon at the street art museum. Though I'm careful not to think about it too much because I don't want to make myself miserable.

"He has a lot of goals, but I know that's a big one."

Espen nods. "There might be a solution that can work for everyone. Come with me."

The next thing I have to do is talk to Dr. Reese. After dinner, I find her in the living room watching TV with Berend. She looks up in surprise.

"Sage, is everything okay? Did you want to watch with us?"

I shake my head. "Actually, can I talk to you about something?"

"Of course. Berend, don't wait on me." She stands and walks to the kitchen table. "He loves that show, but it's not my favorite," she says quietly when we're out of earshot. "I appreciate the distraction."

"You're missing the funniest part!" Berend calls.

She laughs and waves him away. "He's scared that we're going to start talking about research and then I'll lose the whole night."

"Yeah?"

She shrugs. "I was such a workaholic when we first met. I'd go all night and then get up in the morning and do it again. He hasn't forgotten." She looks over her shoulder and smiles fondly at him. "You wanted to talk about something, though? What did you need?"

"I want to talk about Ryland."

Her face grows serious. "Oh. Yes?"

"You know those prints of his you saw in the attic? Well, he created them for a competition. That didn't pan out, but I think I've found another way for him to display them. I'm hoping to show him tomorrow evening and thought you might want to come as well? It would be a nice sign of support for him to have his family there."

She nods. "Of course. I'm sure we can make that work. It's kind of you to do something like that."

I stare blankly at her, realizing that she has no idea how deeply I feel for Ryland. For some reason, I thought she did, that she could smell it in the air or something, but that's ridiculous. I never told her about my feelings in Berlin—I was too busy feeling guilty and mortified.

"I love Ryland," I say simply. "So it's easy to do kind things for him."

She sits back with a look of astonishment on her face. "Sage . . . I know it might *feel* that way right now, but let me assure you that those feelings are fleeting and almost never real. Particularly when you're so young and—"

"Dr. Reese, you've always described me as exceptionally bright, haven't you?"

She nods, her eyes narrowing.

"Then isn't it possible that I could know my own feelings?"

"Unfortunately, feelings are significantly harder to understand than data. I speak from experience."

"I know you do. And I appreciate *everything* you've done for me, and every bit of advice you've shared. Working with you over the last year has given me some of the best times of my life. But, as it stands right now, I'm going to need to step away from your lab."

"I see." Dr. Reese heaves a heavy sigh. "Ryland is an awesome kid. I love him dearly. But just . . . please listen to me when I tell you not to put a boy above yourself and your goals. You will regret it."

Her words and warnings, which at one point would have sent me reeling with fear, wash over me. Sitting here, I feel as confident as I did when I sat down to take my AP chemistry exam. Serene, almost. The only fear I have left is whether I'm too late.

"That's the thing," I tell her. "I'm not putting him above myself. I'm going to have a lot of new opportunities in college, and I plan to take advantage of every single one of them. In fact, I've already reached out to Dr. Lee about working in his lab this year. But if I'm going to do all of this, I need people in my life who want me to succeed as much as I want to. Who support me so much that they lighten the load rather than adding to it. And Ryland does that for me. I hope I can do the same for him." I lift my chin. "I'm choosing myself when I choose him."

She blinks. Her mouth opens and closes. For once, I've actually left my mentor speechless.

"And he feels the same?"

"He did . . . I don't know if he still does." I lift a shoulder and try to ignore the anxiety that surges through me at the possibility that his feelings have changed. "I'd like to find out."

We're both silent for a second, and then she nods. "Yes. If I were you, I think I'd like to find out too."

chapter
29

I stay up till almost three in the morning working on the last part of my plan. This is the part I'm the most scared about. It's very possible that this entire thing is going to implode in my face . . . and that's assuming I can even get Ryland to meet me. But the only other option is giving up, and I am not a quitter.

I'm sluggish for my last day with Diederik, but by now we have a happy rhythm that makes it easier. He eats his bread and bananas and we color and chug trains and paint. And the whole time I stare at the profile of his chubby little cheeks and give him kisses on the top of his head and think how much I'll miss him. I couldn't have imagined thinking such a thing when I first arrived at the airport and he chucked that juice cup across the terminal, but now I feel a dull ache at the idea that I won't be waking up to hear his voice and feel his small hand in mine when we go for walks.

I'm hoping Ryland will stay in the house today so I can talk to him, but he's nowhere to be found. Looks like I'm going to have to get more people involved if I want him to meet me tonight. I suck up my courage and text Dan.

Hey, do you know where Ryland is?

Maybe.
Why?

I've been working on something—a
plan—and I'd really like to show
him before I leave. Do you think you
could convince him to come here?

I send her the address. There's a long pause while I wait for the
speech bubble to pop up again.

Can I trust you?
You've already broken him once.
I'm not sure he can handle a second time.

My stomach squeezes.

Yes, you can trust me.

Fine. But we're coming with him.

By the time Dr. Reese and Berend get back home in the evening,
I'm practically jumping with nerves. I usher them to the door
before they can get settled or take off their shoes, and insist we
take the tram to make sure we get there on time. I'm so scared
this is all going to fall apart, but Espen is waiting for us on the

sidewalk when we get there.

"This is a welcome change." He gestures at my shirt and I look down. I can't quite believe I'm doing it, but I'm wearing the hot-pink *Book of Sage* T-shirt Ryland made me weeks ago. I promised him I'd never wear hot pink in my life, but honestly . . . it's kind of grown on me.

"Is everything okay?" I ask.

"The crew is on break so you have time, but they'll need to get back inside eventually." He lifts an eyebrow. "Do you think this is going to work?"

"I don't know. But I hope so."

It's a very awkward few minutes waiting on the sidewalk for Ryland to show up. Berend keeps giving sidelong looks to Espen, like he can't quite believe what he's seeing, and Diederik is restless to run around and play. Luckily, Ryland and his friends are only a few minutes late. Twitch waves, but Dan and Maiya only peer at me with wary expressions.

Ryland stops abruptly when he sees our motley group. He whispers something to Dan, but she shakes her head and points at me. I take a few steps toward them, hugging a binder to my chest.

He walks forward, awkwardly waving to Berend and his mom, then sucks in a quiet breath when he realizes what shirt I'm wearing. "What's going on, Sage?" he asks in a low voice. "Dan said this was your idea? Why are my mom, Berend, and *Espen* here?"

"It'll make sense in a second." I look at Ryland's family on my right and his friends on my left. "I really appreciate you all coming, but can you give us a few minutes?" I ask them. "I need to talk to Ryland first and then I'll come get you."

Berend nods happily, seemingly content to play with Diederik, but Dr. Reese eyes Ryland and me with caution. The girls nod and Twitch gives me a subtle thumbs-up.

Espen ushers us in. The restaurant has seen better days. In fact, it looks pretty rough. The floors have been torn up, there are holes in the walls, and construction materials and tools sit around.

Ryland looks around incredulously. "Sage, what the hell is going on? Have you lost your mind?"

"Probably." I glance at Espen.

He taps his wrist like it's a clock. "I'll do what I can to keep everyone away until you're done." He walks out and Ryland and I are alone.

"What *is* this place?"

"Espen's next project. He's remodeling it right now, but it sounds like it's going to be a really cool restaurant when he's done."

"Sage—"

I hold up a hand. "I spoke to him about your pieces and we agreed that you can't sell them for souvenirs. And we talked about how much you wanted to be a mural artist and he brought me here and . . ." Gingerly, I put down my binder and walk to the long wall that runs along the right side of the building. "I thought this could be your first mural. You know Espen, he's going to want something over the top, with screaming colors, vibrant settings . . . maybe a few cats. I was thinking you could transform your competition pieces into a huge mural."

He blinks quickly. "My pieces?"

"You created them so each one flows into the next. So maybe you could paint them so they spread over this entire wall? I don't know much about art, and I'm sure this would be a ton of work, but . . . it's something, right? It's not exactly the side of a building like you talked about, but it would be your first commissioned mural. And think of all the people who would see your art every night."

Ryland walks up to the wall, skimming his hand across it. "And Espen's okay with this?"

"Definitely. Though there was some talk about using all neon colors. . . . I'll let you negotiate that one."

Ryland chuckles softly. He drifts down the length of the room and I can see the light coming on inside him just like it always does when he's thinking about his art. It lights me up as well. I know Espen is probably going to come back soon and there's still more to say, but I give Ryland another second to imagine what he could create here. Plus, that gives me one more second to prepare before I share the other part of my plan.

"This is really great, Sage." Ryland walks back to me. "Thank you. But I don't want to be some obligation or homework assignment you need to take care of before you leave. I can take care of myself."

"I know you can. I just thought . . . maybe we could do even better things together."

His eyes flash at my use of his words from Berlin. I take a deep breath, pick up the heavy binder from the ground, and hand it to him.

"For you," I say. "But like you said, there's no obligation."

He looks at me curiously and opens the cover. His eyes go wide. "What . . ." He flips through a few of the pages, looking up at me and back down at the binder. "Transportation, apartment prices . . . ," he reads in a whisper.

I try to push down my nerves. He's reading the glossary at the front. I thought it might be nice for him to have the different sections—hotels and apartment complexes, listed by price and by location, transportation options, a section on art galleries, studios, and classes—listed at the beginning so everything is easy to find.

He flips deeper into the binder. "What is all this?"

"It's . . . my most recent research project." I take it out of his hands and point to some of the maps. "If I'd had more time then it would have been nicer, but I organized it a few different ways to help you make sense of it, and I color-coded it, but then I ran out of sticky notes, so—"

"*Sage.*" His voice is very quiet. "What *is* this?"

"It's information on Baltimore. Places to live and work close to Johns Hopkins. In case . . . you know . . . you wanted to visit there sometime." My hands are shaking and I push the binder back toward him more roughly than I mean to. "Or stay."

"To be with you?"

My throat is thick and it's impossible to look him in the eye, so I stare at his T-shirt. He's wearing his *Walking Interruption* one. I hope it's a good sign that he's still willing to wear shirts inspired by me.

"I know you probably don't want that anymore, and I totally understand. And you have to do this mural, of course, I'm not suggesting that you wouldn't do it. It's important."

He flips through a few more of the pages, sneaking more glances at me as he does. "You put all this together for me?"

I nod.

"And my mom?"

"I already told her that I'm not going to work with her anymore."

"What? When? Sage, this is all amazing, but I don't want you giving up your future for me. I've made my peace with it. Or, well, I'm trying to."

"And what if *you're* my future?"

He takes a ragged breath. I can see hope and caution warring for dominance in his expression.

"I want us to both have the best possible futures," I whisper. "And I'll accept it, truly, if you decide that means you need to stay here. But I'm tired of choosing between my research and you. I think it's possible to have both. I'd like to try to have both . . . if you want to try with me?"

I finally let myself look at him, and see that his eyes are bright with joy now. He carefully puts the binder down and takes my face in both of his hands.

"Yes, I want to try. More than anything in the world."

And then he kisses me.

I wrap my arms around him, barely able to believe this is happening. My heart races and my fears from moments ago fade into nothing as he pulls me tightly to him. I wasn't sure I'd ever experience this again, and now I never want it to end. I don't care about the tools or mess, I'd stay in this construction site with Ryland forever if Espen would let us.

Minutes pass—long, glorious minutes—but eventually there's a noise to the right and someone clears their throat.

"I gave you as much time as I could, but they were quite curious to come inside."

Ryland and I slowly pull apart to find the entire group standing behind Espen. All of Ryland's friends are grinning, especially Dan, and Berend looks adorably confused and amused all at once. Dr. Reese surveys us with wide eyes.

"You both look happy," she says.

Ryland and I glance at each other and smile. "Very happy," I say.

She smiles with us. "Then so am I." She scans the room. "Though I'm also confused. Didn't you say Ryland was going to showcase his art at a restaurant, Sage? Why are we in an abandoned building right now?"

"This is not an abandoned building," Espen huffs. "*This* is the site of my new restaurant."

"And the site of my first commissioned mural," Ryland adds. "Thanks to Sage."

I beckon everyone forward. "I thought it was fitting to have his friends and family here to see this. I think this project is going to be really special."

He pulls me closer and kisses my temple before turning to the group. "Okay, let me tell you what I'm imagining."

chapter
30

I take one more look through my dresser and under my bed before zipping up my final suitcase. Today is the day—I'm heading back home. I'm a mixture of heartbroken to be leaving Ryland, Diederik, and the whole of Amsterdam, and excited to get back to my own family. Mom, Wren, and I have decided on a mother-daughter day when I get back so I can tell them all about my trip . . . and Ryland. Wren let that slip to Mom, I guess. And I have plans to hang out with Ellie, Dev, and Huan next weekend as well. I know they're dying to hear everything and I'm looking forward to seeing them so much that I won't even mind the *extreme* teasing I'm about to endure.

It's probably not smart, but I decide to check my new school email address before I shut down my laptop for the trip. I haven't checked for a response from Dr. Lee since I wrote him the email. I wanted to avoid any possible bad news, but I'm also anxious to see what he says. And if he isn't interested in meeting about a position in his lab, then that's okay. Johns Hopkins is a big school and I know I'll find my place.

Sure enough, there's a reply from him, time-stamped yesterday. I take a deep breath and open it.

Hello, Sage,
Thanks for reaching out about your interest in the work we're doing here. I would love to speak to you about a possible position. I think you could be a good fit.
Dr. Reese just emailed to sing your praises and she's a great judge of character.
Let me know your class schedule and we can find a time to meet.
All best,
Dr. Lee

I blink and reread the email. We're meeting about the position? And Dr. Reese wrote him yesterday? A slow smile spreads across my face. If she's writing other professors to recommend me, then maybe things are going to be okay between us. I sincerely hope so, because I plan to be in her life for a long time.

I hear steps in the hall and close my laptop just as Ryland comes into the room. His cheeks are flushed, probably from carrying my other bags down the stairs to the car. Like last time, Dr. Reese is going to drive me to the airport. But unlike last time, Ryland is coming too. We're trying to spend every second together before I fly home.

He comes up behind me and wraps his arms around my waist. "I still can't believe you're leaving today. Why couldn't we have figured things out earlier in the week?"

I turn around to look at him. "Sometimes brilliance takes time."

"So, dating me is now defined as brilliance?" He nods. "Yes, that checks out. I approve."

"You're going to make a T-shirt of that, aren't you?"

"You better be ready to wear a neon tie-dyed version of it as soon as it arrives at Johns Hopkins. And take a selfie to prove you've done so."

I wiggle from his embrace and point down at the *Book of Sage* shirt that I'm wearing today. "I don't know why you'd doubt me."

"I don't know why I would either." He kisses me softly and I debate barricading the door and staying here indefinitely. "I had some more inspiration about the mural after you went to bed last night. I think it's going to be really amazing."

"Yeah? I'm so glad."

After Espen kicked us out of the construction site/restaurant, we quickly shrugged off the others and wandered through the streets, alternating between talking and kissing (heavy on the kissing). Then we came back and spent our last evening in the attic. Ryland is staying to work on the mural for now. I wouldn't hear of him blowing it off. Plus, he'll need time to convince Dr. Reese about the move to America, though at least his father is supportive of it. I'm fine with the timing. I'll need to get settled at school and focus on my first semester of classes. We'll talk as much as we can until he's able to come, though I'm going to have a lot of work to do. But I'm not worried about that either—Ryland already understands. And that's how I know we're going to be okay.

"Speaking of art, I have a present for you." He releases me and ducks into the hall. "I thought about mailing it later as a surprise, but I don't want to pay for shipping."

"This already sounds incredibly romantic."

He grins and holds out a small art print. I look at him expectantly and take it. It's a drawing of the attic with me standing at the center.

"To hang in your dorm room."

I suck in a soft breath. "When did you make this?"

"Well . . . I've been working on the sketch for a while now. It's my first sight of you."

"Didn't you yell at me the first time we met?"

"You'd moved my paints. It was the only reasonable reaction, no matter how cute you were."

I elbow him, laughing. "I love it." I gaze at the print again and take a breath to steady myself. "And I love you."

His eyes widen and he plucks the print from my hands and lays it on the bed. "I love you too," he whispers, and wraps me in another kiss. Everything feels so perfectly right in his arms.

When we finally step away from each other, I take out my phone and pull up the pictures of his clutter from that first night in the attic.

"We still have twenty minutes before we need to leave, and the attic's only gotten messier since I arrived. Maybe there's still time for a quick cleanup?"

He tosses my phone on the bed and kisses me again.

acknowledgments

Writing *Hot Dutch Daydream* has been one of the best experiences of my life. Which is not to say that it was easy, because writing is never easy, but I've loved every moment of it anyway.

First, thank you to my amazing editor, Elizabeth Lynch, for believing in this book and making it shine. I also want to thank Catherine Wallace, who first heard my premise and gave me great advice. I am so grateful to everyone at HarperCollins who helped in the making of this book, including Chris Kwon, Alexandra Rakaczki, Annabelle Sinoff, Mitchell Thorpe, Jessica White, and Lana Barnes.

As always, thank you to my wonderful agent, Tara Gonzalez, for your support and encouragement. Thanks to Elizabeth Adams for speaking to me about oncology research and answering all my questions, as well as to Sanne Zwart for all her help with the Dutch in the book. Thank you to Jacqueline Li, for illustrating another gorgeous cover. You are a genius!

Writing during a pandemic is a challenge, and I am thankful to all my writer friends who cheered me along, including

Diane Mungovan, Becky Gehrisch, Keely Parrack, Holly Ruppel, Laurence King, and Debbie Rigaud, as well as everyone I've met through SCBWI, the 21ders debut group, EMLA, and PitchWars. Sabrina Lotfi and Carrie Allen, thank you for cheering me on and for your thoughtful critiques of this manuscript. Thank you to Mazie Neville for being both an early reader and such a tremendous supporter of my writing. Rachel Lynn Solomon, thank you for so graciously taking me around Amsterdam during my research trip. I'm so glad we got to experience KattenKabinet together! Kathryn Powers, thank you for always reading my work no matter how busy you are and for eating too much Chinese food and pie with me. Debbi Michiko Florence, your daily encouragement and belief in my writing means more than I can say.

Thank you to my friends for reading and for sharing your parenting stories to help inspire the Diederik scenes: Melissa Beers, Kristy Reel, Courtney McGinty, Rosalee Meyer, Anna Yocom, Kristin Supe, Beth and David Camillus, and Emmett Williams. A special thank-you to Maggie Stevenson for not only helping to inspire *Hot British Boyfriend* by telling me about Harlaxton Manor, but for hashing out the plot details of *Hot Dutch Daydream* over tea and finger sandwiches when we were there in 2019. I knew this book was something special from that first day.

Thank you to my parents for always encouraging my writing and being so supportive. And to Liam, my little reader, for loving my cooking and for understanding when Mom needs to write.

To Mike, thank you for everything. For being there during the ups and downs of writing, for encouraging me to fly to Amsterdam on a whim, for the flowers and presents and all your support.

You are hands down the best book-themed gift giver and the best husband I could have hoped for.

Finally, thank you to all the readers, bloggers, and bookstagrammers who supported *Hot British Boyfriend* when it came out midpandemic, and to all who are reading right now. This book wouldn't exist without you! I know your time is precious, and you chose to spend it with my characters. I'm forever grateful.